BOOKS BY HELENA NEWBURY

Helena Newbury is the *New York Times* and *USA Today* bestselling author of seventeen romantic suspenses, all available where you bought this book. Find out more at helenanewbury.com.

Lying and Kissing

Punching and Kissing

Texas Kissing

Kissing My Killer

Bad For Me

Saving Liberty

Kissing the Enemy

Outlaw's Promise

Alaska Wild

Brothers

Captain Rourke

Royal Guard

Mount Mercy

The Double

Hold Me in the Dark

Deep Woods

No Angel

First Edition

NO ANGEL

A STORMFINCH SECURITY NOVEL

HELENA NEWBURY

NEW YORK TIMES BESTSELLING AUTHOR

For Sarah, who never stops amazing me

1

OLIVIA

GABRIEL KAIN. A MAN SO WICKED, SO TEMPTING, SO DAMN SEDUCTIVE, he'd give Lucifer himself a run for his money. Appropriate, then, that I'd meet him in hell.

We were in a heatwave and in south-east Arizona, that meant the temperature was pushing a hundred and twenty. Through the window of the infirmary, I could see the heat haze shimmer over the parking lot. It was noon and by now, the asphalt would be softening and the cars would burn your fingers if you touched exposed metal. But inside, it was much, much worse.

The concrete buildings of the prison soaked up the heat and trapped it. My infirmary had air conditioning but the cells didn't, and the air there became as thick and heavy as soup. Over a thousand men, all maximum-security prisoners, panted and cursed as they struggled to breathe. And as the temperature rose, tempers frayed. There'd been four serious fights so far that week.

The door buzzer sounded and I hurried over and thumbed the intercom. "Yes?"

It was one of the guards, Louis. A lot of the guards in this place are thugs, but Louis is a sweet old guy in his fifties. "Got two injured for you, Doc," he told me. "One's not too bad, one's got a knife wound."

"Bring 'em in." I unlocked the door and ran to get supplies while Louis and the other guards hustled the two prisoners onto gurneys in separate exam areas. Whatever the two of them had been fighting about, we didn't want it to restart here.

I gave the first patient a quick look: a split lip, a cut above his eye: he'd live. "Check him over," I told my nurse, Alicia. "I'll take the other one."

As I started towards the other exam area, Louis blocked my path. "Uh, before you go in there...just be careful with him, okay?"

I tensed. "Is he violent?"

"No..."

"Grabby?"

"No, he's..." Louis sighed. "It's *Gabriel Kain*."

I frowned. I didn't know the name but then I'd only been at the prison a few months. *Who?*

Louis shook his head and stepped out of the way. His expression said, *you'll find out.*

I pulled back the curtain.

There's something that happens to all men in prison, a cold fog of despair that settles into their bones and leaves them hunched and fearful. It hadn't happened to this man. He was grinning, *proud.* He wore his orange prison jumpsuit like it was a thousand-dollar Armani. He didn't lie on the gurney, he *lounged* on it like a billionaire in a VIP terminal waiting for his private jet.

He'd been chatting away to one of the guards but, as the curtain opened, he turned and looked me in the eye and—

I was looking right into *bad.*

Pure. Unadulterated. Wickedness.

His eyes were the richest, warmest hazel I'd ever seen. But it wasn't the color that made them so hypnotizing. It was the way they glittered. I could feel the intelligence working away behind those eyes, a tireless, efficient machine. He was assessing everything: the guards, the room, *me*...he wasn't just planning, he was three, four, *five* steps ahead. I could actually feel the schemes forming as he gazed at me. Looking into his eyes felt like falling: I plummeted headlong into those rich hazel depths until I was so deep I was helpless. And what shocked me was that part of me didn't want to escape because...

Gabriel Kain was absolutely, completely, blink-twice-and-curse-under-your-breath *gorgeous.*

A lot of the prisoners kept their hair shaved short, so it couldn't be grabbed in a fight, but Gabriel had let his hair grow into soft black curls, as if he wasn't scared of *anyone.* A couple of curls had fallen forward to kiss his forehead. He had his head tipped slightly forward and those glittering hazel eyes were gazing at me from behind those dark locks. I had a sudden, crazy urge to reach forward and brush them back, like a bird daring to groom a lion.

He was a little older than me: mid-thirties, at a guess. His jaw was ruggedly, brutally hard, and as I watched, he lifted a hand and stroked his chin with his thumb as if in thought. He hadn't shaved for a few days, and I stared at his dark stubble as his thumb rasped across it, self-consciously imagining how it would feel against my cheek.

His lips twisted into a smile and suddenly, I couldn't look away from them. A pouting lower lip to tempt you in and make you part your lips in expectation. Then a hard upper lip to take control of the kiss and just freaking *own* you.

Scoundrel. A weirdly old-fashioned word, but it's the one that leapt into my head. Gabriel had a scoundrel's lips. Lips made for stealing kisses.

I mentally shook myself. *He's an inmate.* But the thought was muffled, like I was hearing it from three rooms away. *He's injured. You're meant to be examining him.*

I tried to snap out of it. I really did. But before I could...he spoke.

"Well, well, well," he said softly. "Look at you."

I heard that voice and I was *lost.* It was as warmly intoxicating as bourbon. Refined, but there was something underneath, a delicious rough growl, as if he'd come from humble roots and educated himself. He spoke with absolute confidence and the syllables flowed together in dark poetry, wrapping around my body and drawing me in closer.

For a second, I felt something lift and swell inside me, innocent and shiny as a silver helium balloon. Then reality set in. *Look at you? No one looks at me. He's joking, you idiot.*

The silver balloon popped, and as silver fragments drifted downward, they turned to heat that scalded my cheeks. I ducked my head and looked at the wound, wishing my hair wasn't pulled back into a bun: I wanted it to fall forward and hide me.

The wound was low down on his abdomen: his orange jumpsuit had been slashed open and there was a wet, red stain around it. The jumpsuit's zipper didn't come down low enough for me to take a look. *He'll have to take it off.* I willed my voice to be level and then opened my mouth to speak—

But the words never came out. Because when I glanced up to make eye contact, Gabriel was looking down at me, frowning. Concerned. Curious. And sort of stern, as if he was...*angry?*

Angry at whatever had popped that balloon inside me.

I swallowed, staring into those deep brown eyes and suddenly, I was getting that lift all over again, rising right up from my toes to my chest. This time, it tugged me upward until I thought my feet were going to leave the floor.

He gazed at me, studying me in a way no one ever had before. I didn't understand. I don't draw attention. I'm the opposite of that. But those eyes were so intense that I didn't dip my head again. I let him look.

And he gave a tiny little nod. His face relaxed. *That's better.*

I bit my lip. I could feel his gaze raking over my face, taking in every detail: my hair, my eyes...he paused on my lips, looking at them for a long time. Then his eyes flicked up to meet mine and he smiled as if he liked what he saw. I felt my face heat in a whole different way.

What's going on?! I tore my eyes away from those glittering hazel pools, feeling half drunk, and drew in a shuddering breath. "Please take off your jumpsuit."

That softlower lip pouted and his mouth twisted into a smirk.

"Why, Doc, we only just met. You don't want to move a little slower? A good pinot noir, maybe some Bach...?"

Pinot noir? Bach? Most of the inmates here had gang tattoos and needle marks. Who *was* this guy? And that voice... There was a golden ripple of humor running through it, a playful teasing that went straight through all my normal barriers of cool professionalism and left me flustered and breathy. It felt like all my clothes were held on my body by a single red ribbon and his words were plucking at the bow.

"You're bleeding," I said weakly.

"I've had worse." There was an irrepressible energy to him: I could feel it buzzing in the air, filling the room. He was excited as a child: all this was just a game to him. "What's your name?"

"Doctor Truesdale will do fine. Please take off your jumpsuit."

"That's okay. I'll figure it out." He stretched out on the gurney, hands behind his head. He was injured and no doubt in pain: how could he be so relaxed? "You keep this place cleaner than a preacher's conscience and you're smart enough to be a doctor. Hardworking and clever...that probably means your folks were the same." God, that *voice*. It was like a shaft of sunlight, warmly caressing me: I wanted to roll naked in it. "They'd want something class-*ic* and class-*y*, a short name, to balance *Truesdale*. And pretty, to match you."

Pretty?! My hair isn't golden or auburn or chestnut or any other color someone would write songs about. It's black and long and it tangles like crazy. My skin's deathly white and refuses to tan, so I have to huddle indoors through the long Arizona summers. I'm not lithe and toned, I'm all boobs and hips and I inherited my dad's broad shoulders. On him and my three hulking, handsome brothers, they look strong and impressive but on me, they look awkward. And combined with my curves...I always feel like there's too much of me.

"I'm guessing a vowel at each end," said Gabriel. "*Anna. Erica.* How am I doing?"

My name is Olivia. "Not even close." I lied. Louis caught my eye, silently asking if I wanted some help. But I shook my head: I was determined to deal with this myself. "Take off your jumpsuit," I told him firmly.

Gabriel grinned, a gleam in his eyes. Then, shockingly fast, he sat upright, surging up from the gurney and bringing his face right up to mine.

I bit back a curse and almost jumped back. But I knew I needed to reassert my authority so I forced myself to stay there, staring at him from just a few inches away. For a second, he looked thrown. Then his eyes crinkled, and a slow smile spread across his face, like he was impressed. And finally, his eyes narrowed with lust. As if the fact I'd stood my ground made him want me even more. Heat zig-zagged down my body and exploded in my groin.

"Emma," he tried, staring deep into my eyes. Then as I blinked, startled, "No, not Emma..."

Dammit! He was the prisoner. How come it felt like he was the one in control?

His eyes...that was the problem. Every time I looked into his eyes, I forgot everything else. And while I was helpless, I could feel that frighteningly quick mind whirring away, reading all my secrets.

I managed to break his gaze and stared pointedly at the zipper of his jumpsuit. Then I crossed my arms to hurry him along.

He lifted one hand to the zipper and it was like watching a magician: his hands *flowed,* lazily confident. They were tanned a rich caramel, with just a dusting of dark hair across the backs. Powerful hands...his palms dwarfed mine and he had long, thick fingers. Hands that would feel warm and safe but that were dextrous enough to do wicked, wicked things—

I caught myself and flushed. *What's wrong with me?!*

He shrugged the jumpsuit off his shoulders and reached behind him to push it off his arms. The hard slabs of his pecs strained against his white tank top and his shoulders were smooth caramel spheres that looked as big as my head. He was *big*...big enough that even I felt small. Tattoos covered his upper arms, unusual ones: some sort of vine that wound around his muscles like a lover's embrace.

"Angela," he tried.

This time, I did my best poker face.

"No, not Angela," he muttered thoughtfully.

How is he doing that?

He pushed the jumpsuit further down his arms. As the hard swells of his biceps appeared, I saw more traditional tattoos, images and words, all connected to the vines, but I wasn't close enough to get a look at what they were. I was self-consciously aware of how much I wanted to be closer, how I wanted to read every letter, know everything there was to know about him. *Stop it! He's an inmate, for God's sake.*

But not like any inmate I'd ever met. He was big and tough, but I didn't get a thuggish vibe from him at all: he was smart as hell. He didn't seem dangerous: not to me, at least. I'd met plenty of prisoners who were in for rape and murder and I didn't see that cold cruelty in his eyes. I could be wrong, of course, but if Gabriel was in for something like that, Louis would have warned me about him in a whole different way. So, what *was* he in here for?

The jumpsuit slid down his thickly muscled forearms and then it was falling to hang around his waist. Gabriel lay back on the gurney and his eyes met mine.

"Olivia," he said.

I didn't have time to try to look inscrutable. My mouth hung open dumbly. *How?*

"Olivia," he repeated, tasting the name on his tongue. Then he smiled and, for once, it looked like an honest smile: no games, no tricks. He just looked...fascinated by me. Which made no sense at all. My brothers are the gorgeous ones: my whole life, they've been breaking hearts all over Phoenix. Most people forget the Truesdales even *have* a daughter.

I looked down at his abdomen and, as gently as I could, I lifted his tank top away from the wound to take a look. It must have hurt at least a little, but he didn't even flinch.

I could see right away that the wound wasn't serious. The other guy must have been swinging wildly, not stabbing, because the cut was a diagonal slash across his abs, long but not deep. It had probably helped that he seemed to be carved out of rock down there, the hard ridges of his six-pack warm against my gloved fingers. He obviously spent a lot of time out in the yard pumping iron, but he didn't look like the other guys who lifted a lot, all angular and bulging with veins. Gabriel looked strong but...*functional,* as if the muscle was *for* something. I'd seen that look before, but I couldn't remember where. *Did he used to be an athlete? Is that it?*

"What's the verdict, Doc?" Gabriel asked. "Am I gonna make it?"

That voice: teasing and gentle but filthy as hell...it burned away any coherent thought in my brain and soaked down through my body, burning like hard liquor, and leaving me flushed and giddy. I fought to focus. "You'll need stitches and a shot of antibiotics," I told him. "But you'll be fine." Then I frowned. *But you already knew that, didn't you?* I was seeing other scars now, knife wounds and what looked like a burn. He'd been hurt plenty of times before. He knew what was serious and what wasn't. That was why he'd been so relaxed this whole time. But had all those injuries happened on the outside, or in here?

Then I saw something that had *definitely* happened on the outside. A puckered, circular scar. The entry wound made by a bullet. *Who is this guy?*

"Is the other guy okay?" asked Gabriel.

That teasing, warm growl vibrated through my whole body. My gaze shot up to his face and then I was lost in those hazel eyes all over again and had to struggle to think. *The other guy.* The guy he'd been brought in with.

"Why do you care?" I asked. "Weren't you trying to kill each other?" It came out angrier than I intended. It just frustrates me, when the inmates turn on each other. As a doctor, I want to get them all out of here alive.

Gabriel shrugged, his expression unreadable.

"I'll check," I told him, and pushed through the curtains and out of the exam area. As soon as they closed behind me, I stopped and closed my eyes for a second. It felt like I was waking from a dream.

The air felt cool against my skin and I could think again. Did all of that really happen?

I opened my eyes and hurried over to where Alicia was tending to our other patient.

Alicia is my nurse and in the two months I've been at the prison, she's become my best friend. She's everything I'm not: she's delicate and small, barely coming up to my shoulder. She's all tight and toned from spin classes and boxercise and her skin has this flawless, golden tan. She has long blonde hair and when it isn't pinned up for work, it falls in a silky river down her back. Most of all, she's *fun.* When we go out for drinks, she's like a human firework, drawing all the male attention with her hair flicks and giggles. Meanwhile, I sit there slowly tearing the label from my beer bottle, brooding on whether I've ordered enough bandages and if I should up the insulin dose for the old guy in C block.

It's fair to say that I find it hard to switch off.

Alicia turned and grinned as I arrived. "All good here." She'd given the guy an ice pack to hold against his split, swollen lip and closed up the laceration over his eye with a butterfly stitch. "I was just thinking that I should check him for a concussion. He says he hit the back of his head when he went down."

I nodded. "Good call." Alicia's way too good to be working in a place like this. I've been helping her with applications to some of the big hospitals in Phoenix. Any day now, one of them's going to snap her up and I'll lose her.

Alicia moved me away from the patient. "*Sooo...*how was he?" she whispered.

I blinked at her.

"*Gabriel Kain!*" God, she was starry-eyed as a teenager glimpsing her favorite band. Did everyone know who this guy was but me? *What the hell did he do?!* I was dying to ask but I was embarrassed at the way I'd reacted to him. Now that I was away from him, the spell was broken and reality was setting in. He must have just been teasing, or maybe he just flirted with everyone like that. Besides, he was an inmate and a patient.

"Charming," I said with a shrug, as if I hadn't really thought about it. "His wound's not bad, I need to stitch him up, then he'll be out of here."

Alicia stared longingly toward the curtain and gave a little sigh of regret. Now she really *did* look like a teenager. The band was leaving...and she didn't even get an autograph.

I watched her for a second, biting my lip. This is a hellish place to work. If I could give her a few minutes of fun... "You know what? Why don't *you* do the stitches on Mr. Kain?"

Alicia turned to me, eyes huge. "Really?" When I nodded, she threw her arms around me and squeezed me tight, then shot across the infirmary to Gabriel's exam area.

I went back to the other patient. It felt like balance had been restored to the universe. Now they could both have some harmless fun and everyone was happy.

So why did I feel a kind of cold, gray ache in my stomach, like I'd just missed out on something important?

I shook it off, picked up a flashlight and started the concussion check on Alicia's patient. I hadn't realized until now how young he was: he couldn't have been more than nineteen. And he wasn't much bigger than Alicia. It bothered me that Gabriel had preyed on someone so much smaller than him. I knew I should stay out of it, but as I moved the flashlight back and forth, I mumbled, "What happened between you and Gabriel, anyway?"

He frowned. "Gabriel didn't do this. This was Packard's guys. Gabriel pulled 'em off me and got knifed for it."

I stared at him. When they were brought in together, I'd just assumed they were fighting each other because that's always how it is: good samaritans are thin on the ground in here. Gabriel *saved* him?! I turned towards the curtain. On the other side, I could hear the low growl of Gabriel's questions and the happy chatter of Alicia's answers, like a lion talking to a songbird. Why hadn't Gabriel told me what really happened?

I'd never know. That ache again, worse than before.

I turned back to the kid and finished my exam: no concussion. I told the guards they could take him back to his cell, turned around and—

Alicia was standing there, arms crossed, a sly smile on her lips.

"Did you finish already?" I asked.

She shook her head. She was looking at me as if...*impressed?*

"What?" I was utterly confused.

She walked slowly past me and spoke out of the side of her mouth so the guards wouldn't hear. "He wants *you.*"

I stared at her. *What?!*

She passed me a suture kit and I took it, my fingers numb. Then I started across the room towards the other exam area. It felt like the linoleum was tilting crazily under my feet. He'd had gorgeous, sexy Alicia to flirt with and he wanted *me? What the hell is going on?*

I pushed through the curtain and—

Gabriel was stretched out on the gurney, hands behind his head, looking like a rock star sunning himself on some private beach. He gave me a big, warm grin when he saw me. "Ah, my favorite medical professional." His tongue played with *favorite,* a sinuous caress that left that innocent word sounding anything but. And he made *medical professional* respectful but gently teasing. As if he liked the fact I was so proper and buttoned down in my white coat...because it meant he could unbutton me.

For a second, I thought I saw something else in his eyes. It was only barely visible, under all that cocky confidence, but...he looked relieved. Like he'd been worried I might not come back.

Then it was gone and his gaze was running slowly down my body. The way he did it, it didn't feel furtive or creepy. It was confident and unapologetic. His gaze moved so slowly, so deliberately, that I swore I could feel those big hands cupping my shoulders, sliding down to my breasts, gliding over my waist, my hips... I stood there breathless, lost in it for a second. Then reality fought back and I flushed and shook my head. *This man's a prisoner and you're staff. And he's a patient and you're his doctor.* The rules were crystal clear: I'd be fired in a heartbeat if anything remotely inappropriate happened. And this was *me:* I'll walk half a block to find a crosswalk, rather than jaywalk.

But every time I looked into Gabriel's eyes, the rules felt fuzzy and distant. *What's the matter with me?!*

I tried to focus on something familiar, *safe.* "I need to numb the area," I told him. "So I can suture you." I grabbed a syringe of Lidocaine. "Little scratch," I warned, and injected him. He didn't even flinch, just kept watching me.

I fetched a table, set it beside the gurney and laid out the suture kit. I pulled over a stool and sat down. Checked the suture kit and then *re*-checked it. And then I was stuck: the Lidocaine would take a few more minutes to work and I'd run out of medical stuff to busy myself with. When I finally looked up, I found those hazel eyes still patiently watching me.

And I knew it was time. I knew this was the moment I had to ask what I'd been wanting to ask since the first moment I met him. I just didn't know how. What if my instincts were wrong about him, what if he *was* in for rape or murder? He was in a maximum-security prison, it wasn't going to be tax fraud, how was I meant to—

"Olivia," he said gently, "just ask me."

I swallowed and bit my lip, a little thrown. Partly by him knowing exactly what I'd been thinking. Partly by how good it sounded, hearing him say my name. I've always thought *Olivia* sounded kind of old-fashioned and awkward but in his warm growl, it sounded...beautiful.

"Why are you—" I began. "Why did they—" I took a deep breath. "What did you *do?*"

Gabriel smiled. "I stole four hundred million dollars."

I had to replay his words in my mind to make sure I'd heard right. Four *hundred* million? Four hundred *million?* "I—" I started, but then found I didn't have any words to follow up with. "I—*What?!*" I couldn't even visualize that many zeros except...did he mean some kind of cybercrime? Something involving the stock market, maybe. "With a computer?"

"No," he said, deadpan. "Not with a computer."

"You stole four hundred million dollars in *cash?!*"

"No, that would be ridiculous. I stole four hundred million dollars in gold."

I blinked at him. "*That's* why you're in here?"

His lips twisted and he looked mock-thoughtful. "There were some paintings. A vase. Some jewels. But I'm pretty sure they were mostly annoyed about the gold."

Suddenly, it all made sense. That fierce intelligence, combined with the hard body, the scars and the cocky charm. What else would he be but a professional thief? Gabriel Kain was the gorgeous highwayman who stole your purse and left your panties wet.

"I didn't know they put thieves in maximum security," I said weakly.

"They don't. But I escaped from the first three places."

I shook my head in disbelief. "The Lidocaine should have worked by now," I said. I circled my finger on his abdomen, trying not to think about how good his warm skin felt through my glove. "Can you feel that?"

"Feel what?"

I carefully cleaned the wound, then picked up the needle and suture and began to stitch. Meanwhile, my mind was racing. A thief. Now I understood that badness, that scheming, cunning wickedness that rolled off him in waves. He was a man you could never, ever trust.

Or at least...that's what he wanted everyone to think. I glanced up at him and saw him grinning down at me. He *liked* that reputation. He wore it proudly. But...

"The other guy," I said casually. "The one you were brought in with. He's going to be okay."

He nodded, still grinning.

"He told me it wasn't you who beat him up. He said you saved him."

His grin crumbled and, for once, *he* broke eye contact with *me*. "It was in my interest," he said. "Someone gets killed, more guards get put on and that's a pain in the ass for all of us."

"You sure that was the only reason?"

He still wouldn't look at me. But I wouldn't back down: I waited in silence until, finally, he had to look. We locked eyes and, for just a moment, his cockiness was gone. "Don't make me into something I'm not," he warned. He looked away again but it didn't matter: I had my answer.

A few moments later, I tied off my last stitch. "All done," I told him.

He nodded and gave me a wolfish smile: his confidence was back. Then he looked down at his wound. "It's so *neat,*" he said. "The edges are perfect."

"Well, I didn't want you to scar." It was just what I'd do with any patient. But Gabriel looked at me in shock, as if it was a long time since someone had done something caring for him.

I dressed the wound and then stood up. "One more thing. You need a shot of antibiotics. Whatever they cut you with, I doubt it was sterile. Stand up, please."

He got to his feet. I'm not short but he was taller than me by a full six inches. We'd somehow wound up only a foot or so apart and with him topless, there was suddenly a wall of hard muscle right in front of my face.

I swallowed. "Um. It has to go into a big muscle."

He grinned and flexed his chest, his biceps. Smooth caramel perfection, so close I could feel the warmth coming off his body.

I knew he was playing with me. He'd had antibiotic shots before. "An *even bigger* muscle," I told him. "Turn around and drop the jumpsuit, please."

His grin grew wider. He turned his back, shook the jumpsuit down around his hips, hooked his thumbs into his boxers—

With one quick push, his clothes were in a tangle around his feet and he was naked in front of me. He looked back over his shoulder at me, still grinning, utterly at ease. I cleared my throat and tried to be coldly professional. I'd seen plenty of male patients in the nude before. But...none of them had that broad, powerful back that led down in a perfect vee to a tight waist. None of them had an ass like *that,* the cheeks hard and dimpled, or the thickly muscled thighs. And then, as I leaned around him to pick up the syringe, I caught a glimpse of what was swinging *between* those thighs, and I felt my face go beet-red.

I quickly swabbed his ass cheek with an alcohol swab. "Little prick," I warned.

He grinned. "Now Doc...we both know that ain't true."

We stared into each other's eyes for one, two, three breaths...then I jabbed the needle into his ass cheek and pressed the plunger. "You're done," I said, stepping back.

He started to dress. While I waited for my face to cool, I looked at his tattoos. I could see them better now, and they weren't vines, exactly. They were more like rose stems, covered in thorns. They grew from his upper back and the ink looked older there, soft-edged and faded. It got newer and sharper as the stems encircled his shoulders and biceps. I walked around to the side so that I could see the tattoos on his arms, the more traditional ones. Before, I'd thought the stems connected them together, but now...it looked more like the thorny plant was choking them, swallowing them up until you could barely see them.

Just as he pulled the jumpsuit up over his arms, I saw something I recognized. Without thinking, I grabbed hold of the fabric, stopping him. He looked round at me, first confused, then with a flirty grin.

Then he saw what I was looking at and his face darkened. He jerked the fabric out of my fingers and pulled the jumpsuit up.

But I knew what I'd seen. An eagle, perched protectively atop a globe and anchor. "You're a Marine," I breathed.

He zipped the jumpsuit closed. "Not anymore."

"You saved that kid," I said quietly. "My grandfather was a Marine. He used to say, once a Marine—"

"Yeah, well, not me." Gabriel nodded to the guards that he was ready to go and they stepped forward to collect him.

"Why are you so scared of being a hero?" I blurted.

"You're in the wrong place, Doc," he told me as they led him out. "There ain't no heroes in here."

2

GABRIEL

PUSH.

The steel bar, chipped and scratched with use, rose towards the sky, weight plates clinking. I brought it down to my chest, the muscles shining with sweat, then pushed my feet into the dirt, ground my shoulders into the bench and—

Push.

The wound on my abs hurt every time I moved. It had only been two days since my trip to the infirmary and I knew it was dumb, lifting weights with fresh stitches. But I also knew that the wound wasn't bad, that Olivia's stitching would hold, and that it would be more dangerous to show weakness in a place like this.

Push.

There were two reasons I lifted. One was the old military routine: you always try to stay in some sort of shape, so you're always ready. I didn't have anything to be ready *for,* not for the next seven years and nothing I had planned after that involved anything more strenuous than reaching for my next mojito. But I couldn't seem to shake the habit.

Two: lifting put me in the center of the yard, right where

everyone's paths crossed. It made it easy for people to stroll over and talk. And even in prison, information is power.

I've always been good at talking to people. Understanding their problems. Figuring out a deal. Back in the Marines, when they needed someone to negotiate with one of the local warlords, or convince a village elder to let us use their well, they'd call on me.

In here, I was one of the few people who managed to get along with all of the prison gangs. Some didn't like me talking to the others but all of them needed me, so there was an unspoken agreement that I was like Switzerland, neutral and protected. They needed me because I was the guy who could get anything...for a price.

Anything except drugs. I'd seen enough guys get hooked, after they left the Marines: it didn't feel right. Drugs were controlled by an asshole called Packard, a former bodybuilder who'd used steroids for so many years, he'd lost all his hair and was prone to mood swings. He'd killed two guys since he'd been here. He should have been in solitary, but everyone knew he was giving the warden a cut of the drug money. I stayed away from him...until yesterday, when I'd had to stop his goons killing that scrawny kid.

I paused in my lifting and shifted uneasily on the bench. Saving him had just been good business. That's what I'd told Olivia. That's what I told *myself.* But...

But she'd looked at me like it meant something. Like I was a hero. And just for a second...I'd wanted to be the guy she thought I was.

Olivia. The thought of her unleashed a flood of adrenaline and I heaved the bar up again.

In the days since I met her, I'd been finding excuses to be near the infirmary, in the hope of catching a glimpse of her. I'd taken work details there, volunteered to run errands over there, and when all else failed, I'd just sneaked over there. I'd been bawled out three times by guards and once I'd almost landed a trip to solitary. That had made me question what the hell I was doing, hanging around like some lovesick teenager.

But when I'd finally seen her from down the hall, it had all been suddenly worth it. She'd been telling the warden how she desperately needed more money for drugs, or some of the older prisoners were going to run out of their heart medication. The warden had got right up in her face, snapping that he really didn't give a shit if a few of the old timers croaked. But Olivia had stood her ground, glaring up at him, unafraid, and finally the bastard had cursed and muttered that she could have the money.

I'd stood there leaning on my mop, burning her image into my memory.

My favorite thing about her was her hair. So black that even the few wisps that escaped her tight little bun were striking against her porcelain skin. I could tell just from looking at it that it was silky. I wanted to take one of those little wisps and stroke it gently between thumb and forefinger, savoring the feel of it, and then I'd slide my fingers into the tightly-drawn-back hair at the side of her head, burying them in its softness. There was something about the fact she wore it up: it went with the white coat and that unwavering professionalism. She was so damn buttoned up...it had taken everything I had to resist the urge to pull out her hair clips and let that whole bun just unwind, let all that soft hair spill down her back so I could run my hands through it, gather it up, and use it to gently guide her in for a kiss.

Come to think of it, maybe her lips were my favorite thing about her. Some women have these tight little pursed mouths, but Olivia had these full, wide lips...she didn't seem to wear much makeup and her lips were this beautiful, delicate shade of pink. Sometimes, when I'd smiled at her, they'd twitched once, twice, before she smiled back, as if she wasn't sure if she should or not, and it was adorable. A couple of times, I'd almost forgotten what I was going to say, watching those lips twitch. And I *never* do that. Then I'd glanced up and looked in her eyes and—

Her eyes. Wait, her *eyes* were my favorite thing about her. The irises were a very pale green, almost gray-green. They made me think of a frozen forest, the colors muted by frost but just ready to burst into life as soon as the sun hits it. Goddamn beautiful.

It was her curves, though, that sealed the deal. She had just the sort of body I loved. Full, heavy breasts. Flaring hips and an ass I could grab with both hands. An old-fashioned body. In fact, I knew exactly what she reminded me of. A few years before the gold heist, I'd stolen a couple of Pre-Raphaelite oil paintings from a castle in Switzerland. If you put Olivia in a filmy dress and let all that gorgeous hair hang loose down her back, she'd look exactly like one of the women in those paintings. And that milky, porcelain skin made me think about what she'd look like naked. Already I was imagining soft, pale breasts, the nipples that same delicate shade of pink as her lips... Yeah, her curves were definitely my favorite thing about her.

I guess I had a lot of favorite things about her.

It wasn't just the physical stuff, either. She was so...*good*. You could tell she genuinely cared about her patients, even though we were a bunch of animals. She'd even taken the time to suture my wound so it wouldn't scar: there were doctors on the *outside* who wouldn't have been that careful. That goodness drew me in like nothing I'd ever experienced.

There was something else, too. She blushed a lot—and I loved making her blush—but there was something in the way she'd looked at me, in the way her breathing had quickened, when we got close. Behind all that buttoned-down professionalism and flushed cheeks, there was something raw and wild waiting to get out. A sexuality that would blow any man's mind...it just needed to be unleashed.

I wanted to be the one to unleash it. When I did, I'd start making my way down the long, long list of filthy things I wanted to do to her and with her. As I grunted and pushed at the barbell, muscles burning, I thought about Olivia up against the wall of the infirmary, white coat and blouse hanging open, my hands cupping her breasts as I pounded between her thighs. Or Olivia on her back on my bunk, legs wrapped around me as I fucked her slow and deep. Or— especially easy to imagine, as I lay on the bench—Olivia riding me, grinding down onto me as I licked and sucked at her nipples.

What was weird was, there was another feeling running under that attraction. When I thought about how she'd reacted, each time I told her she was pretty, the way she'd ducked her head and hunched her shoulders...I got mad. This woman had been overlooked by the idiots on the outside, made to feel like nothing just because she didn't fit some super-skinny ideal. I wanted to find those men and beat seven shades of hell out of them.

I wanted to fuck her. But I wanted to protect her, too.

I frowned and pushed the bar up to the sky again. What the hell was someone like Olivia doing in this hellhole, anyway? She was too innocent, too *soft*, for a place like this. Silky, soft hair, those pale, soft curves, even her voice was soft and calming. Something must have happened, for her to wind up here. I couldn't understand why she'd stay, or how she'd managed to tough it out.

The moment I'd stepped out of the infirmary, I'd started asking around, finding out everything I could about her. She'd only been here a few months, but already the inmates all loved her. I'd heard lots of stories about how gentle she was, when she patched guys up, or how she'd helped guys through withdrawal as they tried to get clean. And then there were the guys who wouldn't say *why* they'd seen the doc, only that they had and that she'd been good to them. They wouldn't look me in the eye, and I knew what they were talking about: some predator had cornered them. Olivia had helped them through that, helped them feel like survivors, not victims, and that spoke volumes about her.

She was an angel, right in the middle of hell. A wholesome reminder of the world I used to be a part of. And I couldn't stop thinking about her.

Boots shuffled in the dirt near my head and a shadow fell across me. I knew from the slow, plodding footsteps that it was Bruno, one of the guards.

Here's the thing about prison. The biggest problem isn't the years or the months or even the weeks. It's the seconds. The sound of a wristwatch will drive a man crazy in here, every *tick* another second of the outside world that you're missing. That *tick-tick-tick* is your son's birthday, your daughter's graduation, the last breath of the parent you never squared things with. There's a reason they call it *doing time*.

There are two rules to staying sane.

One: never have anyone you give a shit about.

Two: have something that makes doing the time worthwhile.

They wanted to give me life but they couldn't definitively prove I was the mastermind behind the theft, only that I was heavily involved, so they had to settle for twenty-five years. They seized almost all my assets and I blew every cent I had left on a top lawyer, leaving me broke. But it was worth it: given that no one was hurt during the robbery, the lawyer managed to get my sentence down to ten years, no parole. So far, I'd served three. And the gold I stole?

They never found it. It's sitting there waiting for me. Waiting for the day I get out.

Four hundred million dollars divided by ten years works out to forty million dollars per year, or over three million dollars per month, or—and this was my favorite—seventy-six dollars and ten cents *per minute.* I was making more money than most CEOs.

All I had to do was find ways to pass the time and there are always plenty of those. Big, complicated organizations pride themselves on having rules that lock everything down tight. But there are always gaps in security, opportunities to be taken. It was true in the Marines and it's true in jail. You just have to know where to look.

"How'd it go last night?" I asked Bruno without turning around.

Bruno's six-foot-five and for the last two years he's been trying to work up the courage to ask out this little five-foot-nothing waitress at the coffee shop he stops at after his shift. "I told her that her eyes were nice," said Bruno uncertainly.

"'Nice?'" I put the barbell down. "No, no, it was *like stars,* Bruno. Like stars that light up the whole room!"

"I feel dumb," said Bruno. "I can't say it how you say it."

"Well, that's something we can work on, big guy." For the next half hour, as I lay there lifting weights and the sun beat down on us, I coached Bruno on sweet talk. And this is why Bruno makes sure I get the sought-after work details, like painting the ceiling in the air-conditioned admin office, and not working in the laundry where the temperature pushes one-twenty. Arrangements like this, with guards and gangs and individuals, are how I got a TV in my cell and the pick of the best food at mealtimes. All the little perks that make prison bearable. You need them when you're looking at ten years and every day's the same.

A guard's voice rang out from across the yard. "Kain! Visitor!"

My brows knitted. I slid out from under the barbell and slowly sat up, sweat rolling down my chest.

I hadn't had a single visitor since I'd been in here. Who the hell would come to visit *me?*

~

A few moments later, I sauntered into the blessed cool of the air-conditioned visitor's area. A guard pointed me to booth number five and I dropped into the chair, still mopping sweat from my face. Then I frowned at the guy sitting on the other side of the Plexiglass. He wore a suit and I'm enough of a connoisseur to know that this one cost a lot. But even though it was tailored, it didn't look quite right on him. There was a brooding intensity about him: I couldn't imagine him sitting in meetings. And there was something unusual about his look. The heavy eyebrows and strong jawline put me in mind of somewhere old and mist-covered: warriors swinging swords and carrying off maidens. But it wasn't Scandinavia: his hair was black, not blond. And Germany didn't feel right, either. He was from somewhere else, somewhere more unusual. I had a feeling I'd seen his face before.

The man picked up the phone on his side of the divider and I did the same. "Keeping fit, I see," he said, nodding at the towel.

American, but there was no mistaking the accent that ran underneath. Irish. *Northern* Irish. And suddenly, I knew where I'd seen him: on TV. Standing next to the most powerful man in the world.

It's very rare that I'm taken by surprise, but this was one of those times. "You're Kian O'Harra," I said slowly.

He nodded, watching me closely.

Some years back, someone tried to kill the President's daughter, Emily Matthews. And it turned out that their plans went a lot further than that. The guy who'd saved her—who'd saved the whole country, according to some—was her Secret Service bodyguard and lover. The man who was sitting in front of me right now.

I wondered if he was still seeing her. I hadn't bothered to keep up with the news in here.

I came right out with it. "What the hell do you want with *me?!*"

Kian put his elbows on the table and leaned forward. "I'm putting together a team. For when the government has a problem and can't do anything officially. Or when someone's in trouble and the normal agencies can't help, or won't help. A mix of specialists, all with particular skills." His eyes gleamed and his hand tightened on the phone. "I've got a former Marine sniper who spent six years living in the wilderness: best shot I've ever seen. An Army Ranger turned bounty hunter who can take anyone down in close combat. There's this former SAS guy: put him behind the wheel of a car and no one, *no one* is going to be able to catch us. And then there's my brother... he's never served but he's got his own special skill set."

"A jarhead, a ground-pounder, a Brit, a civilian...that'll never work."

"Oh, it'll work. The pieces are all there, I just had to find the right guy to make them into a team."

"You're not leading them yourself?"

Kian grimaced as if that was a sore point. "My face is too well known. I'll be running things from behind a desk. I've got someone special to lead them in the field. He's just what they need."

I leaned back in my chair. "What've I got to do with any of this?" I tried to sound nonchalant but I could feel my heart speed up. Because really, there was only one reason for him to be telling me all this.

Kian looked me right in the eye. "I want you on the team."

And there it was. There was a moment of disbelief and then it hit me, the feeling I'd kept locked away for so long, I'd convinced myself it was gone but it suddenly tugged like cloth snapping taut in the wind: the thought of serving again, of being a part of something again, of having guys I'd die for and who'd die for me.

Then I came to my senses. I wasn't that guy anymore.

"You got the wrong man," I muttered. "I'm a thief."

"You're *the* thief," Kian corrected softly. "The Bank of Indonesia. The National Gallery in London. The Vatican Museums in Rome. You know how to get in and out of places. You see angles no one else would see. You lie, you cheat, you con. The sort of people we'll be up against don't fight fair. I need someone on the team who doesn't play by the rules. And I need your connections, your contacts. Our jobs will be off the books: we won't have the government to back us up. I need someone who knows who can get us guns in Sao Paulo, who can sneak us across the border into China. I need someone who knows every dirty cop in Paris, every Russian mafia boss in New York." He leaned back in his chair. "That's *you*."

It *was* me. I had to glance away so he didn't see the pride in my eyes. "In case you hadn't noticed," I told him, "I'm a little indisposed." I gestured at my orange jumpsuit, at the concrete walls around us.

He looked me right in the eye again. He was good at that: there was something about him that made you want to trust him, and I don't trust anybody. "The government has authorized your release into my custody, conditional on you joining the team for ten years. He leaned forward and stabbed at the tabletop with his finger. "You can be out *today*. You can be *free*."

The magic word. It didn't matter how cushy my cell was, prison is prison. I could be *out*.

But it would mean ten years with Kian's team. Three years longer than I had left to serve. I couldn't just take the deal and then disappear after a few weeks: they'd never stop hunting me and I didn't want to spend the rest of my life looking over my shoulder. I'd have to do my time with the team and *then* go retrieve the gold and live the high life. Ten years of following orders again.

Of having teammates again. Of fighting for something again. I felt that tug, stronger than before.

Then I crushed it. That wasn't me, not anymore. I shook my head.

"It's a second chance," said Kian urgently. "That's more than most—"

"Not interested," I told him. And I went to hang up the phone.

Kian jerked his tie loose and started unbuttoning his shirt. When the buttons wouldn't cooperate, he growled in frustration and ripped them free, then awkwardly peeled his suit jacket and shirt back to reveal his shoulder. I stared at the eagle, globe and anchor tattoo. I hadn't realized he was a Marine, before he was in the Secret Service.

"This means something," he snapped. "It used to mean something to you, too. I've seen your file. You were a good man. You cared about—"

"I told you, you got the wrong guy." I stood up. "I'm not a soldier anymore. And the only person I care about is myself."

I hung up the phone and stalked out of the room without looking back.

3

OLIVIA

I CHECKED THE CLOCK ON THE WALL AGAIN. HIS WOUND CHECK appointment was for nine am and it was two minutes after. Any minute now, the door buzzer would buzz. Any minute.

This is crazy. He was a prisoner. A criminal. My *patient.* But this morning, I'd spent twenty minutes deciding which blouse to wear.

It had been a busy week. As well as all the routine check-ups and medication reviews, we'd had a guard who'd passed out from heatstroke. Then an inmate had tried to get himself a hospital visit by drinking a bottle of White-out stolen from the admin office. Finally, someone had been brewing prison hooch: I'd had three inmates with serious alcohol poisoning and the guards were now tearing the prison apart trying to find the still before someone went blind.

And yet whenever things had quietened down for a moment, my mind slid straight back to Gabriel Kain. To those glittering, hazel eyes that felt like they knew my every secret. To that rich, warm growl of a voice that made every syllable vibrate through my body. It wasn't just thinking about him, either. I kept seeing him. Sometimes it was in the admin area, when I went out there to sign for a delivery or talk to one of the guards. Gabriel seemed to be there more than any inmate had a right to be. Sometimes it was around the prison, when I got called out because someone was too ill to safely move. And sometimes...

Sometimes, I'd go to the window in the back room of the infirmary, the one that looks out over the yard, and I'd watch him lifting weights, his muscles pumping in slow rhythm, his bare chest gleaming with sweat.

Get a hold of yourself! But I couldn't forget him. He'd invaded my mind and, at night, he ruled my dreams. I woke each morning, panties damp, still feeling his hands on my breasts, his hips between my thighs.

I had to know more about him. I'd gotten in contact with the Marine Corps to request his file, but they kept bouncing my request around different departments and I wasn't sure they were ever going to get back to me.

I told myself that I'd built him up too much in my mind, after that first meeting. He'd become a fantasy, a folk legend. *When I see him again, it'll be a letdown.*

The door buzzer buzzed. I whirled around, startled, and my arm swept a stack of papers off my desk. They drifted down like snow, littering half the room. *Shit!* I crouch-ran in a zigzag to the door, grabbing papers as I went. "Yep?" I asked, breathless.

"Gabriel Kain for his wound check."

I swallowed. Self-consciously smoothed my hair. I pressed the door release, the guard pushed open the door and—

It wasn't a letdown.

Gabriel strolled in from the hallway and he didn't look like a prisoner being transported by a guard. He looked like a rock star arriving at a gig, accompanied by his security. He was utterly relaxed, coolly appraising everything around him. God, the man had *presence.* You couldn't not look at him and when he walked into a room, the room was suddenly full.

Then he turned and looked at me and—

Those beautiful, hazel eyes lit up. I felt that thing in my chest lift and swell again, rising skyward. Reality caught up and tried to tug it back down to earth but it bobbed out of reach. He was looking at me like I was the best thing he'd ever seen.

Then he did something he hadn't done before. He looked away for a second and drew a breath, almost as if he was trying to control himself. But this was Gabriel: I couldn't imagine him ever being out of control.

He looked at me a second time and this time it was different. This time it was smoldering and hypnotic. I felt like I was being dragged towards him: it took everything I had just to stay in the same spot. The look he was giving me flared hotter and hotter, until it felt like my clothes were being burned right off my body.

"Everything okay, Doc?" asked the guard.

My head jerked around and I had to blink a few times before I remembered how to speak. "Yes. *Yes!* Everything's fine."

"You want me to stay?" he asked.

The prisoners don't get much in the way of privacy or dignity, I figure the least I can do is let them discuss their medical problems with me without a guard listening in. So I don't ask for a guard to be present unless the prisoner's known to be dangerous. And Gabriel wasn't.

At least, not dangerous in *that* way. The thought of being alone with him made my stomach flip-flop.

"No, thank you," I told the guard. "We'll be fine."

The guard nodded. "Regs say the door stays open. And I gotta cuff him." He went to cuff Gabriel's hands.

"I'll need to examine his abdomen," I told him.

The guard waited while Gabriel shrugged his jumpsuit down to his waist, then stripped off his white tank top. Then Gabriel obediently held his hands out in front of him and the guard cuffed them. Gabriel's face was a careful mask: he looked nonchalant, almost bored. And this whole time, he still hadn't spoken. It was as if he was waiting for us to be private and that idea made me go heady. *God, what's happening to me? This isn't a good idea. Tell the guard you've changed your mind—*

Too late. The guard ambled out into the hallway to chat with the other guards.

And we were alone.

The room felt instantly different. I was aware of every little noise: the quick little breaths I was taking; the slower, calmer sound of Gabriel's breathing; the rattle of the handcuff chain as he adjusted his position. My face flushed and I looked everywhere but at him. Then, finally, my eyes flicked up and I was looking right into those incredible eyes. He'd dropped the nonchalance and the raw need in his gaze took my breath away. He looked like a wolf again, single-minded and hungry. Hungry for *me*. And at the same time, there was a...*flutter*. An urgency, a hint of nervous energy that didn't fit with his cocky confidence.

Then he glanced down at his naked chest and grinned. "So, Doc, when do I get to see *you* naked?"

My face flushed. I swallowed and it turned into a hot throb that went right down my body, leaving every inch of my skin super-sensitive. I didn't trust my voice so I simply pointed him towards an exam area. I slid the curtains closed behind us and then we were alone *and* private.

I should have been nervous. He was a male prisoner, he was bigger than me...that's why the guard had left the door open, so he could hear if I yelled for help. But there was something about Gabriel: an aura. Sure, he was a thief, a trickster, a master manipulator. You couldn't *trust* him. But I knew he'd never hurt me. I couldn't explain it, but I was sure.

Gabriel sat down on the gurney, swung his legs up and stretched out. He gave me another of those wolfish smiles and I suddenly realized I was smiling back at him. *Have I been doing that every time?* I quickly forced my face straight. His smile turned into a smirk.

I bent over him to examine his wound.

"Did you always want to be a doctor?" he asked.

Be professional. Don't flirt. But answering a question was okay, right? "Yes," I told him carefully. "My father's a doctor." I gently started cutting away the dressing. "What about you?"

"What about me, *what?*"

"How did you..." I gestured at his tattoos, his prison jumpsuit: his life.

"How did I become a thief?" I was looking at his wound but I could hear the grin in his voice. "You want the heart-rending tale of how my life went astray?"

I finally looked up at him. And nodded.

"Aw, hell, Doc, my life didn't go astray. I've *always* been bad." He pinned me with those amazing eyes, God, the raw intelligence there, the sense that his brain was going a million miles an hour. "When I was seven, I stole flowers from the buckets outside florists, took them downtown and sold them to commuters to take home to their wives. In middle school, I paid the smart kids for their homework and sold it at a profit to the others. In high school, I stole the test answers every year until the final test, and I only stopped then because I was too busy sleeping with my teachers." He chuckled, a gloriously warm sound that I felt deep in my chest. "My folks named me after an angel. They should have picked someone from the other side."

He gazed at me and I felt myself falling into those amazing eyes. "Did I grow up poor? Sure. But so did everyone in my neighborhood. My dad was a barber: we did okay, compared to a lot of folk. I wasn't bad because we were poor, I was bad because it was *fun.*"

I stared at him. He was the complete opposite of me. I slavishly followed the rules; he took pride in ignoring them. I'd always wanted to help others; he only helped himself.

Or at least, that's what he was determined to make everyone believe.

"And then you joined the Marines," I said quietly.

He glanced down at the Marine Corps tattoo on his arm, the one that was almost obscured by the thorny plant surrounding it. Then he looked away and shrugged, as if it was no big deal. But the atmosphere changed: I'd ventured into something forbidden and suddenly, he was closed and silent. Our easy banter was gone and I wasn't ready for how much that hurt.

Checking his wound only took a few moments. There was no sign of infection and it was healing up nicely. I cleaned it and put on a fresh dressing and then, technically, we were done: I could call for the guard to take him back to his cell. But I couldn't leave things like that.

"You've got a lot of scars," I said, trying to extend an olive branch.

He looked down at himself and I saw a hint of his usual smirk, but he didn't speak.

I touched an unusual, triangular scar on his neck. "What happened here?"

His lips slowly twisted into one of those wonderful grins and a huge rush of warmth lit up my core. He was back. "That's from when I got caught by some Russian mobsters in Chicago. I'd been offloading some emeralds on their turf and they thought they deserved a cut. They tied me to a chair and did the whole *heat up a knife on the stove* thing. But we worked out a deal." He traced the scar thoughtfully with his fingertip. "Eventually."

"What about this?" I nodded at a small scar, almost hidden by his hairline near his left ear, but he just frowned, not sure where I was looking. "Here," I clarified, and without thinking, I touched it. Something like an electric shock ran up my arm and I swallowed.

"That's from when an arms dealer in Kazakhstan broke a bottle over my head."

"Looks like you got it sewn up," I mumbled thoughtfully. "The stitches are a little, um..."

"Crooked?" He grinned. "I did it myself, in the mirror."

I blinked. "In that case, you did a very good job." He stitched *himself* up? It brought home what a lonely life it must be, being a thief.

He twisted around and slid off the gurney, then turned his back to me and used his cuffed hands to push his jumpsuit and boxers down over his ass. High on the outer side of his left thigh I saw—

"Teeth marks?" I asked.

He nodded. "Breaking into a museum in Italy. I roped down from a skylight and...well, things went wrong. The alarms go off, the guards run in, and the guy on the roof who's meant to be pulling me up gets the ropes tangled. Then this big beast of a dog bounds up and sinks his teeth into my leg. I'm swinging back and forth, hollerin' to be pulled up, and I swear the dog thought it was a game."

I noticed something else: a roughly circular wound right in the center of one perfect ass cheek. It looked almost like a puncture wound. "What's this?" I touched it. God, they were so *firm*. I went a little heady.

"*Oh...*" His lips twitched into a smile I hadn't seen before: a darkly secret one, as if he was remembering something intimate. That smile hit me like a shot of eighty-proof rum, sending heat flashing to my face and rippling down through my body. I wanted to know. And I felt a tiny, irrational stab of jealousy.

"That," he told me, "is from the wife of a French smuggler. She didn't tell me she was married." He looked thoughtful. "Their relationship was...complicated."

"What did she *do* to you?!"

He turned to face me, his jumpsuit still pushed down to his upper thighs. I glimpsed the washboard ridges of his abs, then the deep diagonal line of his Adonis belt that led my eyes down further. Curling dark hair and—

I tore my eyes away and looked up into his face, my mind full of what I'd just seen. *Thick. So thick. And OMG long.*

He gazed back at me, proud and teasing, enjoying my embarrassment. Then he finally hitched his jumpsuit up to his waist. "I was fucking her, on a four-poster bed. And she was cursing away in French and scratching at my back and she had her legs up in the air, kicked out wide." He was still staring right into my eyes, his own eyes like molten sapphires. "And then she came—pretty loudly, as I recall —and she dug her heels hard into my ass."

I swallowed and tried to keep my voice level. "That doesn't sound so bad."

"She was wearing stilettos."

I winced.

Gabriel started to chuckle, then full-on laugh: a big, honest laugh that I really liked. "She's screaming in joy, I'm screaming in pain... then her husband runs in, sees me on his wife, grabs this antique sword off the wall and comes at me with it. He's yelling in French, *she's* yelling in French, I'm running around naked trying to keep away from him..."

I clamped my hand over my mouth. "Oh my *God!* What happened?"

Gabriel gave a wry grin and shook his head. "She kisses her husband and makes a big speech about how he's the only man for her, he kisses her, they fall onto the bed and...well, I became surplus to requirements. Like I said, their relationship was complicated. I grabbed my clothes and made myself scarce. They came downstairs a half hour later with their arms around each other and I did the deal I came there to do."

I slowly shook my head, amazed. My face had flushed and my groin had tightened, imagining him having sex. I was self-consciously aware of how inexperienced I was, compared to him. I'd had boyfriends, but not many: the combination of three big, overprotective brothers and my awkwardness about my body meant I hadn't dated much in high school. Then at college and med school, I'd buried myself in my studies, unable to switch off, while everyone else was hooking up. I was inexperienced in *life,* too, compared to him. He'd had adventures in Kazakhstan, Italy, New York... I'd barely ever left Arizona. We were so utterly different: he didn't care about the rules, whereas I diligently obeyed every regulation, checked every box...

And look where that got me. Anger and shame made a hard knot in my stomach. The job I loved had been ripped away from me and I was stuck here, barely able to make a difference.

Most of the time, I don't let what happened at the hospital get to me. I can't, or I won't be able to function. And however much I hate the prison, I have a job to do. But right then, it *did* get to me. I missed my old life. I missed the ER, I missed all my friends, I missed being able to actually help people...

All the stuff I kept crushed down inside me rose up. I felt my eyes go hot and quickly looked away.

"What's wrong?" His voice had changed completely. He wasn't teasing anymore. "What happened?"

I shook my head and blinked furiously, willing my eyes to stay dry. I needed to stay in control, be professional. But I could feel the memories threatening to break free—

With one stride, he closed the distance between us. Then his cuffed hands came down over my head so that his arms were around me. He gently pulled me to him, his joined hands snuggling into the small of my back, and suddenly I was full-length against him in a hug.

"What—What are you doing?!" I said into his chest.

"Making you feel better," he told me. His cuffed hands ran lightly up and down my back. And—

And it *did* feel better. It wasn't sexual, despite this being Gabriel, despite the fact my cheek was pressed to his bare chest, despite the fact that the only thing stopping his jumpsuit falling all the way to the floor was the press of our bodies. He wasn't being cocky or teasing. The embrace was warm and kind, like he...*cared.* The memories slowly settled back down into the darkness and my eyes cooled. Just for a second, I allowed myself to relax against him and a feeling swept over me, so strong it took my breath away. I felt so safe, so protected...I never wanted it to end.

Then I came to my senses. I was pressed up against a prisoner, against one of my *patients.* I shook my head and ducked out of his arms, and he reluctantly lifted them so I could escape.

I turned from him and walked away. "You're done," I told him. "I'll get you back in for another wound check in a week. I'll get the guard."

"Olivia!" His voice was low, so as not to be heard by the guard, but there was an urgency to it that made my chest ache.

I kept walking.

Behind me, I heard the jangle of the handcuff chain as he reached for me, then the metal clink as the chain snapped taut: I heard him curse under his breath and his footsteps as he hurried after me. "Olivia!" he hissed.

The open door to the hallway was down at the far end of the infirmary and I kept going, focused entirely on it. I'd get the guard, Gabriel would return to his cell and life would go back to normal.

Gabriel muttered something behind me and then there was a strange noise, a metal scratching, and his footsteps slowed, as if he was preoccupied with something. A click. Then his footsteps resumed.

I reached the doorway. I could hear the guard talking to other guards in the hallway just outside. I opened my mouth to call for him...

A hand landed on my shoulder and spun me quickly around. Gabriel's thumb lightly pressed against my lips, warning me to be silent. That's when I registered the handcuffs, open and dangling from one finger of his other hand. I looked up into his face. He had something between his lips: a twisted paperclip. He turned his head and spat it out, and there was a metallic clatter as it landed in the trash can.

He followed my eyes to the handcuffs, then spun them nonchalantly around his finger in a shining circle. He leaned down and put his lips to my ear. "How do you think I escaped from the other places?"

He held out his hand. "Trust me," he mouthed. *Trust him*: a thief, a con man, a master deceiver...

I wasn't worried about what he might do. I was worried about what I might do. Wide-eyed, I looked over my shoulder at the door...

And then I took his hand. He closed his fingers around mine, my hand almost disappearing in his, and his warm grip felt so good I wanted to weep. He led me gently back down the room and into the curtained-off exam area.

"Couldn't leave it like that," he told me. "Couldn't not see you for a week, knowing you were upset."

I felt like I was on a cliff edge, pinwheeling my arms as I teetered on the brink. Behind me was the nice, safe world I'd always known, the one with rules and limits. The one that had always felt so right. In front of me was a yawning dark chasm filled with nothing but danger. I'd already lost the job I loved. This place was my last chance, literally the only place that would take me. If anything went wrong here, I'd never treat another patient again. It should have been simple.

But when I looked up into those molten hazel eyes, all I wanted to do was hurl myself forward and fall.

"Why?!" I asked helplessly. Why was he so concerned about me? He barely knew me, we'd met twice—

He let go of my hand and his hands lifted to my shoulders. Just before they touched, he hesitated, his fingertips hovering a fraction of an inch away from my white coat, as if trying to slow himself, as if he was worried that if he didn't, he might hold me too tight. Then his hands pressed against me, the heat of him throbbing through my clothes as if they weren't even there.

He gazed into my eyes and the lust I saw there made me draw in a shuddering breath, my nipples peaking and hardening, my groin tightening. But there was something else in his eyes, too. An urgency, almost desperation. His fingers tensed on the backs of my shoulders once, twice. His lips parted to say something—

"Doc?" The guard's voice...and it wasn't coming from out in the hallway, it was inside the infirmary. "You about done? We're outta time, I gotta get Kain back to his cell."

His footsteps approached, moving fast. All the other exam areas had their curtains pushed back: he could see we were in here and he was heading right for us. That's when I remembered that Gabriel's cuffs were off. I looked up at him in horror. He reacted quickly, getting a cuff around one wrist. But handcuffs aren't designed to be put on by the person wearing them and when he tried to fit the second cuff, it slipped off his wrist.

There wasn't enough time and when the guard came in and saw them half off, Gabriel was headed to solitary, or for more years on his sentence.

The curtains opened...

I jumped in front of Gabriel, shielding his hands with my body.

The guard looked at us: at my flushed face, at Gabriel standing behind me. It certainly didn't look like I was examining him. "Everything okay here?" he asked suspiciously.

I froze for a second. I had to report Gabriel *now*. If I didn't speak up and the guard saw his cuffs off, I'd be in trouble too. I opened my mouth to speak—

"Fine," I heard myself say. "Everything's fine. We just finished."

The guard looked from me to Gabriel and then back to me. Like Louis, he'd worked here a long time. He'd had years to hone the art of sniffing out prisoners' lies and staring them down until they confessed. Meanwhile, I was a rank amateur at lying. *What the hell am I doing?* Every cell in my law-abiding body was telling me to tell the truth. I could say that Gabriel had told me to lie, that I was scared of him...

But then Gabriel would be in even more trouble. I lifted my chin and stared resolutely back at the guard.

The guard frowned. He knew something was up, but I was staff, not a prisoner, and he couldn't prove anything. "C'mon, then, Kain, let's go."

Gabriel didn't move. And I realized the problem: even hidden behind me, he hadn't been able to get the handcuffs on again. The room was dead quiet and the guard would hear the metal rasp as the cuffs ratcheted closed.

I took a deep breath and then bent over, coughing as loudly as I could. I coughed so hard my throat hurt, so hard that tears came to my eyes. The guard stepped forward, concerned, but I waved him back: *I'm fine, I'll be okay in a second.* I didn't dare stop because I didn't know if Gabriel had fixed the cuffs yet: was I making enough noise? What if the guard—

Gabriel stepped out from behind me and came around to the front. "You okay, Doc?"

Through watering eyes, I saw that his hands were neatly cuffed in front of him. I straightened up, my chest aching. "Yeah," I croaked, wiping my lips. "Yes, thank you."

The guard gave me one last suspicious look and then he led Gabriel away. Just as they left, Gabriel looked back over his shoulder at me. He looked surprised, impressed...and he gave me a little nod of gratitude. Then they were gone.

I tottered over to the wall and leaned there, cold sweat trickling down my spine. We'd so nearly gotten caught. *Oh my God.* I'd have been fired. Gabriel would have had his sentence extended.

That must never happen again. The safest thing would be for us to stay far, far apart. Part of me was already making plans to get Alicia to handle all of Gabriel's visits from now on, or at the very least to be present whenever he was, so that there was no temptation.

But another part of me was remembering his hands on my shoulders and wondering what he'd been about to say.

∾

The next morning, as I walked into the infirmary, sane, logical Olivia was back in control. This thing with Gabriel Kain was dangerous for both of us and it was *over*. I was going to forget all about him and—

There was a big manila envelope waiting for me in my mail tray. The address in the corner said it was from the United States Marine Corps Records Office.

I eyed that envelope all day, as I ran around doing my work. When my shift ended in the evening, I sat at my desk, debating. I could just toss the envelope in the trash. But I had to know.

I slid out the file. It was *thick,* stuffed with so many extra pages that the binding was stretched. I made a cup of coffee, opened the file, and started to read.

The top sheet was his basic information. Gabriel Elias Kain. Joined the Marine Corps at eighteen: there was a photo of him, fresh-faced and buzzcut, but still with that cocky, scheming intelligence glittering in his eyes. Then it got into his career and...

I lost myself reading for a full hour. He'd veered wildly between being a highly decorated Marine and almost being kicked out of the Corps. On one page, he'd be praised for coming up with some clever plan to infiltrate a village held by insurgents. On the next, he'd be reprimanded for smuggling thirteen cases of beer into a forward operating base. Just as he was about to be promoted, he'd be caught in bed with the General's daughter. But just as he was about to be court martialed over some mysteriously missing supplies, he was commended for negotiating peace with a local warlord. The Corps wasn't sure if it loved him or hated him. They only knew they needed him.

He'd received a Purple Heart after being injured on the battlefield and two Silver Stars for volunteering for rescue missions to get back Marines trapped behind enemy lines. I'd been right: the man was a hero.

Later in his career, he'd joined the Marine Raiders and from then onwards, the rest of his file gradually became more and more redacted, until each page was just a mass of thick black lines with only the occasional word left teasingly intact. Right up until the last few pages.

The penultimate page informed me that Gabriel Kain was dishonorably discharged from the Marine Corps seven years ago. That was it: that was what had happened to knock him from his path in the Marine Corps—disreputable and always with some scheme, but an outstanding soldier—to the path of a professional thief, one who'd eventually gotten caught and wound up here. I turned the page, my heart in my mouth—

It was redacted. *Completely* redacted. They hadn't even blacked out individual lines: the entire page apart from the first line was covered in a huge black block. All I could see was that it happened in Syria.

He was so valuable to the Marines, they'd been willing to forgive all of his capers and side-hustles. For them to dishonorably discharge him, he must have done something much, much worse. Had I been completely wrong about him?

I needed to know. But Gabriel's next wound check wasn't for a week, and I didn't have an excuse to see him before then.

I looked around. It was after eleven and the only light in the infirmary was my desk lamp. We'd had *lights out*: the cell blocks were in darkness.

I could sneak over there. The thought just slid into my mind and I sat up straight, shocked. I had a pass key that would get me into Gabriel's cell block, but it was strictly forbidden for me to wander the prison on my own. If I was caught, I'd be in serious trouble.

But I couldn't get the idea out of my head.

It's only a week. Don't be an idiot!

What I needed to do was get in my car and go home to bed. *Right now.* I stood up. Grabbed my purse. Hurried down the hallway to the junction and turned right, towards the parking lot...

My steps slowed. Stopped. I cursed under my breath. *What the hell has that man done to me?!*

I turned around and hurried towards the cell blocks.

~

I was used to walking the hallways as staff, as one of the ones setting the rules. Now, scurrying between the shadows, knowing that if even one guard saw me, I'd lose my job, it felt very different.

I slipped into Gabriel's cell block and eased the heavy door shut behind me. Immediately, the heat pressed in around me and I shook my head in dismay. *How do they sleep, when it's like this?!* Tomorrow, I'd beg the warden again for air conditioning in the cell blocks.

The only light came from the moon, shining in through a skylight, and I had to wait a few minutes for my eyes to adjust. All around me, I could hear men snoring and mumbling in their sleep. My stomach knotted. If one of them woke and saw me, and started a commotion...

I crept along the metal walkway, just feet away from the sleeping men, glad that at least I wore sneakers for work and wasn't trying to do this in heels. Then up the metal stairs to the next level, wincing at every creak. 304, 305...*there*. 306. Gabriel's cell.

It was utterly dark, inside: I couldn't see anything. "Gabriel," I whispered, as quietly as I could. Nothing happened. I tried again, a little louder. "Gabriel?"

I thought I saw a twitch, in the darkness. But then, nothing. I swallowed. "*Gabriel!*"

A rustle of sheets. I narrowed my eyes, trying to see through the blackness. Then suddenly, he was looming up in front of me, barely a foot from my face. "*Olivia?!*"

He'd stripped down to his boxers to beat the heat. The moonlight turned his caramel skin silver, the hard curves of his muscles gleaming. He gripped the bars and pressed his face between two of them, getting as close as possible so he could whisper to me. "What are you *doing?*" His eyes darted left and right, checking for guards.

"I had to see you," I told him, gripping the bars as well. "Before next week."

I watched the emotions play across his face. First, worry: he was so cocky, when he was the one taking the risk, but he didn't want *me* getting caught. Then anger at himself: he scowled at the floor for a moment, maybe regretting ever starting this. And then, finally, he looked into my eyes...and the anger was melted away by a deep, burning need. He slid his hands up the bars and his fingers wrapped around mine. I swallowed, going weak at his touch.

"What happened in Syria?" I whispered.

His whole body slumped: for a moment, it felt like the only thing keeping him upright were our joined hands. He hung his head and my chest ached. The last thing I wanted to do was cause him pain.

He lifted his head and looked at me. "Why?"

For a long time, I couldn't find the words. Then: "Because I need to know if I'm right about you."

He glared. Looked away. His hands loosened on mine and, for a moment, I was sure he was going to pull away and go back to his bunk. He looked back at me, his eyes glittering in the darkness, *furious* with himself. It was like he was trying to work up the anger to go. I gazed right back at him, willing him to stay.

At last he sighed and his expression softened. His fingers curled around mine again and squeezed tight. I felt something lift inside me, rising so high I couldn't speak. Gabriel leaned forward and rested his forehead against the bars, his eyes closed. And in a whisper, harsh with pain, he told me what happened.

"Syria was a mess: lots of different factions fighting. We've got troops there, trying to sort things out and help out the groups we support. Problem is, the Russians are doing the same, with the groups *they* support, and we both have troops and ships there, all within a few miles of each other."

"We're on patrol off the coast, in a little inflatable boat called an RIB, and I see something in the distance. It's a boat—just a raft, really —full of refugees, trying to get across the bay to flee the fighting. Except the sea's rougher than they planned for and the raft's breaking up. They're going under." He sucked in his breath. "So I get on the radio and ask for permission to go get them. But they say *no*, they're in waters controlled by the Russians, the Russians will have to get them: they've got a destroyer nearby."

"So we wait, and watch, but either the message doesn't get through to the Russian captain or he doesn't react to it. We can see the destroyer and it doesn't move. And meanwhile this raft's going down fast. I'm looking at it through binoculars and I can see it's a family on board. Kids. I get on the radio, tell them we *have* to go get these people. But the brass are terrified that something's going to happen with the Russians that'll lead to World War III. So they tell me *no*, under *no circumstances* are we allowed to enter Russian waters. But by now there are people in the water. Kids of five or six. So..."

"You went in anyway," I breathed.

He lifted his head from the bars and looked at me. "As soon as we cross that line on the map, all hell breaks loose. The destroyer turns and heads for *us* and starts firing warning shots. A Russian helicopter starts buzzing us. And meanwhile, we're trying to get to the people in the water." He shook his head. "To this day, I don't know if that Russian captain didn't know what was going on, or if he was using the whole thing to score political points with Moscow. But the Russians claimed we'd knowingly entered their territory, that it was an act of war, etcetera, etcetera. We were surrounded by Russian boats and had to let ourselves be taken. We spent a full day as 'guests' of the

Russians before Washington managed to smooth things over and get us released."

"And the refugees?" I asked.

"We saved them," he said with pride. "Every one of them."

I stared at him. I'd been worried that he'd committed some huge crime. "*That's* why they dishonorably discharged you?" I asked, aghast. "For saving lives?"

"Something that big happens, *someone* has to take the fall for it." He shrugged. "I disobeyed a direct order and nearly started a war." But I could see the pain in his eyes. He'd lost something, that day, something he loved. He was *born* to be a Marine and he'd had that ripped away from him, just for trying to do the right thing.

I understood now. He'd always been cunning, he'd always been about bending the rules, ever since he was a kid. But the Marines had let him use those skills for good. Then they'd taken all that away from him and he'd turned to crime, instead.

A metal *boom* made us both jump. The sound of a door banging shut, below us. I looked down, through the mesh floor of the walkway. *Oh God!* A guard had just entered the block, beginning his patrol! And as I watched, he headed towards the stairs. He was coming up to this level, and when he did, he'd see me.

Gabriel squeezed my hands. "Go over there," he whispered urgently, nodding to the right. "Wait in the shadows. It's Earl, he always goes to the left first. When he does, go down the stairs behind him."

I stared at him. Of course he knew which guards patrolled when. Of course he'd memorized their patrol routes. This was *Gabriel*. I nodded quickly but I couldn't let go of the bars. I was frozen in fear.

Below us, I heard Earl start to climb the stairs.

"You can do it," whispered Gabriel. He looked right into my eyes and—

I believed him. I pushed the fear down inside me and *went*, scurrying off to the right and then ducking down in the shadows. Seconds later, the guard appeared at the top of the stairs. It *was* Earl. But which way would he turn?

Earl paused for a moment, hitched his pants a little higher on his beer belly...and wandered off to the left. I let out the breath I'd been holding. When he was halfway along the walkway, I crept to the stairs and hurried down, then retraced my steps back to the door and out of the cell block.

I could feel Gabriel's eyes following me the whole way.

4

GABRIEL

I COULDN'T GET HER OUT OF MY HEAD.

I was lying on my bunk in a Z shape: head and shoulders up against the wall, knees raised, a sketchpad leaning against them. Olivia gradually appeared out of the strokes of my pencil: her tightly pulled-back hair, her soft lips, those big, innocent eyes...

I don't have much of a talent for sketching, but you can get good at anything if you sink enough time into it, and time was one thing I had plenty of. In three years, I'd learned magic tricks, a little Italian and how to draw people.

I'd wanted her since the first moment I saw her. Pure animal lust, simple to understand. But there were other feelings, too, ones that unsettled me. It had started with that protective urge but it was spreading and growing, waking parts of me I thought I'd shut down years ago. I didn't just want her anymore. I...*liked* her. I liked the fact she was so good, so innocent. Naive, almost: she even thought that I could be redeemed, that I was a good guy who'd just taken a wrong turn in life.

I shifted uncomfortably on the bunk. That was wrong, of course. Ridiculous. But a traitorous part of me liked hearing it. Wished it were true, even.

I shook my head, annoyed. What I needed was to seduce her. Fuck her. Then she'd be out of my system and everything could get back to normal.

"She's hot," said a voice above me.

I looked up. Tobias Larson, my cellmate, was leaning down from the top bunk, looking upside down at my sketchpad. I grunted in response, not in the mood for talking.

Larson twisted his head for a better look, then frowned. "Wait, is that Doc Truesdale?" He looked at me. "You know, there are guys who'd pay good money for a picture like that. 'Specially if you continued it on down, got her boobs and everything in."

I turned to him, a big swell of protective fury rising up inside me. I'm not sure what was on my face, but Larson put both hands up defensively and silently withdrew to the top bunk.

What's wrong with me? I slammed the sketchpad closed. The heat hadn't let up and every breath was a struggle: it was too damn hot to do anything but sit in my cell. But I had to do *something*. I'd go and make my rounds, find out who needed what and what they were willing to bargain for it. That would get her out of my head.

I set off through the prison, nodding to gang leaders, stopping now and then to chat with people. Straightaway, something felt...*off*. I couldn't put my finger on it but there was a tension building, like fans before a big game. I did a loop of the prison and with every step I took, the feeling got stronger. I began to walk faster, unsettled. Had I missed something, this last week, while I'd been distracted by Olivia? What was it?

Just as I reached the commissary, the first alarm sounded: faintly, from somewhere else in the prison. Everyone looked at each other, worried and uncertain.

Almost everyone. One group of prisoners reacted instantly, turning and moving in the same direction. Shivs and socks loaded with quarters emerged from sleeves. I recognized the men: Packard's guys.

More alarms started blaring. The one in our area went off and guards ran in. But as soon as they entered, Packard's men swarmed them, overwhelming them and grabbing their batons. They ran off, whooping and cheering. And other prisoners, frazzled by the weeks of soul-sapping heat, ran to join them.

It became a mob and then a crowd. I was carried along by the crush of bodies. As we neared the next cell block, I could hear a roar in front of us, like we were approaching a waterfall. As the crowd carried me inside, the noise became deafening. This must be where the disturbance had started because the whole block was in uproar: everyone out of their cells, stamping and yelling. Feet clattered on the walkways as more and more men raced downstairs to join the growing crowd. I looked around and found Packard, stripped to the waist and yelling, his bald head gleaming and his eyes bulging. He was whipping the crowd up into a frenzy, drawing in more and more men.

A riot. That's what the tension in the air had been. Packard had organized his men to start a riot, knowing that once he got the ball rolling, others would join in. I was mad at myself: I should have known about this. Any other week, I would have. But the question now was: *why?* What did Packard have to gain from a riot?

I caught movement out of the corner of my eye. In a hallway off to the side, a guard was edging forward, his baton drawn. He was pale-faced and sweating, just a kid, really. I pushed my way through the crowd and got to him before anyone else saw him. "What are you doing?!" I hissed.

The guard swallowed. "I've gotta go in there and try to—"

"Those guys will kill you!" I pointed behind him. "Double back through that hallway and hook up with the rest of your people. Go!"

He hesitated...then turned and ran. I let out a breath: one problem dealt with. But I still didn't know why Packard was doing this. And the crowd had started to move, a tide of people surging out of the cell block. I pushed my way back into the crowd and grabbed one of Packard's men by the front of his jumpsuit, the two of us carried along by the flow of inmates. "What's the plan?" I demanded.

The man's pupils were tiny: he was high, probably on something Packard had given him. He tried to struggle out of my grip, but I just held on tighter, then lifted him right off the floor. "The—The warden," he stammered. "We're going to take the admin building and Packard's gonna give the warden what's coming to him."

I dropped him, my mind spinning. Packard and the warden had fallen out. Knowing the warden, he'd probably demanded a bigger cut of Packard's drug money. Packard's response was to kill him, but the warden's well protected. The only way Packard could get to him was to take over the whole place with a riot. I shook my head in dismay. I didn't have any love for the warden ,but I didn't wish him dead and a lot of guards were going to get hurt or killed, guys who were just doing their jobs, like Bruno and Louis. But there wasn't much I could do to stop a full-on riot, especially with Packard's drugged-up thugs leading it. The best thing to do would be to go somewhere safe and just wait it out. I started figuring out a route back to my cell.

Then I froze, becoming a stationary rock in the river of prisoners rushing past me.

They were going to take the admin building. The infirmary was in the admin building. *Olivia!* The thought of her in the hands of these animals...

By now, the riot was in full swing. The yelling and screaming was an ear-splitting roar, curls of burning toilet paper were drifting down from the upper levels and smoke billowed from burning mattresses, making it even harder to breathe in the stifling heat. It was like the seventh circle of hell.

But hell is exactly what I'm suited to. I started ramming my way through the crowd, hurling people out of the way when they wouldn't move.

They weren't getting her. They weren't getting my angel.

5

OLIVIA

WE'D ALL BEEN TRAINED FOR THIS, OF COURSE, WHEN WE STARTED work at the prison. *Stay calm,* we'd been told. *Lock the door. Help will come.*

But training doesn't prepare you for the noise. There's no sound in the world like an advancing crowd, hyped up and blood-hungry, out of control. They hooted, they bellowed, loud enough to shake the windows. Then, every few moments, we'd hear a scream as a guard was injured and then a roar of triumph from the crowd...and the sounds would move closer. They were winning, advancing second by second. Alicia and I looked at each other in terror: we could actually feel the floor vibrating from the hundreds of feet racing towards us.

Lock the door, they'd said. I'd locked it, but I wasn't sure if it would hold, not against hundreds of determined men. *Help will come...*but through the window in the door, I could see guards in riot gear running *away* from us, down the hallway, towards the warden's office. Had they forgotten us, in their panic? "Hey!" I yelled. "In here!" But they didn't hear me, over the noise of the riot.

"Oh God," said Alicia behind me. I turned to look at her. She'd gone sheet-white and looked as if she might throw up. She was

probably imagining what would happen if those men got in here. I
was doing the same.

The roar of the crowd got louder. They were seconds away from
us now, just around the corner. There had to be something we could
do... I searched the room for an escape route but the only windows
faced onto the exercise yard. Even if we could break them and climb
down, the rioters were out there, too.

Then I saw the drug lock-up. It's a tiny room, no bigger than a
closet. But because it's where we store all of the controlled drugs, it
has a metal door, and unlike the door of the infirmary, it doesn't have
a window in it, making it even stronger. I doubted the prisoners could
get in there, at least not easily. I grabbed Alicia's hand and pulled her
over there.

Then I cursed under my breath. The door locked from the
outside. Someone would have to stay out here to lock it.

Alicia realized the same thing at the same time and turned to me,
her face falling. Then she saw the expression on my face. "Wait," she
said. "No! Don't!"

I ignored her, opened the door to the drug lock-up and pushed
her inside. Then I slammed the door, locked it and slid the key under
the door to her.

"*Olivia!*" she yelled, and banged on the door. "No!"

I turned to the infirmary door just as the rioters arrived. I
screamed as they threw themselves against the door, rattling the
handle. Faces pressed against the window, spittle spattering the glass
as they yelled obscenities at me. *Oh God,* there were so many of them.
I started to panic-breathe. *The door will hold, right? The door will hold.*

One of them rammed a fire extinguisher against the door, trying
to batter it open, but the lock held. But then he thought to try the
door's window. On the first hit, the reinforced glass spiderwebbed,
but held. Another hit and it began to cave inwards. I went cold with
fear. *Oh Jesus.*

Another hit. The crowd whooped. I pulled open a supply drawer,
and with shaking hands, I grabbed a scalpel.

Another hit. The glass was almost out of its frame now. I backed away from the door, but stayed between it and the drug lock-up. Whatever happened, I had to keep them away from Alicia. I looked at the scalpel in my hand, trying to imagine stabbing it into someone.

The fire extinguisher slammed against the glass a final time and it fell from its frame. Instantly, arms reached through the hole, searching for the lock. *Please, no—*

The lock opened and the men surged into the room. I slashed the air with the scalpel, keeping them at bay for a few seconds, but there were too many of them: one got behind me and suddenly I was grabbed and lifted almost off my feet, an arm wrapped around my waist and another around my neck. The scalpel was pulled from my grasp.

Packard stormed in. "Get the drugs!" he yelled. Two of them started trying to force open the door to the drug lock-up, but as I'd hoped, it held. And Alicia was smart enough to stay silent: they didn't know she was in there.

Packard turned to me. "Where's the key?" he roared. He was amped up on adrenaline and he looked to be high, too, a dangerous combination.

I swallowed. "I threw it down the drain," I lied, nodding to the drain cover in the corner of the room.

Packard's face twisted in rage and his hand cracked across my cheek. My head snapped to the side and the room spun and swam. "*Bitch!*" he yelled.

"Fuck the drugs," said the man behind me. "We can have some fun with her." His groin was pressed against my ass and I could feel him getting hard. *Oh God, no...*

That's when I saw Gabriel.

He was stalking through the crowd towards me, his head lowered and his eyes flashing with rage. He barely seemed to see the other men, he just stared straight ahead, right into my eyes, and flung aside whoever got in his way. His hair was damp with sweat and his jumpsuit was torn and spattered with blood but he was coming, and no one was going to stop him.

Three of Packard's men ran at Gabriel and my chest contracted in fear. But Gabriel moved so fast I could barely follow it: a knee to the groin, an elbow to the face, a kick to the back of the leg...it was brutal and efficient, unlike anything I'd ever seen, and the men crumpled and fell.

Packard roared and ran at Gabriel, fists swinging. He was huge: there was no way Gabriel could win in a fair fight.

But Gabriel wasn't interested in fighting fair. He grabbed the discarded fire extinguisher and swung it in an arc that connected with the side of Packard's head. Packard crashed to the floor, out cold.

The man who'd been holding me let go and tried to run. Gabriel grabbed him and flung him against the wall and he collapsed, groaning. The other men backed away from us, terrified.

Then Gabriel's hands were gently cupping my cheek. Some of my hair had escaped its bun and he pushed a lock of it back from my face, his eyes locked on mine. "Are you okay?" he asked breathlessly. "Are you hurt?"

I was too overcome with emotion to manage words. I shook my head. With their leader gone, the rioters pulled back from the infirmary and the noise of the crowd faded away. For a few moments, Gabriel and I just stood like that, staring silently into each other's eyes. As the adrenaline drained out of me, my legs went shaky with fear and I had to grip his shoulders to keep from falling. He hooked an arm around my waist, supporting me.

My eyes fell to his torn, bloodied jumpsuit. Then I looked up into his eyes, shaking my head in wonder. How many men had he battled through, to make it here?

He looked right into my eyes. *As many as it took,* said his expression.

I'd never felt so protected. All the feelings that had been building for the last week welled up inside me.

I saw his eyes flick down to my lips. I drew in a trembling breath.

He lowered his head towards mine—

Guards in riot gear flooded the room. The rioters had retreated and the guards were retaking the prison. When they saw Gabriel holding me, they grabbed him and tore him away from me, hurling him to the floor.

"No!" I yelled. "No, he saved me! He wasn't involved!"

But the guards were running on adrenaline and hungry for revenge after seeing so many of their friends injured by the rioters. Their batons rose and fell.

I lunged forward, trying to reach him, but another guard pulled me away.

Gabriel didn't resist, didn't hit back. As the blows rained down, his eyes stayed locked on mine, as if nothing mattered but ensuring that I was okay.

6

OLIVIA

I GOT ALICIA OUT OF THE DRUG LOCK-UP AND FOR A FEW MOMENTS, THE two of us just held each other. Someone made me a hot drink and tried to get me to sit still and sip it, but there were people hurt: they needed us.

The rest of the day was a blur. Over twenty guards had been injured and about the same number of prisoners, some of them seriously. No one had died, thank God. Alicia and I worked like demons, triaging people, treating the ones we could and sending the ones we couldn't to hospital.

It took hours for the guards to round up the stragglers and get everyone back to their cells. Just as everything quietened down, the warden appeared.

Warden Thwaite is in his sixties, with gunmetal-gray hair shaved into a military buzzcut, although I don't think he's ever served. He's big—his office is full of trophies from his high school football days—and he's intimidatingly tall.

He was showing around a group of people I'd never seen before, all of them in suits, and they were muttering questions and noting things down on clipboards. They glanced around the infirmary for a few moments and then the warden hustled them away.

"Department of Corrections," a guard explained when I asked. "Looking into what caused the riot."

I nodded. That made sense. Maybe some good could come of all this. They'd want to know what the riot was about, and that would lead to Packard, and how he'd sold drugs in the prison and given the warden a cut. The warden would go to jail and maybe we'd get someone who treated the prisoners like human beings.

I shouldn't have been so naive.

Around six in the evening, Alicia was talking to one of the guards while she treated him. She suddenly came over to me and pulled me aside, her face pale.

"What?" I asked, worried. "What is it?"

She took my hands and squeezed them. Bit her lip. "They're pinning it on Gabriel," she whispered.

What?!

The warden couldn't have the real reason for the riot come out. So before the team from the Department of Corrections showed up, he'd gathered all the guards and got them singing from the same hymn sheet: the riot was led by Gabriel Kain. The story was that he'd started the riot as cover, so he could break into the infirmary and steal drugs.

And the Department of Corrections people were buying it. Why wouldn't they? Gabriel was a notorious thief. They'd put him in solitary for a week and were talking about adding five years to his sentence. The guards were all backing up the warden's story: they knew he'd fire them, if they didn't. The few decent guards like Louis and Bruno, who might not play along, had been sent home "to rest." There was no one to tell the truth.

Except me.

But if I did this, I'd be out of a job for sure. And this place was my last chance, literally the only place that would hire me as a doctor after what happened at the hospital. I could get another job, but I'd never practice medicine again.

My stomach contracted to a hard ball of ice and sank to my feet.

Being a doctor was all I'd ever wanted. It was my *life*. I couldn't lose that.

Movement outside in the hallway caught my eye. The Department of Corrections team were saying their goodbyes. All I had to do was sit tight for another few minutes. My hands hurt, and I realized I was digging my nails into my palms. My eyes went hot. I could *not* give up being a doctor.

But I couldn't let Gabriel serve five extra years for something he didn't do, either.

I took a deep breath and then strode out into the hallway and over to the DoC team. "Excuse me?" I said. "There's something I need to tell you."

7

GABRIEL

I was doing push-ups, counting them out in sets of twenty. It made the bruises on my ribs and back ache, but it gave me something to dump the rage into.

A guard had told me what had happened. Five more years. *Five. More. Years.*

I guess I shouldn't have been surprised, but this was a low trick, even for a piece of shit like the warden. I'd done the right thing, for once, and my reward was another half-decade in this hellhole.

But I knew that if I had the chance to go back, I'd do it all again. I'd saved Olivia and that was worth doing the time for. I thought of her as I heaved against the ground, sweat dripping from my torso. I'd heard about how she'd protected the nurse. She was brave as hell, maybe braver than she knew. Even in the middle of all the chaos, she'd looked goddamn beautiful, that dark hair half out of its bun, those soft pink lips parted. And that feeling that had come over me when I'd seen someone about to hurt her...it was frightening how powerful it had been. It killed me that they'd dragged me away before I'd had the chance to kiss her.

Footsteps outside. Then a metal scrape and click as someone unlocked my cell. I got to my feet, my bruises making me wince.

The door opened. A guard was there but I barely registered him because standing next to him was—

Olivia wasn't in her white coat, for once. She was in a gray skirt that hugged those luscious hips and a dark green blouse. It was fitted and the thin cotton hugged the contours of those gorgeous breasts. She looked fantastic. But why was she in street clothes, and why was she holding a box? Had they got her cleaning up after the riot?

"We've only got a few minutes," she said softly. "I'm meant to be gone already."

Gone? I frowned, then took a closer look at the box. There was a mug in it, and a picture of someone. Desk stuff. "Olivia," I said, my voice tight with worry, "what did you do?"

She swallowed and looked at the floor. When she looked at me again, her eyes were shining with tears. "They know Packard did it. The warden's being investigated. Your sentence isn't being extended. And you're being released from solitary." She blinked and sniffed. "Take care of that wound, okay? Stop by the infirmary in a week, Alicia can check it."

"No," I said, shaking my head. I reached for her, but the guard looked at me warningly. "No, you can't—I'm not worth this."

"Yes you are," she said firmly. "Even if you don't believe it."

We stood there for a moment, staring into each other's eyes. There was so much I wanted to say and I could see her trying to find the words, too. *This* cannot *be how we say goodbye.* I wanted to grab her, pull her to me and kiss her but the guard was right there, watching me.

She took a tiny, half-step forward, as if she was thinking about grabbing *me.* But then she stepped back, almost as if to remove the temptation. "Do me one favor," she said.

My voice was choked. "Anything,"

"Do something good with your life, when you get out."

I sighed and shook my head. There she went again, thinking I was something other than a thief. "I thought I told you: I'm no hero," I muttered.

She bit her lip in a way that made my heart break. "I thought I told you, you are."

Then she turned, blinking back tears, and walked out of the room. And the reality of it sunk in. I was still in prison—only for seven more years, thanks to her, not twelve. But now it was going to be seven years of missing her, knowing I'd never see her again.

8

OLIVIA

For two days, I let myself wallow in it. I moped in bed, ate a full pint of caramel ice cream and cried until I didn't have any more tears. Everything I'd worked for was gone...*forever.* I'd never do what I loved again.

And I'd lost *him.*

I tried to tell myself that it couldn't have turned into anything, that he always would have been off-limits. Maybe that was true. But I knew I'd never meet a man quite like him, again.

On the third day, I forced myself to roll out of bed and start making phone calls. I needed a job.

I found a few positions with medical insurance companies. They wanted someone to evaluate claims, with the focus on turning down as many as possible on technicalities. I tried to imagine being that person, and couldn't. There were a few companies looking for someone with a medical degree to make their dubious diet products sound official. I couldn't picture doing that, either. If I couldn't practice medicine, I at least wanted to help people.

Then I found a position with a charity that funded field hospitals in South America. They needed someone with medical experience to keep an eye on how their money was being spent. Corruption was a problem in some countries and it would be easy for someone to siphon off funds by overcharging for drugs or supplies. There'd even been cases where doctors, nurses or even whole medical centers had been found not to exist.

The phone interview went well and I was asked to Phoenix to visit the charity's office there. It turned out I was a good fit: I'd been responsible for supplies at the hospital and at the prison, so I knew my way around an inventory. The job paid even less than the prison, but at least I'd be doing some good.

There was only one problem. My potential new boss explained that while most of the job was about sifting through accounts, the only way to *really* check one of these places out was in person. I'd need to visit each field hospital every six months or so: just a quick forty-eight-hour trip, to meet the doctors and check it was all above board. And one of the hospitals was due its check in just a couple of weeks.

"Where is it?" I asked.

He leaned back in his chair. "Ecuador."

My stomach knotted. I didn't know much about Ecuador but I remembered hearing about political unrest and government corruption. And maybe it wasn't Colombia or Mexico, but there'd been drug cartel violence there, too. It sounded dangerous...and very far away. I'd lived almost my entire life in Arizona. I'd only left the US twice. *I am not cut out for this.* I started working out how to tell him *no*.

Then Gabriel's hazel eyes gleamed in my mind. He'd been all over the world. *He* wouldn't be scared of this. He'd just waltz in there, cocky and confident, and get the job done.

Maybe I needed to start taking a few chances.

I took a deep breath. "I'll do it," I said, and shook my new boss's hand.

~

I got my immunizations, started a course of anti-malaria pills, bought a pair of sturdy boots and, three weeks later I was gazing open-mouthed out of the window of a plane as we descended towards Quito. Towering, snow-capped mountains loomed ahead of us. To one side, they sloped down towards flawless golden beaches and a sparkling blue sea. On the other side, they dropped away towards a rolling emerald carpet draped with mist: the rainforest. I'd had no idea Ecuador was like this.

The airport was modern and gleaming. I grabbed my bag and hurried through the terminal: one of the doctors was meant to be meeting my flight and I didn't want to keep him waiting. But as soon as I hit a flight of stairs, I started breathing fast, and by the time I was at the top, I was panting. *I didn't realize I was this out of shape.*

In the arrivals area, I glimpsed a handwritten sign that said *Dr. Truesdale*. The man holding it wasn't at all what I expected. He looked to be about my age, with faded jeans, a black leather jacket, and a mop of thick, curly black hair. He saw me looking and dipped his head so that he could look at me over the top of his aviator sunglasses. "Dr. Truesdale?"

His voice was low and warm, and it had a playful energy to it. I nodded.

He shook my hand and took my bag. "I'm Marcos Rojas. I run the hospital along with Dr. Guzman." He beamed at me, a wide, honest grin, and I found myself smiling as well. He slung my bag over one broad shoulder. "Come, come, I'm parked outside. Good flight? How are you feeling?"

"Fine," I lied, still out of breath. I was sweating, too.

Marcos stopped, cocked his head to one side and nudged down his aviators, looking at my dripping forehead. "It's the altitude," he said immediately. "It'll take you a few days to adapt. Try not to rush around too much and tell me if you go light-headed. Let's go!"

He set off towards the parking lot, talking non-stop about the hospital, the local wildlife I might see and the food I should try while I was there. He was laid back and friendly and his enthusiasm was infectious: I decided I liked him. He showed me to a dust-covered Toyota Landcruiser and gave me a huge bottle of water. "Drink this," he told me. "It'll help."

As we sped away from the airport, a police pick-up roared past us, siren wailing. The cops in the back looked more like soldiers, with black balaclavas and machine guns. Marcos saw me looking and sighed. "Ecuador's peaceful but Colombia's right next door and the cartels move drugs through our ports. And sometimes through the forest." He gave me a reassuring grin. "They've never bothered doctors, though. Certainly not foreigners."

The journey took about five hours. Marcos was a good traveling companion, full of stories. Once out of the air-conditioned airport, he'd stripped off his leather jacket. He was wearing a blue and white shirt underneath with the sleeves rolled up and each time he turned the wheel, I could see his smoothly tanned biceps stretching out the cuffs. He had nice eyes, too: deep, chestnut brown and warm, like his voice, and when he smiled—which was a lot—he got dimples which were sort of adorable.

We eventually pulled up in a small community near the edge of the rainforest. Marcos introduced me to Dr. Guzman, a very tall, slender guy with a silver beard who was in charge of the hospital.

I spent the rest of the day looking around the collection of tents and ramshackle buildings: their lab was a converted shipping container. The place didn't look like much, but it was obvious they'd poured heart and soul into it. They'd even painted an animal mural in the hut that served as a children's ward.

Late that night, Marcos showed me to my room. "Well," he said, "goodnight."

There was silence for a moment. Which with anyone else wouldn't have seemed strange, but this was Marcos: he'd barely stopped talking since we left the airport. And he seemed nervous, which was unusual for someone as relaxed as him.

"Goodnight," I told him, confused. And started to close the door.

"*Unlessyouwantanightcap,*" he blurted. "I have a bottle of rum in my room, I could go get it."

That's when I noticed how he was glancing at my legs. Realization hit. "Um, thank you," I said. "But it was a long flight. I should probably sleep."

He looked crestfallen, but rallied quickly. "Some other time?"

"Maybe some other time," I allowed. I closed the door and leaned back against it, flattered but a little shocked. How had I missed that? And what was I going to do about it? Marcos was pretty good looking and I was single...would a fling with him while I was here be such a terrible thing?

But when I thought of Marcos's tanned, smooth biceps, my mind skidded off into thoughts of Gabriel's arms, covered with those twisting, thorny vine tattoos. When I thought of Marcos's soft brown eyes, innocent as a puppy's, I couldn't help but think of Gabriel's glittering hazel ones, full of mischief.

Marcos was fun and friendly and good looking. He was a doctor, not a criminal. He was everything I should want. Right?

I groaned and fell into bed, pushing the decision off into the future.

I spent the next day talking to patients, checking records and going through the hospital's supplies. As I finished up, I let out a silent sigh of relief. I'd been dreading discovering corruption and fraud, but everything was how it should be. I'd be able to tell the charity its money was being well spent.

Just as I was finishing up, Doctor Guzman ran into the supply cupboard and started grabbing items and throwing them into a bag. "Marcos and I need to go out on a call," he told me. "There was an explosion in a village." His face was drawn with worry. "Many people are hurt." He went to the blood store and took out three pints of O-neg. "We should be back tomorrow, we can drive you back to the airport then."

"Take me with you," I said.

He looked round at me in confusion.

"I'm—I used to be an ER doc. I can help." Then, when he hesitated, "Come on, I know I'm not licensed here, but it's an emergency!"

"It's not that. The village is a few hours away, deep in the forest. There's cartel activity around there. And I'm responsible for your safety."

"I'll take my chances," I said firmly, and threw a suture kit into the bag.

Guzman stared at me for a second, debating...then he nodded and we ran for the door.

∾

We piled into Marcos's Landcruiser and were soon barreling down dirt roads. As we crested a hill, I looked in wonder at the forest as it spread out ahead of us. Mile after mile of unbroken green, with only the occasional slash through the canopy where a river or dirt track cut through it. No wonder the cartels moved drugs through here. There was no way the authorities could patrol an area this big.

Dr. Guzman saw my wide eyes. "There are still groups of an indigenous people called the *Shuar* living around here: that's how isolated this area is."

Night had fallen by the time we pulled up at the village. To make matters worse, it had started to rain: a hissing, constant deluge that ran down your face and got in your eyes. The locals rushed around us and hustled us towards the most seriously injured. I was suddenly very grateful that I'd picked up some Spanish, working in Arizona.

The village's generator had exploded, throwing out burning fuel and deadly metal fragments. Several people had burns and lacerations but the most seriously hurt were a man and woman who'd been right next to the generator when it blew up. The man's leg had been sliced open in several places and I suspected he might lose it. The woman was bleeding internally and had already lost a lot of blood. Marcos and I examined her in one of the huts while Dr. Guzman worked on the man. "She needs exploratory surgery," I murmured to Marcos. "We need to find where she's bleeding from so we can stop it. Can we get her to a hospital?"

"No time." He nodded at the sky. "This rain will turn the roads to mud. It'll take three, four hours just to get her back to our field hospital and we're not equipped for surgery. Maybe six hours to get her to somewhere that is."

I gripped the edge of the table, the anger and frustration building. When I got home, I was going to start donating to the charity myself. Marcos and Guzman were doing their best, but they could do so much more with more money. This woman was going to bleed to death, when any decent ER could save her...

My jaw tightened. *No.* I wasn't going to let that happen. "We'll do it here," I told Marcos.

He blinked at me in amazement, then nodded. And as the rain hammered on the roof, we put on surgical masks and gowns and went to work.

It was a slow, painstaking process. Her belly had been peppered with razor-sharp fragments of metal and they each had to be carefully extracted until we found the one that had hit an artery. If I went too fast and pushed one quarter-inch deeper, I could cause *more* bleeding. But the portable blood pressure monitor we'd hooked the woman up to kept beeping in warning: she didn't have long left.

That's when the lights went out. I couldn't see a thing and I had both hands right inside the woman's body.

"What's going on?" I asked Marcos, trying to keep my voice level.

"The lights were running on the backup generator. It must have run out of fuel." I heard his clothing rustling as he dug something out of a pocket. Then a flashlight lit up the room. "Here."

He held the flashlight over the patient and I carried on as best I could, teasing apart layers of tissue and plucking out the shrapnel until—

"I see it!" I told him. "Clamp! Quick!"

I felt a clamp press into my gloved hand. I reached in and clamped the artery. Both of us looked at the blood pressure monitor. The numbers fell and fell...and stabilized. I closed my eyes in relief.

It took another hour to repair the artery and close her up. I knew my work was amateurish by surgeon standards, but it would buy her enough time to get her to a hospital. We staggered outside, exhausted. The rain had stopped and Dr. Guzman joined us. He'd managed to stabilize his patient, too, even managing to save the leg.

"Let's get them in the car," said Dr. Guzman. "We can drive them to the hospital in Quito. We should be there by morning."

Marcos yawned and stretched his back. "I know a good place for breakfast," he said, and looked at me questioningly.

I hesitated. He was cute and nice and...wholesome. I liked him, but...

But when he looked at me, I didn't get that lift in my chest, that feeling like I was floating right off the ground. I didn't feel that scalding, wicked heat rippling down my body.

You're never going to see Gabriel again. It's over.

"Yes," I told Marcos. His face lit up.

We got both patients loaded into the back of the Landcruiser. I ran back inside the hut to get the last bag of gear and was just turning back to the door when there was a scream from outside.

I hurried to the doorway...and froze. Two pickups had pulled up in front of the Landcruiser and a group of men were pointing guns at Marcos and Guzman.

I ducked quickly back inside, then peeked through the window.

Guzman and Marcos were explaining in Spanish that they were doctors and needed to get to the hospital. Guzman had his hands up, calm and patient. Marcos was agitated and impatient. Neither approach seemed to be working. The leader of the gunmen seemed to be talking into a radio, listening to orders. He walked past a set of headlights and I got my first good look at him: he was in military-style camouflage pants and his hair was cropped short, but he was wearing a red tank top and a black and white bandana that covered the lower half of his face.

Cartel. Oh God...

Suddenly, the leader finished his call and nodded to his men. They immediately raised their guns and started shouting at Guzman and Marcos, telling them to kneel down, hands behind their backs. Guzman did it, and they zip tied his hands together, then hustled him towards one of the pickups. This was a kidnapping, and it was happening right before my eyes.

But Marcos wouldn't kneel down. He had his hands up, trying to placate the men. *I'll come with you,* he was saying, *I just need to do something first, okay?* And he started talking to one of the locals, telling them that the keys to the Landcruiser were in the ignition, telling them to drive it to the hospital—

He was worried about the patients. Men were pointing guns at him and he just wanted to make sure someone got his patients to hospital.

The gunmen didn't understand, though. They tried to grab him, and when he backed away, one of them raised his gun and—

A shot rang out. I had to clap a hand over my mouth to keep from screaming. Marcos fell to the ground, bleeding from his arm. They grabbed him and zip tied his hands, ignoring his screams of pain. Then they hustled him towards the pickups.

Marcos would need treatment. He might die without it, especially if they were taking them to some camp out in the jungle. Guzman could treat him, but he'd need dressings...and they were in the bag I was carrying.

The gunmen started to climb into the pickups. *They have no idea I'm here.* If I just stayed where I was, in another few minutes, they'd be gone.

But Marcos could die from that gunshot wound.

I picked up the bag of supplies and ran outside. "Wait!" I yelled. "*Espere!*"

One of the gunmen spun around and raised his gun, then paused and frowned.

"I'm a doctor, like them," I told him. I held up the blue medical bag. "Let me treat him."

The leader came over and looked me up and down. "American?" he asked at last.

I nodded. Maybe he'd let me treat Marcos here and then let me go: Marcos had said they never bothered foreigners.

But the leader seemed to grin beneath the bandana and nodded for his men to take me, too. I was pushed onto the back seat, along with Guzman and Marcos.

And we sped off into the unknown.

9

GABRIEL

I STROLLED THROUGH THE CANTEEN, STOPPING EVERY FEW MOMENTS AT someone's table to do a deal, collect payment or just say hi. Since the riot, the mood in the prison had changed. The warden had been suspended and a temporary replacement had been found who seemed to be harsh but fair. Packard had been transferred to another prison and the drugs trade had dropped away to almost nothing. It would be back, of course, but for now, things were better. The heatwave had ended, too. Life was good. So why wasn't I happy?

I knew why, even if I wouldn't admit it to myself. It was her. Knowing I'd never see her again. Knowing it was because I was stuck in here for the next seven years. Knowing it was my own fault and torturing myself with childish *what-if* fantasies where I met her as a Marine, not a criminal.

A TV high on the wall was showing the news, something about drug cartel violence in South America, but no one was really paying attention. Someone in a group down at the far end of the room had the remote: I saw an arm lift out of the throng of people and a finger push the button. I looked up at the TV just as the channel changed—

I froze. Blinked.

The new channel was showing a game show but just before it

changed, for a fraction of a second, I'd seen...*had* I seen it? Was I going crazy?

"Change it back," I yelled. But the canteen was noisy and either he didn't hear me or didn't care. "Hey!" Nothing.

Panic grabbed my heart and crushed it tight because if I *was* right, I might only have seconds before the news story ended. I sprinted towards the group who had the TV remote and when a table got in my way, I jumped up and ran across it, scattering trays and spilling drinks. "Change it *back!*" I yelled.

I jumped off the end of the table and landed right behind the guy with the remote. "Change it back," I panted. "Please. Just for a second."

He turned around. *Aw crap.* It was Lawrence Treymoor, a three hundred pound, almost seven-foot mountain of a man. He wasn't part of any gang but everyone knew to stay away from him. He'd flatten you if you so much as looked at him wrong. And now he was glaring at me.

"I just need to see the news, Lawrence, just for a few seconds," I pleaded. "Please?"

"I'm watching this." A thick finger stabbed towards the game show. "This shit's educational."

I drew in a slow breath. I was good at talking to people and could negotiate with anyone. But I was out of time. That news story could end any second. I stepped right up to Treymoor and looked into his eyes. "Lawrence," I said, "the woman I'm crazy about may be in trouble and I've got to find out what's going on. Now you can beat the hell out of me if you want to, but I *need to watch the news.*"

I winced, waiting for the first blow to land. But Lawrence just stared at me, nodded sagely and changed the channel back.

As soon as I saw the screen, my stomach dropped through the floor. I was right, it *was* her, her name was right there on screen next to her picture. *Please don't let her be dead.*

She wasn't. She and two local doctors had been kidnapped by members of a drug cartel in—*what the hell is she doing in Ecuador?!*

The news report ended. I ran for the prison library: I had to find out more.

In the library, I grabbed the *New York Times* and *Washington Posts* and started reading. The kidnapping had happened three days ago and had started a panic: charities were pulling all of their workers out of the area, afraid the same thing would happen to them. The Ecuadorean government wouldn't say exactly what the cartel was asking in exchange for the hostages, it just stuck to its *we don't negotiate with terrorists* line. The US's offer of help had been rejected.

They aren't going to rescue her. And when the cartel realized they weren't going to get a ransom, they'd kill her.

I stomped out of the library and out into the yard. A protective fury had filled my chest to bursting: I couldn't stop pacing, my face a grim mask. *How dare they mess with my angel!* She was in trouble over there. Someone needed to help her, and the goddamn government wasn't doing anything, ours *or* theirs. Someone needed to go in there and get her—

I stopped pacing. *Me.* I could go in there and get her. I had the skills. I had contacts over there. I knew the terrain. But—

I looked up at the guard tower and concrete walls. But I was stuck in here. She was going to die because I couldn't get to her.

I turned away, stalking off towards the weights area. Other inmates saw me approach and started forward to greet me, then saw my face and backed away.

The rage was white-hot now, uncontainable. *It can't end like this.* I'd seen what the cartels did to their victims. *No. Not her. Not Olivia.* Jesus, what had she even been doing, in the middle of the rainforest? But I already knew the answer: knowing her, she'd been helping someone. And now she was going to die for it.

And it was my fault. If she hadn't stood up for me against the warden, she'd still be working here. I owed her.

I'd never felt so helpless. As I reached the weights bench, I heaved up the barbell and hurled it at the wall with a yell of rage. It bounced and clanged and the whole yard looked round, but it didn't make me feel any better.

And then, as I stood there panting, I remembered that there was a way I could get out of here. There was a way I could save her.

I closed my eyes and let out a long breath. *No. No, there must be another way.* But there wasn't.

For a moment, I tried to talk myself out of it. But even as my brain was spinning away, my soul had already decided. I'd made up my mind as soon as I found out she was in trouble. I'd felt a fear, a need, that I'd never felt before in my life.

My hands closed into fists. I was going to go get her. And no force on Earth was going to stop me.

I marched back inside, went straight to the payphones and picked up a handset. The operator asked who I wanted to call.

"The White House." I waited, listening. "No, it's not a joke."

~

Just eight hours after I called him, Kian O'Harra was back in the visitor's area, sitting on the other side of the Plexiglass. *How did he manage to get here so fast?*

I picked up the handset and got straight to it. "I'll join your team," I told him. "But I've got a condition." And I told him about the kidnapped doctors. "Our first mission has to be going over there and getting them out."

Kian grimaced. "The team isn't ready yet."

"Then get them ready. You told me these guys were the best."

"They are. But they haven't even met yet. They've got to train together, learn to work together. A month, at least, to—"

I leaned forward. "Look, you put this thing together to help people." I stabbed at the tabletop with my finger. "*She needs our help. Right now.*"

Kian looked me in the eye and...it was as if he understood. He knew what I was feeling. I looked away, embarrassed.

"Okay," said Kian quietly.

I relaxed. It started to sink in. *Ten years.* I was signing up for ten years with this Irishman's boy scout troop. Three years longer than if

I just stayed in here. Three more years until I could be free, and go and collect my reward. But I'd do it, for her.

And then my world fell apart for the second time in twenty-four hours.

"There's one more thing," Kian told me. "The Justice Department has a condition for your early release. They want the gold."

"Wh—*What?*" For a moment, I just stared at him. "I don't know where the gold is!" That had always been the line I'd stuck to. They couldn't prove I had it: that's why I only got ten years instead of twenty-five.

Kian leaned closer, his voice sympathetic. With the Irish accent, he could almost have been a Catholic priest, urging me to confess. "You'd better be lying. Because they think you *do* know where it is, and they'll only let you out if you tell them where it is."

No. No, no, no. I felt sick. I actually thought I was going to throw up. Not the gold. Not *my* gold. I couldn't give that up. That was what had kept me going, through the last three years. That was what I needed to get me through ten years with Kian and his bunch of misfits. *It's mine! I bled, sweated, planned, and lived three years in this hellhole for it!* "You didn't mention this before," I croaked.

"You didn't say *yes* before," countered Kian.

I thought desperately. Could I sign, and then somehow get away with the gold? *Maybe.* But it was a massive risk. Every cell in my body was screaming at me to tell him *no.* I could just go back to my original plan: sit here for seven more years and then come out a free man, collect the gold and walk off into the sunset.

But...I'd be doing it knowing she was dead. And that I could have saved her.

I drew in a long, slow breath...and nodded.

Kian took a piece of paper from his suit pocket and handed it to a guard, who brought it around to my side of the glass. I looked it over: it said, in legalese, that I was admitting to being in possession of the gold and that I agreed to hand it over and serve on Kian's team for a period of ten years. If I didn't fulfill either requirement, I was back in jail for the full twenty-five years they'd originally wanted.

If I did this, my dream of doing my time and walking away a free man was gone forever. Even if I could rescue Olivia and then get away from Kian's team and get the gold, I'd be a fugitive for life. Best case, I'd always be looking over my shoulder. Worst case, I wouldn't find a way to slip away and I'd have to hand over four hundred million dollars.

But I didn't have a choice. Not if I wanted to save her.

I touched pen to paper, hesitated...and signed my life away.

"Where's the gold?" asked Kian immediately. "The Justice Department can take us there right now."

I shook my head. "It's somewhere remote. It'll take days to get there and she doesn't have days. We go and get her, *then* I'll show you where the gold is."

Kian's eyes narrowed. "Tell me where it is. They can send people to retrieve it while we're prepping the mission."

"It's booby-trapped," I said. He looked at me disbelievingly. "It *is!* You think I'd leave four hundred million dollars unprotected?! It's booby-trapped and only I know how to disarm the explosives." I stared at him through the glass. "We rescue her, then the second our chopper lands, I'll take you straight to the gold." He didn't look impressed. "You can trust me!"

He shook his head. "I'd have to be feckin' *insane* to trust you." He studied me for a long time. "I'm going to help you, because I think you're doing this for the right reasons. But if you cross me, you're going down *hard.* Clear?"

This guy was no fool. I'd have to work hard to convince him and his team that I was a good guy, so I could slip away the second Olivia was safe.

I looked around. For three years, the gold had kept me going. Now it might be gone and suddenly, I felt the walls of the prison closing in. "Clear," I told Kian. "Now get me the hell out of here."

10

GABRIEL

An hour later, I was standing outside the prison gates, dressed in the jeans and white shirt I'd been wearing when they arrested me. I closed my eyes and felt the kiss of the wind against my cheeks. It wasn't how I'd planned it, the gold was in jeopardy and I had to get Olivia back. But for a second, I just enjoyed being free and Kian was a decent enough guy that he stood back and let me.

A black Secret Service SUV drove us to the airport and straight onto the tarmac, where a private jet waited. *So that's how he got here so fast.* Another Secret Service guy was waiting at the door of the plane. It was sort of funny that a big guy like Kian would need a bodyguard—

A woman with long dark hair ran down the steps of the plane, jumped off the third step and *wumped* into Kian's chest. He wrapped her in his arms and kissed her, first soft and tender, then hard and hot. I looked off at the horizon. Partially to give them some privacy. Partially because I felt a weird twist of jealousy. I'd never had that sort of relationship: the affection and giggles and gifts on your birthday. And I'd never wanted it. I've always needed to be able to pick up and go if I heard the police at my door. But ever since I'd met Olivia, there was a dumb, childish part of me that dreamed of me and her being like that.

"I'm sorry I can't go with you," the woman told Kian as they unwound from each other. "I've got an early meeting in DC."

Kian kissed her again, squeezed her ass and told her he'd see her tomorrow. It was only when the woman was climbing back into the jet with the bodyguard that I realized who she was. *So he* is *still seeing the President's daughter.* Or, technically, *former* President. Jake Matthews hadn't run for a second term. But the elections were coming up and Matthews *was* running again this time, so maybe he'd be President again. If he pulled it off, he'd be only the second President *ever* to serve two non-consecutive terms.

Kian led me into the terminal and an hour later we were on board an airliner headed for Colorado. I dropped into my first-class seat and gave a little sigh of pleasure as I sank into the gray leather. Everything in prison is hard, designed to withstand a bunch of animals trying to tear it apart. This was like floating on a cloud.

After a quick flight to Boulder and then a long drive out into the sticks, we arrived in a small town. Night had fallen so I couldn't see much, but we seemed to be high in the mountains. "I picked this place because it's out of the way," Kian told me. "Discreet. The roads are liable to get blocked in winter, but I want to get us a pilot so we can chopper straight in and out of here."

Kian pulled up in front of a small apartment block and handed me a key. "You're in 3A," he told me. Then he passed me a piece of paper with an address and a map. "Be here at nine tomorrow morning and I'll introduce you to the rest of the team."

Inside, I found a furnished, one-bedroom apartment. It was basic by most people's standards, but the bedroom alone was the size of my entire shared cell, and it was *mine.* For the first time in years, I had my own, private space. I crashed out on the bed, utterly exhausted.

The next morning, I woke early. When I went to take a leak, I caught myself looking over my shoulder, checking no one was about to jump me. And when I went to leave, I had a weird moment of fear:

is this right? Is this okay? I had to remind myself that yes, I could come and go as I pleased now.

Being free was going to take some getting used to.

I had an hour to kill until I met the team, so I went out to see the town in daylight and get my bearings. We *were* up in the mountains. It was a beautiful summer day and you could see for miles across the lower peaks. Then I turned around and looked the other way and—

Wow.

An immense mountain, covered in dense pine forest. And partway up, there was a thick outcropping of rock that jutted out over the town, hanging there like the sword of Damocles. Scary but amazing in a humbling, *power of nature* sort of a way.

The town was pretty, too. It looked like it hadn't changed much in a hundred years or more, with quaint old storefronts and none of the chain stores you get most places. If I squinted a little and ignored the odd passing pickup truck, I could have been back in the Colorado Gold Rush. People waved to each other as they passed and a few of them nodded politely to me, even though I was a stranger. I rubbed at my stubble, frowning but smiling. I'd spent most of my time in cities, where no one knew each other, or in underworld haunts where no one trusted each other. I wasn't sure I'd ever been anywhere so...*wholesome.*

There was a cafe just a little way down the street and it looked like the locals ate there: a silver-haired cop and a woman in janitor's coveralls were sitting outside, holding hands. I was only planning on grabbing a cup of coffee, but their breakfast smelled so good, I ordered myself some. When it came, it was glorious, nothing like the slop I'd had in prison. Thick, meaty sausages, their skin crispy brown, served with rich, golden scrambled eggs and slices of crunchy wholewheat toast dripping with melted butter. I washed it down with a huge mug of coffee. It occurred to me that I had no idea where I was, other than *in Colorado.* I turned to the cop at the next table. "Excuse me," I said. "Could you tell me what the name of this town is?"

He frowned at me, his natural cop suspicion kicking in. "You don't know which *town* you're in?"

But the woman he was with took pity on me. "Mount Mercy. You're in Mount Mercy."

~

The map Kian gave me led me up a dirt road and into the hills. But I decided I must have taken a wrong turn because there was nothing there but a derelict, red-brick industrial building. I was about to double back when I heard a voice from the forest behind me. "No. You got the right place."

The voice was slow. Not just country-slow, but as if the man speaking was out of practice. Each word felt like a big, heavy chunk of rock that he had to maneuver into place.

I turned towards the voice and...nothing. Just trees. I looked a second time, a third. And then the guy moved and *Jesus,* he'd been no more than ten feet from me the whole time, leaning up against a tree. He'd just been keeping so incredibly still, I'd looked right past him.

He straightened up and I realized how big he was. I'm not small but this guy towered over me: he must have been six-foot-eight and heavily muscled, too. And he was...*wild.* Maybe it was the thick, golden beard and the muddy boots that looked like they were at least ten years old. Maybe it was the rifle slung across his back: not some yuppie toy, but a weapon that had seen so much time outdoors, the wood had faded in the sun. Or maybe it was the way he scanned the building, the road, and me, as if even this backwoods place was a little too much like the city for him, and he'd rather be back among the trees.

There was rustling in the undergrowth and then a blur of tan-and-black fur. An enormous German Shepherd with a fluffy coat bounded over to me and started excitedly sniffing at me. I crouched and offered it my hand. I love dogs, and animals are something you don't get in prisons. I hadn't realized how much I'd missed them.

"He likes you," said the giant as he ambled over to me. "That's

Rufus. I'm Cal." He looked behind him and nodded at a woman just emerging from the trees. "Bethany."

She was pretty, with long black hair and some serious curves. But there was only one woman on my mind. I nodded politely.

The four of us were about to cross the dirt road and check out the building when the roar of a car engine made us freeze. A car slid around the corner, kicking up an enormous cloud of dust and drifting so hard it was almost sideways. We all leapt back but the driver held the skid perfectly: the car glided around the corner like it was on rails. The driver flicked the tail around and the car skidded to a stop parked neatly outside the building.

It was an old Jaguar, with gleaming black paintwork and a polished chrome hood ornament of a leaping big cat. The driver got out and he...*matched,* in some way I couldn't quite describe. I've never seen anyone suit a car so well. He wore a suit, but it was very different to the businesslike gray one Kian wore. This was jet black and stylishly cut, teamed with a snow-white shirt and a black tie. The man stripped off his black leather driving gloves and grinned at the woman climbing from the passenger seat.

She was giggling uncontrollably and she clung onto the roof of the car as if her legs were a little wobbly. The man swaggered around the car, slid an arm around her waist and pulled her in tight against him. The woman's giggles died away and she looked up at him, breathy and expectant. Looking at them, I was pretty sure we were about to see their first kiss.

He pushed her long, blonde hair back from her face and kissed her, full-on and filthy. Either he hadn't noticed we were watching, or he just didn't care. The woman melted into the kiss, then gasped as his hands found her ass.

He kissed her one last time, then released her. They murmured some things in low voices that I couldn't hear and she wrote something on his hand. Then he opened the trunk of his car and took out a bicycle, and she hopped onto it and pedaled off, heading out of town. The man grinned to himself as he watched her go, then turned to us and leaned back against his car. "Let me guess," he said. "Two more for O'Harra's Irregulars?"

Now I knew why he matched the car so well. His accent was British. London, but not the London of gleaming skyscrapers and exclusive restaurants. This was the London where men fought bare-knuckle for money in the cellars of pubs, where market traders hawked not-quite legal goods, where tight-knit communities hung on through all the bombs Hitler could drop on them and then demanded *is that all you've got?*

He strolled over, crouched and gave Rufus an expert scratch behind the ears. "Alright, boy?" Rufus pounded the ground with his paw in approval.

"Danny," the man told us as he stood.

He had black hair, just long enough to be tousled, and bottle-green eyes. I liked him immediately: he was completely unpretentious. I looked down at his hand where a phone number was scrawled in blue ink. I nodded in the direction the woman had cycled off. "How long had you known her?"

Danny considered. "'Bout four and a half minutes. She pulled up next to me at the traffic lights and started giving me an earful about how my car was killing the planet." He grinned. "So I offered to show her what a V8 could do."

I could see him working through Mount Mercy's entire female population, with his cocky charm and that accent. Cal must have had the same thought because he put a possessive hand on Bethany's back as they introduced themselves. Then Bethany kissed Cal goodbye and headed back into the trees. I guessed she and Cal lived not too far away.

We wandered across the street and I cautiously pushed open the door. *Whoah.*

The place had been a factory, once. There was a big open area with marks on the floor where huge machines used to sit, doors off to what must have been workshops, big wooden workbenches and an upper level that I guessed used to be offices. At least half the windows were broken and the floor was covered in dust, dirt, and discarded beer cans from when kids had hung out here. "What *is* this place?" I asked aloud.

Kian appeared out of the shadows. "Our base," he told me. "We've got to have a place to plan, store our gear, and train. This place'll be perfect." He nudged a broken bottle aside with the toe of his polished shoe. "C'mon, use your imagination."

A pigeon, startled by the bottle, flapped noisily into the air. We all followed it with our eyes as it flew out through a car-sized hole in the roof. "Not sure my imagination's that good," I muttered.

Kian bristled. "When I bought the place, I thought we'd have another six months before we needed it."

I put my hands up placatingly: *fair point.*

Kian beckoned someone from the shadows. The guy who stepped forward was the most solidly built guy I'd ever seen: there wasn't an ounce of fat on him but he was *wide,* a walking wall of muscle. He must have weighed two hundred and fifty pounds, even though he was about the same height as me. He had a thick black beard and a Ranger dagger was tattooed across one huge bicep. He was wearing a rock band tank top and he could have passed for a roadie at a gig, or a biker at some outlaw meet. But there was something he reminded me of even more. He stooped very slightly when he moved, his knees bent, and I'd seen that quirk before, in guys who've wrestled: he was so used to keeping his center of gravity low that he did it all the time. He was like a bear, huge and shambling and almost sweet, but I bet he'd be unstoppable if he ran at you.

"This is Colton," Kian told us. "Part-times as a bounty hunter. He's our close combat and prisoner transportation specialist."

"That's a fancy way of saying I hit people and slap cuffs on 'em," said Colton. His voice was a low growl with a definite southern twang: Missouri, maybe.

Kian turned and nodded to someone else. The guy who stepped forward couldn't have been more different to Colton. While Colton was hulking and wide, this guy was stripped down and lean, a panther next to Colton's bear. While Colton was slow and even a little awkward, this guy moved with silent grace: he seemed to flow between the shadows without making a sound. And while Colton was distinctive, with his beard and his accent and his rock band t-shirt, this guy was instantly forgettable. His clothes were dark blues and grays, not shabby but not brand new, either, and I couldn't see a single brand or logo anywhere. I'm good at reading people, but I got nothing from this guy: he was a brick wall. If I'd had to describe him to a police officer, I wouldn't have been able to give them anything useful...and I realized that that was the point. Someone who'd mastered the art of blending in...what was he, a spy?

Then I took a closer look at his face. That was the one part of him that didn't blend in so easily. He had the same look as someone else in the room, those thick brows and blue eyes...

"Your brother?" I said to Kian.

The guy nodded. "Bradan," he told us. He had the same Northern Irish accent as Kian.

At the prison, Kian had said that his brother hadn't served. I didn't like the idea of taking a civilian with us, no matter what special skills he had. But I didn't want to get into an argument about it now.

Kian showed us around. There was a kitchen with a sink full of paint cans, a bathroom someone had stolen all the pipework from and one completely empty room. "This'll be the locker room," said Kian proudly. He looked around. "We'll need some lockers."

I let out a tiny sigh. But I didn't really care how shabby the place was. I'd have prepped for the mission in a toxic waste dump, if it meant getting Olivia back.

Kian showed us a room lined with shelves. "This'll be our storeroom," he told us.

"I can be quartermaster," rumbled Cal. "I'm pretty good at keeping inventory."

Kian nodded gratefully. He showed us an empty area that he said we could use as a gym. I grunted: I'd lifted enough weights in prison to last me a lifetime.

"You know what we could use?" Colton mused. "A boxing ring."

That was it for the inside of the building. Kian showed us out the back and pointed to some wasteland. "We own this whole plot. We can set up a firing range out here." He pointed to a second, smaller building. "And we can make this into a killing house, for training."

We wandered back inside, and in the main room, I looked at the team Kian had assembled. "You said you had someone to lead this bunch of reprobates," I said. "Where's he?"

"That'd be me." The voice was deep and booming, with a confidence and wisdom borne of long experience. And it came from somewhere high above. For a second, it was as if God Almighty had spoken. But then I replayed the voice in my head. *No.* Not unless God was from Texas.

Peering up into the gloom, I saw someone emerge from one of the offices that overlooked the main room. *He was watching us from up there. Gauging us. Seeing how we interacted.*

The man started down the open metal staircase and we all turned to follow him. He walked like he spoke, not exactly slow but unhurried, like he had nothing to prove. Battered brown boots, blue jeans that had been worn smooth with use and a white shirt. What got my attention, though, was the hat: a cream Stetson. *We're being led by a cowboy?!*

He stopped in front of us and stood there like an oak. I'd never met anyone with such calm, unshakable authority before. He was older than the rest of us, maybe mid-forties, with a little silver mixed into his dark hair around the sides. But he looked to be in formidable shape. His skin was tanned from a lifetime spent outdoors and his eyes were crinkled at the corner with smile lines. He tipped the front of his Stetson. "JD. Army. Delta." His voice was warmly reassuring with a broad Texas drawl. He said *Army* with obvious pride and then slipped in *Delta* like it was no big deal.

JD turned to Danny and for a second, the two men just stared at each other in silence. "Good to see you, Danny," he said at last. I could hear the emotion in his voice.

"Fucking good to see you, too, mate." Danny stepped forward and embraced the older man with obvious affection. Meanwhile, my brain was trying to catch up. *Wait, these two know each other?*

Danny finally released JD and stepped back, then glanced

around, a little embarrassed. "JD and I go back a long way. I was seconded to Delta for a while. JD led our team."

From outside, we heard the rumble of a truck engine. A moment later, someone knocked on the door. "That'll be the supplies," said Kian. "Can you give me a hand getting everything inside?"

We all stepped forward but JD put a gentle hand on my shoulder: *not you*. Everyone else trooped outside, leaving me alone with JD. He studied me silently for a moment before he spoke.

"Let's get a few things straight," he told me in that slow Texas drawl. "I'm the only one aside from Kian who knows about the gold and your deal with the Justice Department. Kian told me we're doing this mission and my job is to lead it, and I will. But I don't like it." His face hardened. "I don't trust you. I don't especially like you. I don't know why Kian even wants you on the team. And if you betray us out there and try to make a run for it, I'll slap these on you—"he produced a pair of handcuffs from his back pocket—"and I'll let them put you in a cell for the rest of your days. Are we clear?"

I stared at him for a second. *Great.* Not only was I going to have to get used to taking orders again, I was going to be taking them from a good guy all-American hero. Part of me wanted to walk straight out the door.

But this was the only way I could save Olivia. "Crystal," I told JD.

The others returned, all carrying crates, and JD and I lent a hand. Kian had spared no expense: there were guns and ammo, camping gear, ropes...and uniforms. As Cal started getting everything squared away in the storeroom, Kian told the rest of us to get changed, so we could start training. Since we didn't have a locker room yet, we all just stripped off where we were: we'd all spent enough time in barracks that we weren't shy, and I'd basically forgotten what privacy *was*. Danny and I wound up next to each other and, as he carefully hung up his white shirt on a nail, I saw some brutal-looking scars across his back, from his shoulders all the way down to his jockey shorts and maybe on below that.

He glanced over his shoulder at me. I looked away, but not quickly enough.

"Iraq," he said. "Got captured. A bloke went to work on me with a belt."

I nodded, wincing. The scars were layered: they must have tortured him for months.

I finished pulling on my combat gear and did up my boots. Danny finished a second before me and headed back towards Kian and the others. I was about to follow him when I saw something that made me stop.

Under one of the many holes in the roof, there was a bucket, half full, and I'd seen my reflection in the water. I was in uniform for the first time in seven years. About to go and train with a team, about to go into action. I felt it all well up inside me: the pride, the feeling of belonging...everything I swore I'd eliminated from my soul the day they kicked me out.

No. I tapped the bucket with the tip of my boot and the reflection scattered. Those feelings were just ghosts. I wasn't that guy anymore.

I rejoined the others. "We're getting satellite imagery from Ecuador so we can pinpoint the cartel's camp," Kian said. "And I have a friend arranging fake passports to get us in and out of the country on the sly. It'll be a couple of days 'till we're ready, but we need that time to train."

I knew he was right. Special Ops teams train for months together before their first mission, until they operate as a smooth machine. Apart from JD and Danny, we didn't even know each other. At the same time, I wanted to be out there now, tonight, because I couldn't bear the thought of Olivia in cartel hands for even another hour. It shook me, how badly I needed her safe.

I owe her, I told myself. *That's what it is.*

∽

For two days, we trained. A couple of things became clear.

Firstly, all of the guys were genuine badasses who knew their stuff. They could move quietly, stay out of sight and handle a gun.

Secondly, I was out of shape. The prison yard had been big

enough to do laps but there's nothing more depressing than running towards a concrete wall, so I'd lifted weights, instead. Now I didn't have the stamina of the other guys. I compensated with raw effort, running until I was on the verge of throwing up. If I couldn't keep up, I was putting all of us in danger.

Thirdly, we weren't even remotely close to meshing as a team. We were a mix of Army, Marines and SAS and we all had subtly different ways of doing things. Only JD and Danny had worked together before. They were *close:* they communicated almost without words, each knowing instinctively what the other one would do. The opposite was true of JD and me: after being on my own for so long, taking orders again rankled. And JD really didn't like having me watch his back.

I couldn't blame him, I wouldn't have trusted me, either.

Meanwhile, Cal wasn't the best at communicating. Apparently, he'd lived alone in the forest, barely speaking to another person for years until Bethany had come along, and sometimes it was like he was still re-learning how to talk.

The person I was really worried about, though, was Bradan. He could handle himself as well as the others, but Kian still wouldn't tell us what his background was and there was something...*off* about him. You know when someone's tense and it makes *you* tense? It was like that...times a thousand. Like he was a spring, wound tight, a snake ready to strike. And there were little things he said, or didn't say. Like one night, we all got talking about parties, when we were teenagers. Colton told us about some annual thing they'd had back in Missouri, where the kids jumped hand-in-hand off a cliff into a lake. Danny told us about sweet-talking his way into some posh girl's party in London. But Bradan dodged his turn and I saw a flash of panic in his eyes. As if he'd never *been* to a party as a teenager. What the hell had he been doing, during those years?

There was no time to dig into it. It was almost time to go.

The evening before we flew out, Kian gathered everyone for a briefing. We didn't have a high-tech ops center to hold it in. We didn't even have *chairs*. We sat on crates in the main room, looking at a satellite photo Kian had taped to the wall. I looked around at the scene: at the broken windows and oil-stained floor, at the ragtag bunch we'd assembled. *Are we going to be able to pull this off?* We were Olivia's only hope.

Kian pointed to the satellite photo. "The doctors are being held here, in a cartel camp way out in the rainforest. You'll chopper in, get them out, then hike to the extraction point. That's going to be the hard part. The cartel will be on your tail and you'll have to stay ahead of them for a full thirty-six hours."

"Why'd the cartel kidnap the doctors in the first place?" asked Danny, stirring a mug of tea.

Kian shook his head. "We don't know."

"No ransom?" asked JD, rubbing his stubble. "No demands? Doesn't make sense."

I leaned forward, frustrated. There was no time to get sidetracked. "Doesn't matter why they did it," I said. "We just need to get her back." The others looked round at me and I felt my face heat. "Them. Get *them* back."

We moved on and dug into the details of transport, weapons, and supplies. When the briefing ended, Cal cornered me by the locker-room-with-no-lockers. He gazed at me for a while before he spoke. "This lady doctor, she someone you know?"

I looked away. "She was the doc at the prison I was in. I just want to see her safe. I owe her."

Cal's blond brows furrowed skeptically.

I stared back at him stubbornly. "Being sweet on her would be a lousy reason to run an op."

Cal shook his head. "No. It'd be the best reason." He slapped me on the shoulder and walked away.

I looked down at my shoulder, a little thrown. It had been a long time since anyone had done that.

❧

On the morning of our flight, Bethany came to see Cal off. He knelt and ruffled Rufus's fur, telling him to be good. "I'm worried about him," he muttered to Bethany. "This'll be the longest we've been apart in years."

Bethany looked up at him and blinked, and I could tell she was fighting back tears. "I'll take care of him," she promised. She sniffed. "We'll take care of each other."

Bradan had someone to see him off, too, a woman named Stacey with sleek, dark hair. Whatever was going on with Bradan, she seemed to cut straight through it: as soon as she showed up, Bradan's whole body relaxed and he seemed...*normal*. It was obvious the two were crazy about each other. When it came time to go, I watched as they went from an embrace to holding hands to brushing fingertips, maintaining contact until the very last second.

I felt that pang of jealousy again, like I had with Kian and Emily. *Stupid.* I'd never had that sort of relationship with anyone, always sticking to one-night stands and quick flings. You can't have anything real, not when you know Interpol might break your door down in the middle of the night and you'll have to grab a bag and run.

I turned away from Bradan and Stacey. I had a plan and I was going to stick to it.

I'd get Olivia back, because I owed her.

I'd fuck her, to get her out of my system.

I'd find a way to slip away from the team and then I'd disappear into the sunset with the gold.

Alone, just like I'd always been.

11

OLIVIA

I crept along the hallway, my footsteps swallowed by the thick carpet. I could hear him humming to himself and I homed in on the sound. I pushed open a heavy wooden door and—

Gabriel was wearing black suit pants that hugged his ass and an expensive white cotton shirt turned almost translucent by the sunlight streaming in from the window. I could see the smooth globes of his shoulders, the curve of his pecs and the dark ink of his tattoos. He'd just lifted a painting down from the wall and he held it casually as he gave me one of those wicked grins. "Well, hey, Doc! Come to join me?"

I glanced down at myself. I was in my white coat and sensible shoes, the way I always dressed in my dreams. And that confirmed to my semi-sleeping brain that this *was* a dream, that it had to be. But my brain boxed that thought up and pushed it aside. It *needed* this.

I looked around at the lavish bedroom, at the four-poster bed and antique furniture. "You have to get out of here!" I told him. My jaw dropped as I saw the necklace dangling from his pants pocket, the emerald pendant as big as a duck egg. "You can't just—You can't just *take things!*"

He grinned and tossed the painting carelessly onto the bed. Then he advanced on me, the lust flaring in his eyes. "You know what I'd like to take right now?"

I swallowed, my face heating. "I can't—That's not—"

He walked right up to me, his hands went to the front of my coat, and before I could protest, the top button was undone. He stopped and watched to see what I would do.

I looked up at him, my breath trembling. But I didn't say *stop.*

He deftly slipped another button open. Then another and another. My head went swimmy. We were in someone's mansion: I didn't *do* things like this. But I couldn't control the heat that throbbed up through my body, faster and faster with each button that opened.

He popped the last button. Then, with just two fingers, he hooked the coat up over my shoulders and it slithered down my arms and fell to the floor behind me.

I stared up at him. He stared down at me.

"I'll buy you a new one," he told me.

"A new what?"

He grabbed the neck of my white blouse with both hands and ripped it open, threads tearing and buttons flying. I drew in a shuddering breath and looked down at myself, then up at him. He was gazing down at my heaving breasts in their simple white bra, his eyes narrowed in lust. Then his eyes met mine and the heat pulsing through my body doubled, trebled, turning to slick moisture as it reached my groin.

He leaned forward and hung the stolen necklace around my neck, the gold cool against my heated skin. "It matches your eyes," he told me.

I had no words. I needed to tell him that I shouldn't, I mustn't, I *couldn't,* that I was the sort of person who would still stop at a stop sign even when I could see for ten miles in all directions.

But I didn't.

Because part of me didn't want to be that person anymore.

Then his lips came down on mine, claiming me, spreading me and damn well ravishing me. His hands slid through my hair, pulling the clips free and sending it spilling down into a swishing curtain. My knees weakened and I grabbed his shoulders for support.

He broke the kiss for a second and I felt his whispered words on my aching lips. "I'm going to make you come so hard you see stars."

He grabbed me around the waist and tossed me like a doll onto the bed. I bounced to a stop next to the painting. He was on me immediately, kissing my throat, my collarbone—

A shout from downstairs. With a strangled gasp, I sat upright, pushing him away. The owners were back! My eyes went to the painting, the necklace around my neck—

"It's okay," Gabriel told me, his lips twisting into a grin. "We'll talk our way out of this. We just need to find you a maid's uniform." His eyes went molten at the thought and he leaned in and stole a kiss.

Another shout, closer. Then the daylight outside the window flared, becoming painfully bright. The walls, then the bed, disintegrated as the light hit them.

No! No, no, I want to stay! I grabbed for Gabriel but he was already disappearing, his grin fading last of all.

I groaned, feeling the breeze on my face and the hard-packed dirt under my body. I opened my eyes to see Dr. Guzman sitting against the bars of the cage, his eyes full of sympathy.

The brief escape of sleep was over and I was back in reality, thousands of miles from everything and everyone I'd ever known, held by men who'd shoot me without a second thought if I became a problem.

It had been five days since we were kidnapped. We'd spent that entire time in a bamboo cage, eight foot by eight foot, living on the scraps of food they brought us. The days were sweltering, and we spent them huddled in the one corner of the cage that was in the shade. I was lucky that I'd had a bottle of sunscreen with me, when we'd been captured, or I'd have been fried by now. The nights were barely any cooler and the jungle pressed in tightly on all sides of the camp, blocking any breeze. I couldn't even see the sky, and for someone like me who'd spent her whole life under the big skies of Arizona, that was unsettling and claustrophobic.

At my lowest points, I closed my eyes and remembered the feeling of being pressed against Gabriel's chest, shielded from everything the world could throw at me. I knew it was crazy. Who dreams of being protected by a criminal? But that memory kept me going.

Each day, it got harder. I felt the fear and despair welling up inside me, threatening to spill over. Did anyone know where I was? Did anyone back home even know we were missing?

I dug my nails into my palms and willed the tears back. I wasn't being brave. I just knew that if I broke, I wouldn't be able to put myself together again.

Besides, Marcos needed me.

I stood up slowly, stiff and aching from sleeping on the ground. Together, Dr. Guzman and I checked Marcos's wound...then exchanged worried looks. We'd left the dressing as long as we could, but it needed changing and we'd used up all the alcohol wipes. We had to get something sterile to clean it and dress it with, or Marcos was going to pick up an infection: and out here, without antibiotics, that would kill him.

Guzman cursed in frustration. I gently patted his arm: *this isn't your fault.* I knew he felt responsible for Marcos and for me, too, even though I'd volunteered to go to the village with them.

I turned and looked out at the camp, biting my lip. The men holding us had short fuses. On the first night, we'd made the mistake of talking too loudly and one of the cartel had yelled at us and pointed a machine gun at our heads. Since then, we'd tried to be as quiet and trouble-free as possible. But we needed medical supplies for Marcos, and someone had to risk speaking up. Marcos was hurt. Guzman had a wife and kid waiting for him back in the city.

I had no one.

I timidly called out in Spanish. Dr. Guzman tried to quiet me, worried for me, but I shook my head: I had to do this.

A guard marched over, glaring. I shrank back, my heart sinking. I'd seen him the night we arrived: a guy in his forties with his long hair pulled back in a ponytail and thin, cruel lips. Something about him gave me the creeps. *Why did it have to be him?*

I explained in Spanish that we needed medical supplies but he shook his head: *we don't have any.*

"Boiling water, then," I pleaded. "And clothes, even rags."

He sighed and I thought he wasn't going to help. But then he stared at me, his eyes narrowed in thought...and he unlocked the chain securing our cage.

He motioned me out, and for the first time in nearly a week, I stumbled out into the world. He grabbed me by the wrist and pulled me with him and I hurried to keep up.

In the cage, we'd only been able to see one small corner of the camp. Now I got my first look at the rest of it: it was a mixture of tents, shacks, and old shipping containers, surrounded on all sides by thick jungle. I tried to take in everything I could: in case it could help us escape. But my heart sank when I saw the wire mesh fence topped with razor wire that ran right around the camp and the guards who patrolled, all armed with assault rifles. Even if we could get out of the cage, somehow, we couldn't get past all that.

The guard led me to a wooden lean-to with a sputtering diesel generator. There was a kettle for the guards to make coffee. The guard started it boiling and then muttered something about finding me some cloth. I nodded gratefully, still surprised that he was helping me.

Using the toe of his boot, he scratched an X in the dirt just in front of me. *Stay right there,* he told me in Spanish. *Or—* And he tapped my forehead with the muzzle of his rifle, hard enough to hurt.

I nodded meekly, my stomach knotting in fear. He laughed and strolled off.

I stood frozen to the spot, listening to the kettle's whistle build and build. Then I heard another noise, a low rumble slowly approaching from behind me. A car.

The shack's walls were made of planks, only roughly nailed together. I checked the guard was nowhere in sight, then turned around, crouched, and found a gap where I could peek through the wall.

An SUV was pulling into the camp. Cherry-red, with a white logo on the side I didn't recognize, like two black triangles side by side. The head of the camp—the man who'd been giving the orders, the night we'd been kidnapped—was there to meet it. The black-and-white bandana was pushed down around his neck, and he looked older without it: I could see the silver in his stubble and the wrinkles at the corners of his mouth.

The guy who climbed out of the SUV was much younger and he didn't look like he was cartel. He was in a white shirt and black slacks, with fancy, blue-and-silver framed glasses. He had a couple of armed guys with him: bodyguards? My heart leapt. *He's a lawyer! Or some sort of negotiator, sent by the government, he's going to bargain for our release—*

But there was no introduction, no cautious handshake. The two of them just started a muttered conversation, as if they already knew each other. *What the hell is going on?*

At that second, I heard footsteps behind me. I stood up and whirled around, but not fast enough. The guard with the ponytail was standing there, glaring. He snapped his rifle up and pointed it right at me. *What were you doing,* he demanded in Spanish.

I swallowed, terrified. My whole world seemed to narrow down to that yawning barrel and the sight of his finger, hooked around the trigger. I glanced around, searching for an excuse—

There was an open bag of chips lying on a table, near where I'd peeked through the wall. *I—I took one,* I stammered in Spanish. *I'm sorry, I was so hungry...*

He blinked, then burst out laughing, lowering the gun. For a second, I relaxed.

Then he stepped closer, close enough that I could smell the liquor on his breath. *I'll bring you food,* he told me. *But you already owe me for the hot water.*

Oh Jesus. That's why he'd helped me.

His hands went to the top button of my blouse. I froze, my mind racing. *Hit him?* He'd shoot me. *Run? Run where?!*

A voice barked in Spanish: *What's she doing out of the cage?!* We both turned. The head of the camp was standing just outside the shack, glaring. The guard with the ponytail mumbled something about the hot water. I quickly poured the kettle into a bowl and picked it up, took the shirt the guard had brought me, and let him walk me back to the cage.

After he'd locked me in, the guard grabbed my hand through the bars and squeezed it. *I haven't forgotten,* he told me. *You owe me. Tonight.*

I stared at him, feeling myself breaking inside. Jesus, he wanted me to...and not just once, but whenever I needed more supplies.

As he strolled off, whistling, I felt the tears finally prickle free of my eyes. I turned so the other doctors couldn't see. I knew Dr. Guzman would blame himself and I didn't want him to feel any worse. I stood there holding onto the bars with silent tears trickling down my cheeks.

I was in hell.

And no one was coming to save me.

12

GABRIEL

"THIS IS IT," MUTTERED JD, LOOKING UP AT AN ORNATE BUT SHABBY building.

Thank God. I leaned against the wall and tried to get my breath. We'd been in Ecuador an hour. We'd spent most of that hiking uphill through Quito's winding streets, but I shouldn't be struggling *this* much. "Anyone else feel...weird?"

Colton nodded gratefully. "Thought it was just me."

"I've got a hangover but I don't remember drinking," said Danny.

"It's the lack of oxygen," JD told us. "Because we're at a different altitude."

Danny looked up at Cal. "Must be even worse for you. You were at a different altitude to start with." Everyone chuckled, and JD waved us inside.

The place was an old hotel. It must have been a high-end place once: there was wood paneling everywhere, a chandelier overhead and an elaborate staircase. But now the paint was peeling and the floorboards creaked. The bar downstairs had become a roost for American expats and that was probably all that was keeping the place open. I rubbed at my stubble, trying to get used to being in a foreign country again. For three years, my entire world had fitted into less than a square mile.

The bartender was a local woman in her twenties, with long dark hair. Danny walked in through the door, went over to the bar and slid onto the bar stool in front of her in one unbroken movement. "I'm Danny," he told her with a broad, cocky grin. "And who are *you?*"

The rest of us stopped just inside the door, looking around. We were meant to be meeting the pilot who'd fly us to the camp, a guy called Mitchell Gantz. But the only other person aside from the bartender was a woman hunched over a bottle of beer. Not her first, judging by the empties on the table.

We stood there awkwardly for a few minutes, but no one else appeared. JD leaned on the bar to get the bartender's attention but she was oblivious. Danny was telling her some story in that rough London accent and she was leaning forward, hanging on his every word. JD sighed and elbowed Danny and the pair glanced up.

"Looking for Mitchell Gantz," JD told the bartender. "You know him?"

The bartender blinked, as if waking from a dream. "Gina?" she called to the other woman. "You seen Gantz?"

Gina grunted and took a swig of beer. "Probably stayed up all night playing video games and then fell asleep." Her voice was American and more than a little slurred. She tossed her black, bob-cut hair back from her face and frowned at us. "He flying you out to cartel territory?"

JD marched over, furious. We weren't meant to be in Ecuador and the fewer people knew about our mission, the better. "How in the hell did you know that? Did Gantz tell you?"

Gina shook her head and looked at JD's Stetson. "Easy there, cowboy. No, Gantz didn't tell me. But it's the only thing that makes sense. You aren't tourists. You aren't with one of the oil companies: they've got their own pilots." She raised an eyebrow. "You look like special ops to me."

JD scowled and turned away. But I moved closer to the woman.

I'm good at reading people and I had a feeling about her. "You sound like you know about this stuff," I said gently.

Gina shrugged.

I looked her over. Cargo pants, battered boots. Her arms were toned and lean. And then I saw something peeking out from the sleeve of her black t-shirt: the back legs of a prancing horse. I drew in my breath and looked her in the eye.

She met my gaze stubbornly but said nothing.

I lifted the sleeve of her t-shirt and she didn't stop me. I already knew what I'd find: the horse had the upper body of a man, and he was raising a sword under a moonlit sky. 160th Special Operations Airborne Regiment. The elite helicopter pilots who fly special ops teams into hotspots under cover of darkness. Better known as...

"Night Stalkers," I said aloud. "What the hell are you doing *here?!*"

She shrugged again. She did that a lot.

At that moment, a guy ran down the stairs, stumbling a little on the last one. He was about thirty, with pasty skin and long, straw-colored dreadlocks he must have been growing for years. "Hey!" he said brightly. "You the guys? I'm Gantz. Sorry I'm late. Had this other job. Mission. This other mission."

I could smell weed on his breath and the sickly-sweet stink of energy drinks. I rejoined the others and whispered in JD's ear. "Are you kidding me? He flies tourists around, he's not military."

JD turned to me. "We're not exactly spoiled for choice. Maybe if we'd had a little longer to plan..."

I forced myself to take a breath and tried to see it from JD's point of view. He'd been hired to lead this team and then, before he had time to get them ready, he had to take us all on this hastily planned mission and try to bring us all back safe. If I was him, I'd be annoyed, too. I put up my hands in a sign of peace. "Okay, I get it. But maybe someone with more experience...?"

"Who?" asked JD. Then he followed my eyes to Gina. "*Her?* She can barely stand, let alone fly." He nodded to Gantz. "C'mon, let's go."

I sighed and followed. At the bar, Danny was staring deep into the bartender's eyes, one hand cupping her cheek as he whispered softly to her. When he saw we were leaving, he gently drew back. The bartender grabbed a pen and wrote her phone number on a beer mat, then pressed it urgently into Danny's hands. How long had *that* taken, five minutes? The man was a machine!

At the airfield, we met up with Emilio, an arms dealer I knew from back in the day. He was supplying us with guns, ammo, and anything else we hadn't been able to bring through customs. The rest of the team stayed back while we embraced. "This is new," I told him, giving his black, bushy beard a friendly tug.

"It's been three years, my friend." He slapped me on the arm. "What happened? I heard they caught you." He looked at JD and the rest of the team. "What is *this?!* You're back working for your Uncle Sam?"

"Trust me," I muttered. "It's strictly temporary. In fact, I need your help with that." And I told him what I needed.

We unpacked the guns and everything was in order. JD looked grudgingly impressed, even though he clearly wasn't comfortable hanging out with an arms dealer. "See?" I said. "It helps to have friends in low places."

We geared up, changing into jungle camouflage gear and applying camo paint to our faces. All of us had our own little good luck routine. I checked I had my lucky metal dice: I'd whiled away many hours in prison, betting on those for money or rations. Danny slid a hip flask into a pocket and tapped it twice. JD finally took off his Stetson, slid it into a plastic bag and put it lovingly on top of his pile of street clothes. Colton had a silver Zippo lighter that he flicked open and tested, then shoved in a pocket. Cal sharpened his hunting knife. Only Bradan stood quiet and still. What, didn't he believe in luck? What was it, with that guy?

Just as we were about to board the chopper, Emilio pulled me aside and put his mouth right to my ear so I could hear him over the noise of the rotor blades. "I made some calls," he said. "There's a guy who can get you out of the country for $100,000. When the helicopter brings you back here, say you gotta use the bathroom and run in that building over there. Go out the back door, through the hole in the fence and the guy will be waiting in a car just through the trees."

Slick. I embraced him tightly. "Thank you, Emilio." My gold was still in reach. All I had to do was get Olivia to safety, bring her back here on the chopper, and then run.

And never see her again. I wasn't ready for how much that thought hurt. Then I shook my head. There was no other choice.

We boarded the chopper and Gantz got us in the air. Soon, emerald jungle was rushing past beneath us, and an hour later, we were hovering over a quiet clearing a few miles from the cartel's camp. There was no place to land, so we'd have to be extracted in a different spot, a few days' hike away. JD double-checked with Gantz that he understood. "Here," JD told him, pointing to a mark on the map. "At dawn. Two days' time."

"That's a big ten-four, chief!" Gantz grinned and I winced. The closest this guy had ever gotten to serving was *Call of Duty.*

We roped down, and as the chopper climbed away, the sound of the jungle surrounded us: the soft creak of trees, the chatter of monkeys and the calls of exotic birds. The trees were a little further apart here and shafts of sunlight stabbed through the gaps to light up golden motes of dust and scarlet butterflies. It was heartbreakingly beautiful, and after staring at nothing but concrete for three years, my brain felt almost overloaded. I turned in a circle, amazed. I'd missed out on so much *life,* being locked up.

Cal stood for a moment at the edge of the clearing, looking up at the sky. Then he spoke and everyone looked round: Cal saying something was a big event. "Weather's going to change. Three days, maybe four and we're looking at a storm, a big one."

"We'll be out of here before then," said JD. But his jaw was tight: maybe he didn't like storms.

We started through the jungle, with Cal taking point. I couldn't believe how silently he moved through the trees. We all knew how to move quietly but this guy was a ghost.

JD waved for me to take the right side and I walked with my eyes glued on the trees, watching for ambushes, trusting Danny to do the same on the left and that Colton had our backs. The feeling took me instantly back to the Marines and it felt good.

Then I caught myself and crushed those feelings into dust. I wasn't part of this team. I was just fooling them. I'd get Olivia, we'd get back to the airfield and I'd disappear.

A few hours later, we reached a hill overlooking the camp. We crept as close as we dared and then JD swept the camp with binoculars. He shook his head ruefully: *nothing.* My chest tightened. What if our information was wrong? What if she wasn't there?

Then Cal, who was scouting around the side of the camp, waved us over to him. He passed me his rifle and showed me where to look. I put the scope to my eye. Where...

There! My heart leapt and I forgot how to breathe for a second. She was bedraggled and dirty, and just the most beautiful sight I'd ever seen. The rifle's scope put me so close to her, it was like I could reach out and touch her and my chest ached with the need to do just that.

I panned around a little, trying to see more. There were lengths of bamboo in front of her, in a row—

A cage. I blinked. Then the shock turned to anger, boiling up like lava, filling every part of me. *They've got her locked in a cage?!*

A guard came to the bars with a hunk of bread. Olivia reached out to take it, but the guard pulled it back at the last second, teasing her, motioning her closer to the bars. She glared at him, then glanced over her shoulder at a guy who lay on the floor of the cage. Her shoulders slumped and she stepped forward, pressing herself against the bars. The guard stroked her cheek and muttered in her ear, something that made her shudder.

Bastard! Take your hands off her! I surged to my feet, threw the rifle to Cal and started forward. A strong hand grabbed my shoulder and pulled me back. "Wait!" JD's Texan drawl in my ear. "Wait!"

I shook his hand off, turned and glared at him. But to my surprise, the old hard ass actually looked sympathetic. "I get it," he told me firmly. "I really do. But you race in there without a plan, you could get her killed."

I stared at him sullenly for a moment, then grumbled and crouched back down. All of us looked at the camp.

"They're better organized than I expected," said Danny after watching for a while. "Regular patrols, they've got guards posted...I thought they'd be—"

"...just thugs with guns," rumbled JD. The two knew each other so well, they even finished each other's sentences.

"We can't get in and out without being seen," said Bradan.

"So, it's a firefight then," said JD. "But that cage is a problem. Bullets start flying, the doctors have got nothing to hide behind."

"We need someone on the inside, to keep them safe," I said. I thought for a moment, then dug in my backpack. What I pulled out was electric blue, with an orange sunset and silhouetted palm trees. It was so garish that the others all recoiled.

"Why've you got a Hawaiian shirt in your pack?" Danny wanted to know.

"Camouflage," I stripped off my military gear and started pulling on the shirt. "You ever see a soldier in a Hawaiian shirt?" Danny shook his head. "Exactly. Good way to disappear." I pulled off my pants.and pulled on some khaki shorts. "Now, what have you got in that hip flask?"

It was whiskey. I took a big slug of it, then splashed some over my shirt.

JD stared at me. "That's your plan? Play the drunk tourist, get yourself captured and hope they throw you in the cage? What if they just shoot you?"

"They won't," I said with a confidence I didn't feel. "Not an American tourist. Not without calling up some head honcho cartel guy to check with him. By then, I'll have got the doctors ready to move. I'll make with the secret signal and you come charging in with the cavalry." I showed him a little LED flashlight and then clipped it to my shorts. "Three flashes," I told him.

JD stared at me for a while. I could tell he didn't like it: this was *not* the way he was used to operating. But he didn't have a better idea and this sort of scheme was exactly why Kian had wanted me on the team. JD sighed. "You want a gun? A knife, at least?"

"No. They'll search me." I turned to go.

JD stopped me with a hand on my shoulder. When I turned to him, I saw real concern in his eyes. He didn't like me. He didn't trust me. But he didn't want to see me get killed, either. "Good luck," he said at last.

I felt the ghost of something in my chest, memories of a time when my unit all looked out for each other, a bond tighter than brothers. I didn't know how to deal with that, so I just grunted and hurried off towards the camp.

As I got close, I started singing, loudly and drunkenly. The last thing I wanted was to surprise some guard with a twitchy trigger finger. Even so, when I stumbled up to the front gate, three guys spun around, guns up, and I honestly thought I was going to die.

"Hey there," I slurred, and stumbled sideways a little, as if I couldn't keep my balance. "You know where I can find a phone?"

They looked at each other, then surrounded me and patted me down for weapons. I kept a poker face, pretending not to understand while they discussed in Spanish whether to shoot me. To my relief, they came down on the side of *no*...for now. They didn't believe an American tourist would really get lost, all the way out here. But they weren't about to execute me, either, not without approval from their boss. It's a universal truth: no one wants to get fired.

The sun was fully down now, and they hustled me through the darkness to the cage, unchained the door and pushed me inside. I saw a shadow rise from the opposite corner, walk forward into the light and—

It was her. After days of travel and planning and training, it was *her,* in the flesh. The feelings surged up inside me and I closed the distance between us in three big strides, carried on a wave of protective need. My hands cupped her cheeks, thumbs stroking through her hair, and suddenly I couldn't speak.

She stared at me, open-mouthed. "What—How are you *here?!*"

I struggled to make my voice work. "Well, I heard my favorite doc was in trouble."

She looked up at me and those pale green eyes suddenly shone with tears. I couldn't stop myself. I wrapped my arms around her and crushed her to me.

I drew in a shaky breath as I rocked her against me. *Jesus,* it felt good. All that time at the prison unable to touch her, my feelings growing and growing and now... God, I was overwhelmed, drunk on the scent and the softness of her. All the fear of the last week, all the worrying that we'd be too late or that she'd be dead, melted away leaving me weak and shaky. And as the fear left me, a new feeling swept in to replace it, one that was even stronger. My arms tightened around her back.

I'd found her again...and I wanted to never let her go.

When I finally, grudgingly, released her, she stepped back, her eyes still shining but a smile twitching her lips. And she gave me a look of such admiration, such pride, that it damn near broke my heart. She really thought I was a hero. And for a moment, I wished she was right.

She lowered her voice. "Are you here with the military?!"

I thought of our mismatched, thrown-together team. "In a manner of speaking. We're here to get you out."

She nodded towards a guy lying on the floor. "One of us was shot in the arm. He's okay for now but I could really use some better medical supplies to take care of his wound."

I stared at her. She'd been through hell and even now, her first thought was for her patients. Did she realize how brave she was? I showed her the LED flashlight. "Three flashes and the cavalry come in, guns blazing. When I give the signal, we all need to get down on the floor, then be ready to run when they open the cage."

I was just about to give the signal when I saw three guards marching towards the cage. *What?!* They'd been away less than a minute. Not nearly enough time for them to get the head of the cartel on the phone, if they even *had* a phone here. I'd been relying on them having to pass the message through a radio network and wait hours for a reply.

"Gabriel?" whispered Olivia, her voice tight.

The plan had gone badly wrong. They were going to drag me out of there and probably execute me.

I turned to Olivia. "Kiss me, Doc."

She took a half-step back, her cheeks flushing and her eyes huge. "W—what?"

My chest ached: it was one of those classic Olivia reactions, shocked and embarrassed and turned-on, all at once. God, I loved doing that to her. And this might be the very last time I got to do it.

"Kiss me," I told her again. "Those guys are going to kill me, so if you've got any feelings for me whatsoever, you kiss me right now because this is our last chance and I don't want to leave this world without knowing what it's like to kiss you."

She stared at me, her eyes filling with tears. And then she jumped forward and pressed her lips to mine.

It was my first kiss in over three years. It felt like my entire life had been made of jagged, gray rock, damp and cold as ice and suddenly I'd escaped to a place where everything was soft and warm and filled with her sweet, intoxicating scent. I groaned low in my throat and kissed her harder, sliding my hands around that tightly pulled back hair at the sides of her head, kissing down into her. The kiss became hard and hungry: I opened her, *spread* her, wanted to possess her utterly. At the same time, I was trying to rein myself in because I didn't want to scare her: she was just this sweet, innocent little thing.

Then she gave a little moan, and I felt the brush of her tongue against mine, nervous but excited, hungry for more, and that was *it,* I lost control completely. My hands slid all the way down her back to her ass and I pulled her hard to me, squeezing her cheeks as our tongues danced, both of us panting.

The chain on the cage door rattled. I quickly broke apart from her: luckily, the cage was dark so they wouldn't have seen what we were doing. I heard the cage door creak open and then hands were hauling me out.

"No!" Olivia jumped forward and grabbed at me, trying to cling onto my shirt, plucking at my shorts, but they pulled me out and slammed the cage shut.

They dragged me towards a wooden building on the far side of the camp. I stumbled along, trying to come up with a plan but—

I could still taste her. I could still feel the soft press of her breasts against my chest. I was addicted. I wanted *more*. And whatever happened, I'd got to experience that once.

They pulled me up the steps of the hut. I guessed they used it for sleeping because there were camp beds strewn around and a camping stove. A single chair had been pushed into the center of the room. That wasn't a good sign.

Sitting in the shadows in the corner of the room was a guy with a black and white bandana over his mouth. He snapped orders to the guards in Spanish and they pushed me into the chair. My hands were zip tied behind my back. An even worse sign. They were going to interrogate me.

"Who are you?" the guy in the bandana demanded.

My brain was working frantically now. His English wasn't bad— he was definitely educated. And he had a calmness, an authority, that I wouldn't have expected of a cartel thug. I decided to keep playing it as *stupid drunk tourist*. Hopefully, he was just taking the initiative to impress his bosses and he wouldn't risk killing me.

"Jack Miller," I slurred. "Look, I'm sorry, pal, I didn't mean to wander into anything, I just got lost—"

The world suddenly warped: I could still see but everything looked distorted. There was a tightness all around my face and my mouth wouldn't work. I sucked in air but nothing happened. My whole body jerked in the chair in instinctive panic, my wrists pulling at the zip tie, but I couldn't get free. I sucked harder and felt something sticking to my tongue.

A bag. They'd put a clear plastic bag over my head. They were going to suffocate me.

"Stamp your foot when you want to talk," the guy with the bandana told me from the shadows.

I huffed and huffed, but the plastic just tightened against the red O of my lips. I could feel the bag being twisted tight at the back of my head and then tied off with something.

I'd been wrong: this guy was *absolutely* prepared to kill me.

Not being able to breathe is one of the most frightening things imaginable. My body went into animal panic, every instinct screaming at me to give in, to talk.

But if I told them about the team, they'd go out there and hunt them down.

You're not part of the team, a little voice reminded me. *You're just playing them.*

My lungs strained, desperately trying to expand, but the life-giving air I needed was on the other side of that invisible, impenetrable barrier. My leg tensed, ready to stamp my foot.

But there was something inside me that wouldn't let me do it. I told myself it was because if I died but protected the team, maybe they could still save Olivia. But it wasn't just that. There was some part of me that didn't want to betray them.

The world darkened around the edges. The plastic turned cloudy with my desperate breaths, sticking to my cheeks. I felt my head go heavy. *This is it.*

I heard the man behind me jump backwards and crash to the floor. *What the hell?* A half-second later, the sound of a gunshot echoed through the room. He hadn't jumped: he'd been shot.

A second guard fell. The one remaining guard and the guy with the bandana dived for the floor. Someone was shooting through the window with a rifle: I was being rescued. But the bag was tied off: I was still going to asphyxiate. The world went gray and swimmy.

There was a third shot and the bag tugged and then went a little loose against my face. I breathed in and it *worked,* air whistled through the bag and filled my lungs like sweet nectar. I took another breath and another, and the world bloomed with light and color.

The guy with the bandana ran for the door and slipped out. A moment later, the guard did the same and got there just in time to meet Colton coming the other way. Colton threw him to the ground and clubbed him in the head with the butt of his shotgun.

JD was close behind him. He cut the zip tie on my wrists and I clawed the plastic bag off my head and looked at it.

There was a bullet hole in the bag at the top. Someone had shot an airhole to save my life.

JD passed me a radio and I slipped the earpiece into my ear. "Cal?" I asked cautiously. I walked to the window and stared out into the darkened jungle. I couldn't see him, but he was out there, somewhere, lying full-length in the undergrowth with his rifle, watching over all of us. "That was you?"

"Mm-hmm," came the reply.

I poked a finger through the hole. An inch lower and the bullet would have gone through my head. He might be a man of few words, but he was an *incredible* shot. "Thanks," I said, with feeling. Then I turned to JD. "How did you know to come in? I never gave the signal."

"She did," said JD. "Helluva girl you've got there."

I looked down at my shorts. The little flashlight was gone. I thought of Olivia, plucking at my clothes as the guards dragged me away. *Damn,* she thought fast.

Then I heard gunshots outside and my insides went cold with fear. She was still out there, in the cage. I looked at JD in panic. He threw me a gun.

And we ran to get my woman.

13

OLIVIA

In the cage, Dr. Guzman, Marcos, and I were lying flat on our faces as the camp erupted in chaos around us. We could hear screams and shouted orders in Spanish, the sharp crack of gunfire and sometimes the whistle of bullets as they passed close to us: already, one had hit the bars of the cage. Something was burning down at the other end of the camp, silhouetting people as they ran in front of the flames. Flashing the flashlight had worked: Gabriel's team had clearly arrived. But where was Gabriel? Did they find him? *Did they get to him in time?*

I made out a group of people running towards the cage, but I couldn't tell who they were. Wait...the man out in front: his silhouette had a short-sleeved shirt. My chest filled with hope. *Gabriel!*

He was only twenty feet away when someone else ran in from the side and unlocked the cage door. He grabbed my wrist and hauled me to my feet and I tensed as I recognized the ponytailed guard. Then he pulled me tight against him, my back to his chest, and I stifled a scream as a knife pressed against my throat. He turned to face Gabriel, keeping me as a shield between them. *"Stop!"* he yelled in Spanish. *"Or I kill her!"*

Gabriel pulled up short and held up his hands to halt the two men who ran up behind him. I'd never seen him so scared.

The guard backed up, pulling me with him. The blade of the knife scraped against my throat. God, I could feel it right against my jugular. If I so much as swallowed... I closed my eyes and held my breath.

The guard moved sideways along the cage, his back sliding along the bars. In another few seconds, we'd be lost in the shadows. With me as a hostage, Gabriel's team wouldn't be able to shoot: they'd be sitting ducks.

Suddenly, the knife was jerked away from my neck. I staggered free of the guard's grip and turned to see what had happened.

We'd all forgotten about Dr. Guzman. He'd reached through the bars and grabbed the guard's arm, wrenching the knife away from me. The guard was struggling to get free but Guzman's eyes were ferocious, diamond-hard glints in the darkness. He was making up for all the times he hadn't been able to protect me.

Dr. Guzman was in his sixties and couldn't hold the guard forever. But he didn't have to. Gabriel marched forward, and just as the guard struggled free, he slammed his fist into his face. The guard staggered back but Gabriel wasn't done: he hit the guard twice more. The guard slumped to the ground, unconscious, and Gabriel glared down at him, panting in anger. Then he looked at me and those beautiful hazel eyes were searing hot...and protective.

He knew. Somehow, he knew how the guard had been threatening me. Even as I processed that thought, Gabriel stepped forward, wrapped his arms around my back and pulled me to him. My cheek pressed against his pec and it was the best thing I'd ever felt in my life.

"I'm here now," he muttered in my ear. His hands pressed on the small of my back, mashing me to him. "Nobody's going to—" I felt his muscles tense in protective fury. *"I'm here now."*

A wave of relief washed through me, so powerful that my legs nearly gave way. I clung to him, the sound of the fighting fading into the background. It was real, he was *here,* wicked and wonderful. And just like in my dreams, he made the whole nightmare go away.

One of Gabriel's team stepped forward, an older guy with silver in his hair. "Gotta go," he told Gabriel, slapping him on the shoulder. "Colton, get the others."

"On it, boss." A stocky guy with a thick beard hurried into the cage and brought out the other two doctors. I nodded my thanks to Dr. Guzman and grabbed the medical bag. After nearly a week in the cage, the blue fabric was caked with dirt and dust. But we'd need it for Marcos, and if anyone else got hurt.

"You stay right behind me," Gabriel told me. "Put a hand on my back so I know where you are."

I nodded and planted my palm right in the center of his back. The warm solidness of him helped quell the fear in my stomach.

Then we were off, crouch-walking and sticking to the shadows. Most of the gunfire seemed to be coming from the other end of the camp, and as we got closer, two more men in military gear joined up with us. I realized they must have been keeping the guards busy, to buy time for my rescue. *All this for me?*

We crept forwards, the team firing in short bursts that lit up the night and rang in my ears. Bullets whipped past us, terrifyingly close. Again and again, one of the men up front would raise his hand and we'd drop down behind cover. There'd be a crackle of gunfire and then a *move up* and we'd hurry forward again. Then the main gate was looming up ahead of us. We jogged forward—

A cartel member ran out of the darkness to one side of us, gun raised. The soldiers whipped around towards him, but they'd been caught by surprise. I winced and tensed, waiting for the bullets to tear us apart—

The man fell. He didn't cry out, he just dropped like someone had hit his off switch. A gunshot echoed.

"Thanks," muttered the older guy into his earpiece. Someone else was out there, shooting from a distance. We ran through the gate and then we were out, slipping between the trees. We stopped a few moments later and ducked down in a line, our backs pressed against the trunk of a fallen tree.

"You okay?" Gabriel asked me immediately. "Are you hit? Are you hurt?" He didn't wait for an answer. His big hands cupped my shoulders and then traced down my arms and up the insides, checking for wounds. His palms moved down my sides to my waist, thumbs rubbing over my stomach. Then down my legs, all the way to my ankles. His hands started to skim up the inside of my legs. They slowed, and the mood changed...

I caught his hands with mine. "I'm fine," I told him, my voice shaky. He lifted his head to look at me and—God, his eyes were hooded with lust. I went weak.

He seemed to catch himself and realize that the others were looking at us. He drew back.

"Everyone else okay?" asked the older guy, in a carefully neutral voice.

There was a chorus of *okays* and *yups*. When they'd finished, a British voice murmured, "I dunno. Gabe, can you check *me* over?"

Gabriel glared at him and there was stifled laughter. Both of us flushed.

The older guy turned to me. "We've got medical gear to treat your wounded and fresh clothes for you, but that'll have to wait a while. They're going to be coming after us and we've got to put some distance between us and them."

I nodded and my legs tensed, ready to stand up and move. But they all seemed to be waiting for something.

Suddenly, a huge form loomed over us and I choked back a shriek of fear. The guy was *huge,* like seven feet tall, but somehow I hadn't heard him approach at all. Then I saw the rifle slung on his back. This was who they'd been waiting for: the guy who'd been covering our escape.

"Let's go," said Gabriel. And we set off into the jungle.

14

GABRIEL

WE WALKED FAST, TRYING TO PUT THE CAMP AS FAR BEHIND US AS possible. Each time I looked back at Bradan, who was covering our rear, he shook his head: *nothing yet*. But we knew they'd be coming. For the next thirty-six hours or so, until we were extracted, it was going to be a race to stay ahead of them.

As we walked, I thought about how things had gone at the camp. Cal saving my life. Colton taking down that guard hand-to-hand and getting the injured doctor out. Bradan and Danny keeping the bad guys off us. The plan had gone wrong and we'd had some close calls but they were a talented bunch, and I had to admit JD was doing a good job giving the orders, even if he was kind of a boy scout.

At first, it was almost totally dark. My night vision had been ruined by all the bright flashes and the flames back at the camp, and I just followed, relying on Cal up front to know where he was going. But as we pressed on, the moon broke through the clouds and my eyes adjusted.

That meant I could see her.

I'd put her ahead of me in the line: I'd told myself it made sense, now that we weren't being shot at: I could keep an eye on her and any attack was more likely to come from the rear, anyway. But it had another advantage, too. As she hurried along, that perfect, curvy ass in its tight jeans swayed back and forth, hypnotizing me. I kept finding myself moving faster, unconsciously trying to catch up to it.

When I wasn't staring at her ass, I was focused on the back of her neck. She had her hair pulled back into a bun, as usual, but this was the first time I'd been able to see her from behind. Below the bun, there was this beautiful, pale skin, turned silver by the moonlight. It looked so soft...and it was a place she was never normally touched, which meant it would be super-sensitive. I kept imagining kissing her there, twisting my head sideways a little to come in just under her bun and kiss a line that would have her squirming and gasping and maybe giggling if she was ticklish. Then I could finally slide those hair clips out and let her long hair cascade down, nudging it aside as I turned her and kissed the side of her neck, along her jaw and finally her lips...

I must have spent a full hour just staring at that patch of skin. *What's the matter with me?* I'd been in jail for three long years: I'd spent a *lot* of time thinking about women and what I'd like to do with them. But until Olivia, none of those fantasies wasted time on tender, romantic kissing. I couldn't remember the last time I'd felt like this about a woman. I wasn't sure I ever had.

And in a few days, when we made it back to Quito, I'd slip away and disappear...and I'd never see her again. The thought made my heart shrink down into a lump of brittle ice.

It's just an obsession, I told myself. Like when you have a thing for your teacher, or your boss. It was because she was so hot and also so professional, so serious, and buttoned-down. That's all this was. And there was a solution: I just had to fuck her. I'd bed her once and that would get her out of my system: all these feelings would go away. We had two nights together out here: that was plenty of time.

When we'd been on the move for about ninety minutes, JD called a halt and we took a few minutes break. JD opened his mouth to give an order to Danny, but before he could speak, Danny nodded and headed into the trees to check for anyone following us. The rest of us caught our breath and drank water: even at night, it was punishingly hot, this close to the equator.

I went to give Olivia some of my water and found her checking the injured doctor's wound. I watched her work, overcome again by the way she put others first. I'd been right: she'd been far too good for that hellhole of a prison.

Far too good for someone like me, too.

I pushed that thought away and passed her my canteen. She took a long drink, sighed with relief, then looked at me and the rest of the team. "So, who are you guys? Delta Force?"

I looked around at the others. "We're not Delta. We're..." What *were* we? A thrown-together bunch of reprobates and misfits. Cal had lived on his own in the forest for years, Bradan wasn't even military, and I should still have been in jail. "...different."

"Amen," muttered JD.

Danny emerged from the trees and gave JD a quick shake of his head. The cartel hadn't caught up to us...yet.

"I want to thank you," said Olivia, turning slowly to face each one of the team. "For getting us out of there." The other two doctors nodded in agreement.

JD, Cal, Bradan, Colton, Danny, and I all looked at each other. We'd all been running on adrenaline ever since I went into the camp. It was the first time we realized that we'd pulled it off. And just for a second, we felt like a team.

Olivia moved closer to me. "And what about you? How did you get out of jail?"

I swallowed. "I kind of...did a deal. Joined up."

She broke into a smile and it was heartbreaking because her eyes were so full of hope, of relief. "See? I always knew you were one of the good guys."

She thought I was on the right path. She didn't know I was about to double-cross these guys and disappear into the sunset with my gold, the second the mission was done. For the first time, my plan didn't feel slick. It felt dirty. I had to struggle to control my voice. "Yeah. Well. Sometimes I surprise myself."

Her smile grew wider and my self-doubt was burned away by a hot rush of need. God, she was beautiful. I found myself staring at those soft lips, unable to tear my eyes away. She did that thing where she flushed and ducked her head, uncomfortable with the attention. But then she took a little breath and looked at me again and my heartrate rocketed higher. I could feel it crackling in the air between us: neither of us had forgotten the kiss. She bit her lip and that sent me over the edge. I took a half-step forward, about to sweep her up in my arms—

"Hey," came a voice from the darkness.

Both of us looked around, and then down. The injured doctor was watching us from where he sat against a tree. "Just wondering what the plan was," he said.

Olivia stepped back slightly, as if embarrassed we'd been caught, then looked to me for an answer.

I stared at the doctor for a moment before I spoke, trying to remember his name from the TV news report. *Marcos.* I hadn't paid much attention to him until now, but he was younger than me, probably the same age as Olivia. And he wasn't bad looking. He'd made the question sound innocent enough, but I could see the hate in his eyes. He had a thing for Olivia. That's why he'd interrupted us.

My mind spun. Presumably, he and Olivia had been working together when they were captured. Had they been having a fling? Anger surged from deep in my belly, pulsing through my veins and tightening my muscles. *Get away from her! She's mine!* I didn't know how to handle jealousy. I was used to being with women for one night or a couple of days: what did I care if they slept with someone else? But with Olivia...

My hands were trying to curl into fists. I forced them to relax. "We've got a chopper coming to pick us up, but there are no good landing places nearby. It's not all that far to the extraction point but moving through the jungle's slow so it's going to take us another full day to get there. We'll walk for another few hours, then stop for the night. Tomorrow, we'll walk all day, and we should reach the extraction point by nightfall. Then, at dawn, the chopper picks us up."

I turned away for a moment, still trying to control my feelings. Luckily, Colton chose that moment to walk up with military tops and pants for the doctors to change into. It wasn't just about giving them fresh clothes, after nearly a week of captivity: they'd blend into the jungle much better in camouflage gear and that kept all of us safer. I changed back into my own camo gear for the same reason.

The older doctor, Guzman, started helping Marcos into his clothes, being careful of his injured arm. Olivia looked around, then bit her lip nervously when she realized there was nowhere to change.

I nodded at a large tree at the edge of the camp. "Go behind there. I'll keep watch." She nodded gratefully and I took up position on the side nearest the camp, while she darted behind the tree. I crossed my arms and leaned back against the trunk.

From behind the tree, the thump of boots hitting the ground. Then the rasp of denim. I imagined her pushing her jeans down those long, pale legs.

I could sneak a peek. I'm no Bradan, but I can be pretty quiet, and it was dark. She wouldn't know.

The soft rustle of cotton. That would be her unbuttoning her blouse. I could lean around the tree *right now* and finally see those full, soft breasts in just a bra...

I ground my back firmly against the trunk of the tree. *No.* It wouldn't be right.

The devil on my shoulder broke into hysterical laughter. *When did you ever worry about* that?

Fair point. But Olivia believed I was better than that. She was wrong but, when she trusted me like this...it made me want to be the man she thought I was.

I heard cloth unfold and then the sound of clothes being pulled on. *There,* said the devil. *Too late. Happy now?*

I'd missed my chance. Or, maybe, I'd achieved something.

A moment later, Olivia emerged from behind the tree, now in

jungle camouflage gear. She gave me a jokey, nervous little spin. "How do I look?"

The answer was, *sensational.* The pants were just the right sort of tight on that amazing, curvy ass. The top half was too big, so she'd had to cinch it in at the waist to stop it flapping around, and that meant it showed off the ripe curves of her breasts.

I couldn't speak. And when she saw how I was looking at her, she went quiet, too.

I took a step towards her—

"Move out," said JD, from behind me. I looked round to see everyone picking up their stuff. When I looked back to Olivia, she was already hurrying past me to join the others.

I stalked after her, horny as hell and cursing under my breath. But as we moved off, I told myself it was okay. In just a few hours, we'd make camp for the night. That was when I'd work my charm.

I'd fuck her tonight.

15

OLIVIA

WE HIKED FOR ANOTHER TWO HOURS, BY WHICH TIME MY THIGHS AND hamstrings were aching. Gabriel's team looked like they could have gone on all night.

We finally stopped in a small clearing. I had no idea what time it was: the cartel had taken our phones when they kidnapped us and none of us had been wearing a watch, but it felt like it was past midnight.

While the others unrolled sleeping bags, the really big guy started making a campfire. I helped gather twigs and branches and he nodded his thanks. I figured it was about time I started getting to know my rescuers. "I'm Olivia," I said quietly.

He hesitated for a second before he spoke, as if it wasn't something he did often. "Cal."

He wasn't so scary, once you got used to him: he was huge but his deep growl of a voice was surprisingly gentle. As he got the fire going, the glow of the flames lit up his face and I saw the sadness in his eyes. "What's the matter?" I asked.

Cal shrugged, as if it was nothing. Then he muttered, "I miss my dog. Never been away from him for more than a few hours."

I patted his arm. The others joined us around the fire, and for the first time since we left the camp, the tension eased. We were still deep in cartel territory but, for now, we were staying ahead of our pursuers. With two of the men standing guard, it felt like we could relax a little.

I refilled the medical bag from the supplies the team had brought with them: I wanted to be ready if anyone got hurt. Then I was finally able to properly clean and re-dress Marcos's wound with a sterile dressing.

The men unpacked rations they called *MREs* and there was complicated bargaining as they traded the sachets with each other. Gabriel plucked one out for me and set the entree heating in a pot of water over the fire. "Stew," he told me. "It's the least worst."

I was so hungry, I would have eaten anything. And actually, the stew wasn't bad: meaty and hot and very salty. There was a sachet of chocolate pudding, too, and candy bars and cookies. I devoured it all: it was the first proper food I'd had in days.

I started learning names. The older guy who reminded me of a cowboy, with his Texan drawl and his deep tan, was JD. The stocky, bearded one with the country accent was Colton. The Irish one was Bradan: when he'd had a gun in his hands, he'd seemed confident and tightly efficient but now, sitting around the fire, he seemed awkward, almost shy.

And finally, there was Danny: funny and charming, with a rough, London accent and these amazing green eyes. He was full of stories about him and JD: the two of them had served together for years, in Delta Force. "You remember that time in Germany, in the sauna?" he asked, an infectious grin spreading across his face.

"*No,*" warned JD. "Don't go telling them about—"

"We're in Berlin," Danny told us, ignoring him completely. "CIA black op in conjunction with German intelligence, we're following this German banker who's been funneling money to a terrorist group. He goes into this posh health spa. We wait, but he doesn't come out. We start getting worried we've lost him. So, eventually someone has to go in to have a look. JD says he'll do it. So, in he goes...and he finds our bloke in the sauna. Proper European-style sauna." Danny paused for effect. "No clothes allowed."

JD sighed and covered his face with his hand. We all leaned forward, rapt.

"Well, a man's gotta do what a man's gotta do, right? So, in JD goes, sits down in the steam, tries to blend in. But then one of the banker's mates goes in and tips him off that he's being followed, and the guy does a runner." Danny creased at the belly, trying to laugh and talk at the same time. "So, *JD...*"

"I'd had to take my radio off," JD explained. "I couldn't call for backup."

"So, JD comes running through the lobby of this spa," choked Danny, "*butt naked,* chasing after this guy who's *also* butt naked. Tackles him right in front of a busload of tourists. People are screaming. Taking pictures. *To this day,* if you search on the internet for *naked hotel wrestling match—*"

Everyone was laughing now, even JD. It was the first time I'd seen the big Texan smile. "Wait," he said. "Remind me, why was it *you* couldn't go into the sauna?" Danny hung his head, abashed. "He was hungover," JD told us. "He'd hooked up with this German intelligence officer the night before, one of his exes."

I shook my head in amazement, still laughing. The two of them were as close as two guys can be, but at first, I couldn't get my head around the friendship: JD was older, serious and sensible, always doing things by the book, while Danny was clearly the party guy. But as the stories kept coming, I began to see it. Danny lightened JD, acted as his escape valve so that the weight of leadership didn't crush him. And JD reined in Danny's excesses.

JD and Cal took a turn on guard duty, and I found myself talking one-on-one with Danny. He told me about growing up in London, about stealing cars as a teenager. He gradually leaned closer, flashing me those cocky grins... Me being me, it was some minutes before it clicked. *Wait. Is he flirting with me?* Men didn't normally do that. I felt myself flush, flattered but unsure what to do.

And then suddenly, the flirting stopped, like a switch had been thrown. I couldn't work out why until I glanced across the fire and saw Gabriel looking steadily at Danny. Had Gabriel just *warned him off*, like, *she's mine?!*

No one had ever done that to me before and it made a hot bomb go off in my chest, the warmth spreading out to fill me completely. I looked at Gabriel over the campfire and he stared right back at me, the flames dancing in his eyes, making him look even more devilish than usual. I could feel myself weakening, melting...

I hadn't stopped thinking about the kiss. And when I'd changed, on the other side of the tree from him, I'd been self-consciously aware of how close we were. I'd stood in just a bra and panties for a second and some tiny part of me had almost wanted to reach around the tree and pull him round to my side. Then I'd realized how crazy that was—I didn't *do* stuff like that—and I'd quickly scrambled into the military clothes.

The whole time we'd been marching through the jungle, I could feel Gabriel's eyes on me. I knew he wanted me. And I'd spent so long wanting him. Now he was out of prison and I wasn't his doctor, in theory there was nothing stopping us.

Except...he was still a criminal. A legendary thief, a master of the con and the underhand plan. It'd be stupid to fall for him...right?

After the meal, the men sat around talking, while Colton quietly moved around the circle grabbing any desserts that had gone uneaten. They talked about the Colorado town where the team was based: Cal already had a place there and the others were discussing where to rent or buy. From how they described it, it sounded beautiful, and I said so.

"It is," said JD, smiling. "Kinda old-fashioned. Might be why I like it."

"Good place to raise a family," I threw in.

And then I watched in horror as JD's face froze. Then his jaw set and he looked away. *Shit! What did I say?* I opened my mouth to apologize, but Danny caught my eye and gave me a tiny shake of his head. I nodded and we changed the subject, but I was twisting inside with guilt. What happened? Did JD not have a family?

Or worse...did he lose one?

Something else I noticed: Gabriel didn't take part in the conversation about finding a home. In fact, he didn't seem to take part much at all in the jokes and camaraderie. Almost like he didn't want to get too close to the others.

As we were about to turn in, JD and Cal, who were taking first watch, fueled themselves with coffee. Danny, who'd brought his own teabags, sat carefully brewing a mug of tea. "Something's been bothering me," he said as he watched the liquid change color. "Bradan and I went through that whole cartel camp, end to end. And you know what we didn't see any of?"

"What?" asked Gabriel.

"Drugs."

Everyone went quiet. It hadn't occurred to me until now, but Danny was right. I'd been in the cage for a week and I hadn't seen drugs arriving or leaving. But if it wasn't drug-related, what were the cartel doing there?

JD and Cal took up positions to watch over the camp. The rest of us bedded down in a circle around the embers of the fire. I lay down but found I couldn't sleep. Out in the open, I just didn't feel...*safe*. Whenever I closed my eyes, I was back in the cage. We were still in the middle of cartel territory and one of their patrols could find us at any time—

I heard a sound I'd never heard, a leathery flapping, right above me. My eyes snapped open and—

It was hovering maybe a foot from my face, so close that I could feel the powerful downdraft as its wings beat the air. Black eyes gleamed in the moonlight. I filled my lungs to scream but then bit it back: a scream could carry for miles in the quiet of the night, I could alert a patrol and get us all killed—

Suddenly, Gabriel was there, shooing the thing away. It fluttered off into the trees. "Just a bat," he whispered. He bent low over me so that he could talk without waking the others. "Can't sleep?"

I silently shook my head.

Gabriel nodded towards the edge of the camp. I followed him.

A little way into the trees, he found a fallen tree and sat straddling it. I did the same and sat facing him. Maybe it was because I was looking into his eyes, but suddenly, I was very aware of being alone with him. I swallowed. Had this been a plan? Get me alone and seduce me?

No. I could see the need in his eyes but there was concern there, too. This was a genuine attempt to calm me down and help me sleep. I smiled at him, grateful, and that made him look away as if embarrassed.

Doing the right thing bothered him.

"One thing you never told me," he said, "was how you wound up at the prison." Then he cocked his head to one side. "Unless you don't want to tell me."

I hesitated. I didn't want to tell *anyone*. That day was still a fresh crack in my mind that separated my old life from my new one. The edges were razor sharp and just touching them was painful. But...

I realized I did want to tell *him.*

"I was an ER doc," I told him. "At a hospital in Phoenix. A good place. The people I worked with were the *best*...we were like a family, you know?"

He nodded and from the way his lips pressed together, he understood what that felt like.

"The job was my life. You might have noticed I'm a little..." I sighed. "I kind of take work..."

"Seriously?" But his eyes sparkled in the moonlight: kind, not cruel.

I cracked a tiny smile. "Yeah. I never really figured out how to switch off. But helping people is all I've ever wanted to do."

"What happened?"

I sighed. "One day, I went to the drug lock-up to fetch something and one of the other doctors was there, an older guy called Alec Bryce. He was signing for some Oxy, said he needed it for one of his patients: no big deal. Except..." I chewed my lip. It was getting more difficult to tell, the closer I got to the moment. "Except...I happened to see that patient myself, later that night, and he hadn't been given Oxy, or any painkillers."

I looked up to see Gabriel frowning. He was smart: he already knew where this was going.

"All I had to do was leave it alone," I said tightly. "All I had was a hunch. But I was worried. I checked the drug log, checked with patients...Bryce was signing out a lot of Oxy, and claiming it was for patients who weren't getting it."

"He was selling it?" asked Gabriel.

"That's what I thought. Then I started watching Bryce as he worked." I met Gabriel's eyes. "He was high. The Oxy was for *him*."

"Jesus," whispered Gabriel. "What'd you do?"

I closed my eyes and breathed in, long and slow. I was right up against the memory now, and every syllable rubbed my mind against the edges. But I wanted to get it out. "I took Bryce aside," I said slowly. "Told him I knew. He broke down. Begged me not to tell the hospital admin. He admitted he had a problem, said he'd check into a rehab place that night..." I took a shaky breath. "And I believed him."

I could feel myself cracking wide open, exposing my vulnerable insides for the first time since it happened. I almost jumped off the log and ran back to the campfire—

But then I lifted my gaze to meet his. And those eyes that were always so full of schemes and trickery and wickedness...they were warm. Honest.

I could trust him.

I kept going. "I got into work the next day and straightaway, I was called in to see administration. And they told me—" My chest quaked and I had to stop and take a breath, dangerously close to crying. "They told me that Doctor Bryce has come to them, deeply concerned that I've been stealing Oxy."

Gabriel leaned forward, his brow creasing in disbelief: *what?!* I remembered having exactly the same reaction, the day it happened. Then the disbelief turned to creeping, sick dread.

"Bryce told them that he'd discovered the theft the night before, and that he'd been up all night, checking through the logbook," I said. "What he'd actually been doing was *altering* the logbook so it looked like *I* had signed out all the extra Oxy."

Gabriel's mouth moved but nothing came out. For once, he was lost for words. But then the rage began to build, first in his eyes and then in those massive shoulders and powerful arms. He leaned forward, his fingers gripping the log so hard his knuckles went white. "That fucking *asshole!*" he spat.

His protective fury gave me just enough strength to finish. "Bryce had been at the hospital for twenty years: he had a good reputation. They believed him, not me. I would have gone to jail, but the hospital didn't want the bad publicity. They fired me, and word got around the hospitals that it was drug-related. No one would hire me..."

Gabriel's mouth tightened. "Except the prison. *Jesus.*"

My shoulders dropped and I let my head hang forward. Hot tears filled my eyes and started to plop onto the log between us. I gave a ragged sniff, seconds from breaking down completely. It wasn't just that revisiting it all hurt. It was that he knew now. He knew that—

"*Jesus, I'm so stupid!*" I hissed.

He stared at me for a second. "*That's* what you think?!"

"I'm just a stupid, naive—" I shook my head and my voice broke down into sobs. "All I had to do was report him, why didn't I just—"

"You blame *yourself?!*" Suddenly, his big, warm fingers were under my chin, lifting my head to look at him. "*No.* No, Olivia, Jesus...You were just trying to do the right thing. You're a good person. Don't ever apologize for that."

I blinked and looked at him through a curtain of tears, searching his face for deception. But he looked open and honest, his eyes full of concern. I sniffed, unable to speak. I wanted to believe him. *Really?*

His hands gripped my shoulders and squeezed. *Really.*

We looked into each other's eyes and then he grabbed me around the waist and pulled me along the log until our bodies met. His arms wrapped around me and he crushed me to him, one hand cradling the back of my head, my face pressed against his chest. I kept sobbing, but for the first time, it was healing. Each time my chest spasmed and my body jerked against his bigger, stronger one, a little more of the pain left me.

I felt something I'd never felt before, not even with the couple of boyfriends I'd had. I felt *not alone*.

When I was all cried out, he held me for another few moments, his hand slowly running up and down my back, calming me. Then I finally sniffed and untangled myself from him. I was a mess, red-eyed and wet-cheeked, but when I looked up at him, he was looking down at me like I was the best thing he'd ever seen. In that second, he looked helpless, and it wasn't lust in his eyes. It was something more innocent. Something deeper.

I swallowed.

He slid his hand along my cheek, the tips of his fingers brushing through my hair. And then he leaned down to kiss me.

16

GABRIEL

SHE WAS RIGHT THERE, MORE BEAUTIFUL THAN EVER, BLACK HAIR gleaming in the moonlight, soft lips upraised to meet mine. I could have her, right now: kiss her and press her back on the log. Slowly strip her out of the camouflage gear and fuck her right on the fallen tree, one of those long legs either side of the trunk.

But I froze. Just sat there staring down at her, because...

I didn't want to just fuck her, not anymore. Hearing her story had changed something. All the feelings that had been building had crystallized, going from ghosts I could bat away and push through to an unshakeable, solid truth right at my core. I couldn't give it a name but—

I wanted...*more.*

I wanted to be with her. Wanted to be the person she came home to each day.

Stupid, I raged at myself. *Childish.*

But real. Maybe more real than anything I'd ever felt, my whole life.

Only I couldn't have that. In one more day, we'd reach the extraction point. We'd get the chopper back to Quito...and I'd duck through that hole in the fence and disappear forever.

I couldn't just fuck her, as I'd been planning to. It wouldn't *get her out of my system,* as I'd thought: it'd make me want her even more. Worse, I'd be taking advantage of her, just like that bastard Bryce. I couldn't do that to her.

I leaned back. And then, before I could change my mind, I swung my leg over the fallen tree and stood up. I offered her my hand. "We should get some rest," I muttered. "Got a long way to walk tomorrow."

She stared up at me and I had to stand there and watch as it all played out on her face. First bewilderment. Then hurt that I was rejecting her. *No,* I wanted to say, my chest aching, *no, it's not like that, it's for your own good.* Finally, she looked ashamed. She thought she'd gotten it wrong, that I didn't like her. Her face crumpled. *Aw, no. No, no, no, I—*

She stiffly got up, ignoring my hand, and walked past me back to the camp.

I stood there helpless. I couldn't explain...not unless I told her my plan. And I told myself I couldn't do that: what if she ratted on me to JD?

That's what I told myself. But secretly, I knew she would never rat on me. The truth was, I couldn't tell her about my plan because I couldn't bear seeing her face fall when she realized I was still a lying, double-crossing schemer.

I watched as she lay down on her sleeping bag, facing away from me. I sighed, turned my back and lay down to try to get a few hours' sleep. *I did the right thing,* I thought firmly. Better to hurt her now than break her heart later. At least this way, she wouldn't feel used.

All I had to do was keep my distance from her, until we got back to Quito. That was going to be hell, now I'd accepted how I felt about her. Before, I'd just wanted her. Now, I needed her.

It was only for one more day and one more night, though. Then the chopper would pick us up, I'd make my escape and Olivia could find some guy, some normal guy, some *good* guy, and settle down and have kids and all that stuff.

I rolled over and stared at Olivia's back.

This is the right decision.
It sure didn't feel like it.

17

OLIVIA

THE NEXT DAY, I WOKE TO THE DAWN LIGHT FILTERING DOWN THROUGH the trees. I rubbed at my face and silently groaned. I hadn't had a proper night's sleep in nearly a week. Last night, I'd managed just a few fitful hours and now I was exhausted and emotionally drained.

I felt like an idiot. It had felt so good, opening up to Gabriel about what happened. And I'd been so sure about what I'd seen in his eyes, I'd been ready to ignore all my doubts about who he was. But then he'd pushed me away. I must have been wrong.

I sighed, stood up and found my boots. Balancing on one leg, I started to slip my left foot into my boot.

Suddenly, arms hooked under my armpits and jerked me up and back. I let out a yelp: I was dangling, my feet kicking just off the ground and my back pressed to a big male chest.

"Wait," said Gabriel's voice in my ear. I went limp and he set me gently down on my sleeping bag. Then he stepped around me, picked up the boot I'd been about to put on, and gave it a shake.

A brown spider as big as my palm dropped out and scuttled into the undergrowth. I jumped back, shuddering and nauseous. God, I'd nearly—

I glanced up at Gabriel and caught him just as he looked down at me: caring and concerned and so powerfully protective that it took my breath away.

I hadn't been wrong.

Gabriel swallowed, rubbed at his stubble and turned away. "You should check the other one," he muttered as he walked off.

I stood there watching his retreating back, my heart thumping. He *did* have feelings for me. But he was pushing me away: why?

I checked both boots very carefully. Twice. Then I pulled them on and we set off.

～

We made good progress for the first hour but then slowed as we started to climb...A thick mist started to descend: first it was above the canopy, then it was down around the trunks, then finally it was on us: curls of cool, refreshing fog that soaked our clothes and left our faces dripping. "What's with the mist?" I asked Gabriel.

"It's not mist," he told me. "It's cloud. We're high enough that we're walking through clouds."

I looked around in wonder. Everything felt lush and new, the air was thick with the scent of exotic flowers and the vines overhead dripped a constant warm rain on us. The monkeys were out in force, chattering and howling to each other overhead. There were constant bird calls and croaks that had to be from some sort of frog. I'd never been anywhere that felt so crammed full of life. It was like walking through the Garden of Eden. It felt wrong, that we could be in so much danger, somewhere so beautiful. But we knew the cartel must be close. It wasn't just that they might have followed us from the camp. This was their turf, and we could stumble into one of their patrols at any time.

The whole time, I could feel Gabriel watching me. When he was behind me, I'd feel his eyes tracking my every move. When he was in front of me, he'd do these little glances over his shoulder, quickly looking away when he realized I'd seen him. And when we were close together, pushing through undergrowth or scrambling up a slick, rocky path, I'd look up and find him gazing at me as if helpless. He'd break the gaze and look away, scowling, then a second later look again, as if he couldn't help it.

We crested the top of the peak and started descending and the cloud lifted. We stopped around noon for more MREs, supplemented by mangos plucked from the trees. JD sliced one up and we all sat motionless, watching as small white and brown monkeys cautiously approached and then scampered up and grabbed the fruit from his hand.

It hit me that I was way, *way* out of my comfort zone, thousands of miles from my safe, predictable little life in Arizona. But I was seeing things I never would have seen at home.

We started marching again, and as JD rotated his men through different duties, Colton came up from his position watching our tail and joined me in the middle of the pack. It was the first time I'd spent much time around him. He was *big:* not as tall as Cal but wider, a walking wall of muscle with not an ounce of fat on him. He'd stripped down to a tank top to beat the heat and he had the strongest arms I'd ever seen, with huge, thick biceps and hands that looked like they could crush rocks. He wasn't my type but he was hot as hell, in a rough kind of way. With his thick black beard, he almost looked like an outlaw biker. And maybe it was because he was a bounty hunter when he wasn't with the team, but he had a sort of stern authority. *Good,* honorable, but someone who wasn't afraid to lay down the law. It was easy to imagine him slamming some dangerous criminal into the ground and cuffing him. But it was easy to imagine something else, too. If you were a certain sort of woman, one who cheeked him and teased him, he might just—

Tie your hands, throw you over his shoulder and carry you off.

I flushed. Where had *that* come from?

By mid-afternoon, we were all getting tired, walking on autopilot as we followed the person ahead. Suddenly, we stopped. Cal, who was out in front, had put up his hand.

The team all readied their guns. JD crept down the line and sidled up to Cal. "What is it?"

Cal reminded me of a dog that's alerted: he'd frozen in place, only his head moving as he looked back and forth across the trees in front of us. "Someone's here."

JD stared at the forest. "Where?" he asked after a moment.

Cal shook his head, his brow creased with frustration. "I don't know."

JD gave a hand signal and the team spread out in a circle with me and the other doctors in the center. My chest contracted in fear. *They've found us.*

Gabriel muttered to me over his shoulder, "When the shooting starts, hit the ground and stay there."

I nodded.

Danny suddenly raised his gun and gestured towards the trees on his side. Everyone swung their guns that way. Danny crept forward silently...

Suddenly, he stopped. "*Shit!*" he hissed. "JD?" he asked uncertainly.

There was a man in the trees, but he wasn't cartel. He was stripped to the waist and he was holding a long, slender pole in one hand. I had to stare at the arrow-shaped tip of the pole for several seconds before my brain accepted the image. *Yes, that really is a spear.* I suddenly remembered what Dr. Guzman had told me about the indigenous people around here, the Shuar.

"Two more," said Colton, behind me, his voice tight. I looked over my shoulder. Colton had his gun half up, unsure whether to raise it. The men on his side were carrying machetes.

"Another behind us," said Bradan. Then, "More. Another three."

"Two more in front," said Cal. "Got a rifle and a shotgun here,"

"Guns down," said Gabriel.

JD glanced at him. "We're outnumbered," he growled. "We put our guns down, they could rush us."

"They won't hurt us if we don't hurt them," said Gabriel. "This is their land, they just want to be left alone." He took a deep breath and slung his gun on his back, then raised his hands in peace.

I could see JD debating. I'd picked up on the fact that the two men didn't like each other. But Gabriel knew people, he could read them. *Listen to him,* I mentally begged.

"Guns down," JD said at last.

Everyone put their guns away and we all held our breath. The Shuar stayed where they were.

"Very slowly," said Gabriel, "start walking."

We moved off, with Gabriel bringing up the rear. I could feel sweat trickling down the back of my neck and my shoulders ached with tension...but nothing happened. A few moments later, when we checked behind us, the Shuar had melted back into the trees. Everyone let out long sighs of relief and I saw JD look at Gabriel with a newfound respect.

We moved on and thanks to Cal's skill in threading a path through the jungle, we made good time. Just as the sun was setting, we pushed through some trees and—

I stopped, blinking.

We'd emerged on one side of a deep valley. After nearly a week deep in the forest, never seeing more than thirty feet in front of me, suddenly I could see for miles, right across to the other side. Above was an enormous, pink and gold sky decorated with long trails of cotton-candy clouds. I drew in a deep lungful of air. I'd felt the claustrophobia of the jungle for so long, I'd forgotten what it felt like to feel space. And there was a breeze! I could feel it toying with my hair: I'd forgotten what that felt like, too.

Gabriel pointed down. The jungle continued down the sides of the valley, but there was one spot at the bottom that had been cleared. I could see grass and a blocky white building. "That's the extraction point," he told me.

We'd made it. Tomorrow, we'd be going home.

18

GABRIEL

As we descended into the valley, my eyes never left Olivia for a second. This was the last time I'd be close to her. The last time I'd see her lips twitch into a smile, the last time I'd stare at all that tightly pulled back dark hair and dream of freeing it, the last time I'd run my eyes over those gorgeous curves. I tried to burn her into my memory: the shape of her jaw, the color of her eyes.

It wasn't like I could kid myself that this wasn't goodbye, that maybe we'd run into each other again someday. Running off with the gold would put me on a Most Wanted list for life. There were plenty of countries where I could enjoy my riches, but the one place I'd never be able to go back to was the United States. Olivia would be lost to me forever.

Earlier that day, I'd been watching her as she gazed around at the jungle in wonder. I loved that she still had that sense of innocent amazement. When you've spent enough time in combat, you lose that: you start to see the places you go in terms of ambush points and sniper positions. But once I'd seen how Olivia reacted to the jungle, I looked around again with fresh eyes, taking in the purple and pink butterflies and the tiny blue frogs clinging to leaves, and you know what? It *was* amazing.

She was good for me.

About a hundred feet from the bottom of the valley, the path we were following turned to loose gravel and small stones. We had to go slow, testing each foot as we put it down, or we'd wind up tumbling head-over-feet all the way down. When Olivia slipped a little, I lunged and grabbed her hand to stop her falling. The instant I touched her, I felt something inside me *lift*: it was like I could breathe again. It felt *right.*

She steadied herself, then nodded at me gratefully and waited for me to release her.

I couldn't let go. I knew that once I did, I'd most likely never hold her hand again. *God, what's wrong with me?* But it was how I felt. I stared into those frozen-forest eyes, my chest aching...

And let her go.

~

We reached the bottom of the valley just as the sun was slipping below the horizon. As we emerged from the trees, all of us stopped and stared and Colton gave a low whistle.

We were looking at a house. A grand, hacienda-style home, right in the heart of the jungle. The setting sun turned the white stucco walls amber and cast deep shadows under the row of arches that ran along one side of the house.

Years ago, someone had cleared an area of jungle the size of a football field and then built this place at the edge, taming nature against all odds. But the place had been abandoned for decades and the jungle was taking the land back. What had once been a manicured lawn was now long, scrubby grass and the paved paths were overgrown and uneven. Young trees were sprouting up fast at the edges of the cleared area, shrinking it, and vines had grown up the walls and over the windows of the house. In another ten years, the place might not even be visible.

"How?" asked Danny. "There are no roads out here. There's *nothing* out here."

Cal pointed across the valley. "There's a river, listen." And when we all stopped and listened, there *was* the distant sound of water. "Probably brought everything in by boat. That's what I did with my cabin in Idaho."

"But why?" asked Danny.

"Drugs," I told him. "Remember, we're not far from the border with Colombia. Someone high up in the cartel built it so they had somewhere luxurious to stay while they were managing things out here. Then the police or a rival caught up with them and it's been abandoned ever since."

We crept cautiously inside. The entrance hall was huge, two stories with an elaborate stone staircase and a black and white tiled floor. Birds had built a nest in the chandelier that hung overhead. We did a room-by-room sweep just to be sure, but the place was empty. It was in surprisingly good condition too .Anything valuable that could be easily carried out was gone, but the windows were intact, so the place had stayed dry, and the bedrooms still had beds.

"Might as well make ourselves comfortable," said JD. "But no lights." He pointed to the windows: the curtains had long since been stolen. "They'd be visible right up and down the valley."

No light meant no fire, but we had some chemical self-heating pouches and we used them to warm up some MREs. There weren't many left: we'd had to travel light, so we'd only brought enough to last through the mission, plus a little for emergencies. I got chili with beans: edible, but I'd rather have been back at that little cafe in Mount Mercy. It bothered me that I'd never see that place again.

When we were done, and Colton had "tidied up" any uneaten desserts, he and I took the first watch. As the others spread out amongst the bedrooms, we went outside and started walking the perimeter. The sun was fully down now, and with clouds blocking the moon and stars, it was almost pitch black. JD was right: out here, any light would be visible for miles and bring the cartel running. I had to grudgingly admit that he knew his stuff. But I muttered a lot of curses, tripping over vines and banging my shins on rocks, before my eyes adjusted to the dark.

"It's dark as the inside of a cow," muttered Colton, when our paths crossed. "Next time, we could do with night vision gear."

I grunted my agreement, feeling a twinge of guilt. I wouldn't be there for the next mission.

After two hours, Danny and JD took our places and we headed inside to get some sleep. The inside of the house was even darker than the outside. I picked my way carefully up the stairs, feeling as much as seeing, then along the upstairs hallway. I stopped outside the third bedroom on the left.

Olivia was in there. I'd seen her go in just as Colton and I headed out.

I could just go in there, wake her and tell her how I felt. But then what? Lie to her about some perfect future together, back in the US? What would happen when we got back to the airfield in Quito? Just tell her to *wait here, I'll be right back,* then slip through the hole in the fence and disappear forever, leaving her standing there like a jilted bride at the altar?

I couldn't do that to her.

It took all my willpower, but I turned away. The room next to hers was empty. I unrolled my sleeping bag on the bed, pulled off my boots, and crashed out.

I was just closing my eyes when I heard something: a creak and a huge intake of breath, then ragged panting. I'd heard that kind of breathing before, but I couldn't think where. It prickled at my spine, hard to listen to because it was so shockingly vulnerable: the sound of someone in full-on, hysterical fear.

It was coming from the other side of the wall: Olivia's room.

I was up and moving before I was even aware of it, groping for the door handle and feeling my way out into the hallway, then finding Olivia's door and stumbling inside. I homed in on her labored breathing: she was on the bed, and I figured out she was sitting up. "Olivia!" I said urgently. "It's me."

No response. Her breathing got worse: she was hyperventilating now.

The hell with light discipline. I felt in a pocket and found a chemical glow stick. I snapped it, shook it and brought the dim green glow in front of her face. "Olivia!"

She was sitting bolt upright. Her eyes were open but she was staring off into space: she didn't seem to see me or the light. She was having a nightmare, and she was still in it.

Now I knew where I'd heard that kind of panicked breathing before. I'd heard it in tents and barracks and the backs of trucks, anywhere soldiers slept. It was the sound of the bad stuff that gets inside your head and won't come out, for weeks or months or the rest of your life.

"*Olivia!*" Still nothing. I gripped her shoulders with both hands.

She made an unearthly noise, a high-pitched shriek of fear that made my chest ache in pity. She flailed, trying to push me away, and I took a hit across the face. Then her eyes focused and she looked around in wild panic.

I quickly brought the glowstick up to my face so she could see me. "It's me," I said quickly. "Olivia, it's me. You're with me, it's okay, you're with me."

She stared at me uncomprehendingly for a moment. Then she threw her arms around me and clung to me with all her strength, burying her face in my neck.

I crushed her to me. A huge, hot throb went through me, stronger than anything I'd ever felt, primal and fiercely protective. I tried to speak but it choked off my words, so I just squeezed her tight, wrapping my arms around her like I was blocking the entire outside world from touching her. She quaked against me and I felt silent tears wet against my neck.

I rocked her there gently until her breathing settled. Then I eased her gently back so that I could look at her.

She stared up at me in the ghostly green glow of the glowstick. "God. I'm sorry." She shook her head. "I think I'm going crazy."

"*No*," I said urgently. "God, no. With everything you've been through?"

She gave a bitter laugh. "You're all so brave. You just handle this and I'm having nightmares and—"

I took her firmly by the shoulders again. "Olivia. You might just be the bravest person I've ever met." I stared into her eyes and suddenly the words just started spilling out. "And you're good, and you're kind and you're—"

I managed to stop myself speaking but that just made the words pile up in my head. *Beautiful. Adorable. Smart. Special.* Everything I'd been holding back welled up inside me and I wrestled for control. My mouth opened but nothing would come out. I shook my head and just gazed at her...

And then, with a superhuman effort, I stood up.

I'd been doing the wrong thing my entire life. However much I wanted her, however much she wanted me, for once, I had to do what was right.

I turned my back to her.

This is the right thing to do.

I walked to the door.

It's the right thing.

I put my hand on the knob...

And then I cursed, marched back to the bed, and kissed her as hard as I could.

19

OLIVIA

I'D BEEN SITTING ON THE BED, CRUSHED AND GRAY. THEN HIS FOOTSTEPS changed direction and there was just time for my heart to lift and my chest to fill in hope before—

The kiss came suddenly, and in the pitch blackness, my whole world narrowed down to that one sensation. As his lips pressed mine, I could feel every tiny nerve ending coming alive, each one sending a golden spark arcing down through my body. The sparks twisted together, becoming a scorching rush of heat that rocketed down my body and detonated in my groin. I grabbed for him in the dark. Found his shoulders and clung on tight, the fabric of his camo top rough under my fingers.

His lips broke contact and then came back, tasting me, and the second kiss was even better than the first. I gave a soft little moan and my lips flowered open under him. That made him growl low in his throat and pull me tighter against him, every muscle in his body suddenly hard. *That's me?!* I thought, in excitement and shock, *that's me, doing that to him?!*

He cupped my cheeks with both hands, thumbs stroking my cheekbones and fingertips sliding into my hair. He leaned me back, kissing down into me, every press of his lips taking me another inch towards the bed. I was breathless, panting against his mouth, and every time I inhaled, I seemed to go a little more heady: I was getting drunk on him.

This was exactly what I'd been fantasizing about since the first time I met him: I was the lady being seduced by the highwayman, the maiden being corrupted by the rogue. And I wanted it. I'd never wanted anything more.

I felt my head touch down on the bed and then we were lying, him hulking over me with a leg between my thighs. A hot ripple went down my body. *God, this is really happening.*

His tongue brushed my lips, expert and teasing, and I writhed, my ass grinding against the bed. Then his lips spread me wide and his tongue full-on *plundered* me, leaving me quaking.

He laid a trail of kisses down my jaw and down my neck. I'd closed my eyes at some point. Now I opened them again, desperate to see him. He'd dropped the glow stick on the bed, and as my eyes adjusted, its dim light let me watch as he stripped his camo top off over his head. His midsection appeared first, rock-hard and tight with power. Then his pecs, so wide and full they made me feel small. And finally, those big, caramel shoulders and the biceps like melons. I couldn't help myself: as he hunkered down over me, I reached up and stroked my fingers over the warm muscle, going weak inside at the feel of him. I followed the tattoo of thorned vines down to where it encircled his Marine Corps tattoo: the good, surrounded by the bad but still fighting bravely.

He glanced down, saw what I was looking at, and then looked at the window. The glowstick wasn't as bright as a flashlight, but with no drapes the light would be visible for a long distance. "We should probably lose the light," he muttered.

He grabbed it. Then he brought it up to my face and just gazed down at me, drinking me in while he still could. I bit my lip: it was just like that very first time he'd looked at me, in the prison infirmary. No one had ever made me feel special like he did.

He reluctantly wrapped the glow stick in his fatigue shirt and the room went instantly black. For a second, it was disorienting and scary. Then I reached up, and as soon as my fingertips brushed the warm, firm muscle of his bicep, it was okay.

I felt the tension unwind and the darkness started to take on a different feel: it became private and secret, intensely intimate. It made me bolder: I'd been worrying in the back of my mind about being inexperienced but, in the dark, it was easier to just go for it, to reach up and run my hands over his chest and arms, to do what felt right. I still had a mental image of him naked from when he'd stripped off in prison, but now I got to rebuild it from touch, tracing my palms slowly down over his shoulders and back, then his waist. With each inch of warm skin I touched, the heat pulsed through me deeper, stronger, until I was panting and needy beneath him. My fingers reached the rough fabric of his pants and I groped for his belt, wanting to feel all of him.

He stopped me, gentle but firm. "No. First..." —his voice became a low growl of lust— "*you.*"

I swallowed. There was so much pent-up lust in that one word, like he absolutely *could not wait.* The bed creaked as he moved and then the backs of his hands brushed my chin as he started to unbutton my fatigue shirt. For a moment, the only sound in the room was our breathing and the soft pop of buttons easing through cloth. Then his hands reached under my shoulders and lifted me, and I shrugged out of the shirt, then unhooked my bra. As I slipped it off, I couldn't see a thing but I knew he was right there in front of me. For a second, we just sat there, unable to see but knowing our bare skin was only inches apart. I could feel the warmth of his breath on my breasts and hear his breathing quicken as he imagined me—

And then he didn't have to imagine anymore because he was touching me. I caught my breath as his hands found my breasts and traced every soft curve. The darkness made everything more intense: each brush of his hands sent little silver earthquakes straight to my core, where they turned into slick, liquid heat. Then his fingers found my nipples, slowly stroking the base of each one, experiencing every little bump of the areolae before spiraling upwards to the peaks. I took a shuddering breath, struggling to keep still.

He started kissing me again: slow, hungry kisses, devouring me. He filled his hands with my breasts and began rolling and kneading them in time with the kisses, and I groaned and moved with him, arching my back and grinding my hips. Each kiss, each squeeze of my breasts, rippled down to my core and stoked the heat there a notch higher. Each one made me kiss him back harder, press myself against his body tighter.

He gave another of those growls, grabbed the waistband of my pants and then broke the kiss for a second while he rammed pants and panties down my legs and off in one tangle of fabric, leaving me naked and gasping. His hands found my hips and ass, and as they traced the shape of me, I felt myself tense, insecurities rushing back. What if he thought there was too much of me?

He whispered, a hot little rush in my ear. "You're goddamn beautiful, Olivia." He slid his hand up over my hip to my waist. "This curve of you." His other hand slid down my spine to my ass and squeezed. "And this curve." He slid both hands up my body to my breasts, cupped and squeezed them. "And these curves. You know what I think of when I look at you, when I feel you?"

"No..."

"I think somebody should be painting your picture. That's the kind of beauty you have. Minstrels used to write songs about women like you. Guys used to write poems. You're classic, you're timeless."

"I—" That fragile silver balloon in my chest was tugging at its string, wanting to float skyward. "I—But—" I squirmed inside. "But I'm not all...little and slim and—"

His hands gently cupped my cheeks and a thumb brushed my lips, silencing me. "Men start fights over women like that," he told me. "But they start wars over women like *you*."

I felt that silver balloon soar into the heavens. It was such a release of emotion, I just lay there for a moment, unable to speak, my eyes hot. Then I hooked my arms around him and tugged him to me. We kissed and ground together again, my breasts stroking against his chest, and I felt so gloriously *free.*

One of his knees pressed gently between my legs, opening them, and then his hand slid down my body. I drew in my breath as he cupped me and started to rub.

I had no idea what was coming.

He started with slow strokes of his fingers, until I began to grind my hips and helplessly arch up to meet him. Then he brought his thumb into play, circling and teasing my clit, and I suddenly clutched at his shoulders. I had to feel something solid under my hands because everything was dissolving into rolling, silver-tipped waves of pink pleasure. *Oh my God. How is he...?*

I'd never felt anything like it before. He had the perfect hands, big and powerful enough to make me feel small, but dextrous as a pianist's. And he knew *exactly* how to touch me: he touched me like no one else, including myself. The heat in my core was building and building, expanding within me with each touch of his fingers, and I knew I wouldn't last long.

But Gabriel was as cunning in bed as he was in everything else. Cunning and *evil.* He stroked my lips until I was slick and begging, then slowed until the wave subsided. He plunged his fingers into me and teased my g-spot until I locked my legs around his arm, heels digging into the bed, panting, *pleading...*and then he'd stop and wait for me to calm. Even in the dark, he seemed to be able to read me perfectly, judging from my breathing exactly how close I was. I could feel him grinning down at me, his eyes glittering.

Finally, though, he sank lower, taking his weight on his forearms, our faces only a few inches apart, and I knew this was going to be the time. His expert fingers stroked and rubbed, then plunged deep. His thumb began a slow, insistent rhythm at my clit. I grabbed his arm with both hands, urging him on. "Please," I begged.

He gave a filthy chuckle. His fingers hooked a little, finding just the right spot and I cried out. *God, how is he doing this?* Did they teach this at Rogue School? Advanced Female Pleasure 101? I was completely at his mercy: writhing on the bed as the pleasure took hold of me, my legs locked so tight around his arm that he could barely move it. *"Yes!"* I hissed in a voice that didn't sound like mine. *"Gabriel, yes! Please!"*

His fingers moved faster, circling and twisting: he'd done a deal with the devil to grant him magic fingers, that was the only explanation. But I didn't care: I was bucking and thrashing, my head levering back against the bed until my chin pointed at the ceiling. I was dimly aware of him reaching up with this other hand and doing something with my hair and it felt good. Then the pleasure was carrying me up and up, unstoppable. All those waves of pleasure that he'd built up and let slip away were suddenly back, stacking on top of each other to make one thundering tsunami. My shoulders and heels dug hard into the bed and my back arched like a bow. *"Gabriel, yes!"*

The hand that had been in my hair slid down my body and rubbed at a nipple. At the same time, his fingers hooked inside me, his thumb circled my clit and—

A solid wall of pure pink pleasure, crackling with silver energy, slammed into me and carried me with it. The room disappeared behind flaring, brilliant stars and I full-on screamed, it felt so good. I'd never been loud during sex but then I'd never felt anything like *that:* the pleasure was too much to be released any other way. My head tossed back and forth as I rode the waves and now I knew what he'd done to my hair: he'd unpinned it. As I thrashed around, I could feel it gradually unwinding, spreading out into a dark cloud, and it felt freeing.

I finally fell back onto the bed, my throat and chest aching and my whole body weak and shaky. *Wow.* I stared up into the darkness. I couldn't see anything, but I knew for sure that Gabriel was giving me one of those wicked grins. The echo of my scream still throbbed in my ears. "Do you think anyone heard that?" I whispered.

He kissed me. "I think they heard that back in Arizona."

I felt my face going scarlet. But the crushing feeling of embarrassment that normally went with it never arrived. Something had changed inside me. I felt as if I'd been laced into a super-tight corset for years, and Gabriel had just cut through its bindings.

Gabriel nudged my legs apart and settled himself between them. Then there was a rustle of fabric and I realized he was pushing his pants down. A moment later, I felt his cock brush my leg, hot and heavy and *big*. A mental image popped into my mind: him standing naked in the infirmary. I swallowed.

The sound of foil tearing, then the rubber stretching sound of a condom going on. Gabriel moved in closer. I inhaled slowly at the feel of him there, the muscles of his hips like warm rock as they spread my thighs. The head of his cock brushed my sopping folds. He reached up and stroked one of my breasts and then I gasped as he eased himself into me.

It was amazing, indescribable. The feeling of being slowly penetrated, without being able to see a thing. The darkness made every sensation more intense: I felt every hard millimeter, every vein as he filled me, stretched me. I couldn't see how much more there was to go and that made it feel thrillingly endless. I felt his elbows press into the bed on either side of me and then he took both my breasts in his hands, gently rubbing my nipples as he sank deeper and deeper. As he rooted himself, I groaned and hugged him to me, hands roving over the hard muscles of his back.

He began to thrust and I hissed, eyes screwing shut at how good it felt, each slow push compressing the growing heat in my core. He was as good at this as he was with his hands, taking me towards my peak but then slowing, so that I didn't quite crest it. My hands roamed lower, finding the hard curves of his ass and pulling him into me: *God, what's happened to me?* I'd never been confident in bed. Maybe it was the darkness or maybe it was him, setting me free.

He sped up and the room filled with the sound of our bodies slapping together, my soft panting and the growls he made low in his throat. I could feel the climax building, a ball of raw heat that burned brighter and denser with each hard thrust. It grew until it was all I could think about, until it ruled my whole body and I was a moaning, panting mess, weak with pleasure. I began to pull at his ass: *just a little faster!*

But he held back. And then, suddenly, I could see him. The moon had finally broken through the clouds and a shaft of light was lancing through the window and lighting him up, making him look like a statue cast from pure silver. I saw his lips twist into a grin and his eyes twinkled. He *loved* that he could do this to me, hold me on the very edge while staying in control. And before tonight, I would have waited.

But something had changed. He'd let something loose inside me, and it wouldn't wait.

I reached up, gripped his shoulders and rolled us. I saw him blink in surprise and then he went with it, rolling over onto his side and then his back. As I came to rest astride him, he shifted deeper inside me and I let out a moan, palms pressed against his chest, momentarily lightheaded.

Then I began to ride him, pushing against his chest, my hips rising and falling. Now *I* could control the rhythm and I sped up, unconsciously grinding in circles as I got closer and closer. Gabriel cursed and then gave a low chuckle, as if he was delighted at what he'd unleashed.

I moved faster, moaning and arching my back like a cat as the pleasure ratcheted tighter and tighter: I was seconds away now. When I glanced down at him, he was looking up at me in wonder. I looked over at the window and realized that the moonlight had grown stronger: the whole bed was bathed in silver now, and he was staring up at my naked breasts. For a second, I went shy, feeling huge and awkward. But then I saw the look in his eyes: he was just *eating me up* in big, ravenous bites—my face, my hair, my breasts—and my chest swelled with pride.

He pushed aside the tresses of dark hair that were hanging down and palmed my breasts, squeezing gently. His voice was shaky with lust: he was as out of control as I was. "*Olivia,*" he whispered.

I bounced atop him, unable to speak, the climax tightening and tightening and—

It exploded, roaring through me and obliterating everything except him and me. My hips became a blur as I rode the wave, and then he groaned and lunged upwards and I knew he was shooting, deep inside me. My fingers curled around his shoulders and I clung to him as I spasmed and shook around him. Then I slowly collapsed down onto him and put my head on his panting chest, and we lay like that until we fell asleep.

20

GABRIEL

I WOKE UP AND LOOKED DOWN. OLIVIA WAS ASLEEP, HALF ON TOP OF ME. Her naked body was pressed against mine all the way from ankle to shoulder, one arm and one leg were thrown languidly across me and her head was resting on my chest.

It was without a doubt the best thing I'd ever felt.

I glanced at the window. The sky outside had turned from black to deep blue. I figured dawn was about an hour away.

In one hour, the chopper would come. Soon after that, we'd be back at the airfield and I'd slip away forever.

I looked down at Olivia. *What have I done?!* I'd tried so hard to resist because I knew how much it would hurt her, if I slept with her and then left. But when I'd seen her so scared and defenseless the night before, there'd been this overwhelming, protective urge...

This went way beyond just lust now. I was having feelings I didn't dare give a name to.

The last thing I wanted to do was hurt her but now I was going to do exactly that. I'd disappear and it would destroy her.

I couldn't just leave. But what other choice did I have?

I could stay. Give up the gold and stay with the team.

No. Unacceptable. I'd sweated and bled for that money. I'd spent three years of my life locked in a cage. I wasn't going to give it up now. Plus, the idea of working for Kian, of fighting the good fight...

I looked down at Olivia's sleeping face. She was snoring: tiny, peaceful snores, like a kitten would make. She thought I was still the Marine who fights for what's right. But I wasn't that guy anymore.

I couldn't stay. But I couldn't abandon her, either.

I sat there brooding, staring out of the window for a full half hour before some gear meshed just right in my brain. My back straightened and I drew in a long, slow breath.

What if there was a third option?

It was a huge gamble. It made an already risky plan even riskier and if it went wrong, I'd lose *four hundred million dollars,* plus I'd be sent straight back to jail for the full quarter-century.

I looked down at her again. Brushed a lock of hair from her cheek, and made my decision.

"Olivia," I said, gently shaking her. "Olivia? Wake up. I've got something to ask you."

21

OLIVIA

I came awake slowly, grudgingly surfacing from the best sleep I'd had in a week. My sleepy brain half-remembered wild, uninhibited sex with Gabriel. The man still haunted my dreams...

Then I registered the warm muscle under my cheek. *It wasn't a dream.*

I sat up and pulled my sleeping bag over my nakedness, self-conscious in the pre-dawn light. It was weird to finally see the room we'd slept in: there was a huge painting on one wall that must have been too big for the looters to take, and high overhead, a glittering chandelier.

There was a look in Gabriel's eyes I'd never seen before. He wasn't teasing, for once. He looked solemn and uncertain. I'd never known Gabriel to be uncertain about anything.

"I've got a lot to say and not a lot of time to say it," he told me. "Olivia..."

He stopped. He looked like he was groping for words, but that was impossible: this was *Gabriel*. I'd only just woken up and my mind was still playing catch-up. Was this the dreaded morning-after conversation? My chest tightened. The one where he said it had all been a mistake?

"When I met you," he said, "I wanted—I *needed*—to fuck you."

I felt my face heat.

"But the more time I spent around you, the more things changed. I started to—" He sighed and looked me right in the eye. "I started to fall for you. Even back at the prison." He swallowed. I'd never seen him so vulnerable. "I'm crazy about you, Olivia."

A cloud of warm, sparkling bubbles rushed up inside me, threatening to lift me right off the bed. "I'm crazy about you, too," I blurted.

"I kept away from you, when I realized we had feelings," he said. "I didn't want to sleep with you and then leave."

Leave?!

He took a deep breath. "Olivia...I have to go."

I listened, open-mouthed, as he told me about the stolen gold and his plan to slip away from the team and escape.

Reality set in. *I'm going to lose him.* Just as we'd gotten together. "But—" I shook my head, trying to put it into words. "But—"

He took hold of my shoulders. "I know," he said firmly. "Me too." He took a deep breath. "That's why I need you to come with me."

I gaped at him. *What?!*

"When the chopper lands at the airfield, you slip away with me. The guy who's getting me out can get you out, too, I'll pay him double. He can get you false papers, a whole new identity. We'll get out of the country, go and get the gold..." He grinned, his eyes glittering. "Olivia, we'll have *four hundred million.* We can live anywhere we want. Any country you want!"

"*Any* country?" I asked in a small voice.

"Except one," he said gently. "We can never come back to the US again."

"*Never?* Not even in a year? Not even in ten years?"

"It's four hundred million dollars," he said sadly. "They're never going to stop looking for us."

I'd never see my family again. I'd never see my country again.

But I'd be with him.

I got up and walked to the window, wrapping the sleeping bag around me. I was shaking: I couldn't stop shaking. The decision was just too big, and I only had a few minutes to make it. I could hear noises from the other rooms: people were getting up, getting ready to go.

Gabriel got up from the bed and slowly approached. "There are *so many* places I want to show you," he said. "So many new experiences. We can do whatever we want, we'll never have to work again."

I'd be a fugitive, always looking over my shoulder.

But I'd be with him!

I stared out at the jungle. It took a long time for me to make a decision, but much longer to summon up the courage to turn around and tell him.

"I'm sorry," I said, my eyes filling with tears. "I want to. But I'm not like you. I can't."

22

GABRIEL

I THOUGHT I WAS PREPARED. I THOUGHT I WAS BRACED FOR IT. I WAS wrong.

No?! No, as in, I'm never going to see her again?!

I wanted to tough it out but something inside me just broke and my eyes begged her. *Why not?*

But I already knew why not. She was right, she wasn't like me. She was *good,* she followed the rules. She'd probably never gotten so much as a parking ticket. I couldn't ask her to live on the run. It's not a life I'd wish on anyone.

I tried to look away but her eyes were begging me right back, asking their own *why?*

Why couldn't I just give up the gold. Why did I need it so much?

I wanted to explain. I wanted to tell her it was about proving something to the guys who threw me out of the Marines. That it went back further than that, that I'd been trying to prove my entire life that I was something more than just a poor kid from the wrong side of the tracks. But I couldn't put any of that into words. Olivia was the one woman who left me tongue-tied. So, I just said, "Okay. Okay, Doc."

And I turned and walked away so she couldn't see the pain in my eyes.

Outside, everyone was waiting with their gear, watching the sky for the first sign of the chopper. A morning mist was rolling across down the sides of the valley and spreading out over the treetops, and as the sun crept over the horizon, it lit it up gold. It looked like a giant was spreading out some magical comforter made of dreams. It was unspeakably beautiful.

"There," said Cal, pointing. I strained my eyes but couldn't see a thing. Then, at last, I made out a black speck in the sky. As the speck grew, we started to hear the clattering drone of the chopper's blades. No one ever described it as a pleasant sound, but every soldier loves to hear it, because it means you're going home.

The chopper grew until we could see Gantz through the windshield. He was thirty feet from us, descending towards the lawn, when a shot rang out.

Everyone whipped around, checking all directions. "*Contact east!*" yelled Danny, firing into the trees. I looked that way and saw cartel members swarming out of the forest.

"*More! South!*" yelled Cal, and he started firing, too. They were coming at us from two directions. *How did they find us?!*

Another shot rang out and a white spot appeared on the chopper's windshield. I was close enough to JD that I could hear Gantz on his radio. "*They're shooting at me! Jesus fuck fuck, they're shooting at me!*" Suddenly, all of Gantz's bravado was gone: he sounded like a scared kid.

The chopper stopped its descent and rose into the air.

"Gantz! Get down here! We'll cover you!" snapped JD. He started firing, too. All of us were shooting now. Cartel members were running out of the trees on three sides of us, trying to completely surround us. We formed a circle, facing outward, with the three doctors protected in the center.

I could hear Gantz panic-breathing over the radio. The chopper kept rising. It lurched, turned...and started to speed away.

"*Gantz!*" JD yelled. "What the hell are you doing? You can't just leave us here! *Gantz!*"

But the chopper was already shrinking into the distance. JD stared at it in disbelief.

Danny backed up to him, still shooting, never taking his eyes from his rifle's sights. He nudged JD with his elbow. "We can't stay here," he said. "They're going to cut us off."

JD gave the chopper one last glare and then nodded. He jerked his head west, the only option left. "Into the jungle. Run!"

I grabbed Olivia's hand and towed her with me as we raced for the trees. We'd nearly reached them when I got a feeling I hadn't had in a long time. When you're in a team, you develop a sort of sixth sense. I don't know if it's hearing the footsteps of the others around you, or the little glimpses in your peripheral vision; hell, maybe some of it is people's scent. But if you spend enough time with a bunch of guys, the team gets this vibe and you can tell if it changes.

We were one short.

Cal, Danny, JD, Colton, three doctors, and me. Where the hell is Bradan?

I spun around and saw him, standing motionless on the lawn, right out in the open. His gun was down by his side, and he was staring at a stone fountain, of all things. As I watched, a bullet that must have been meant for him took a chunk out of the side of the fountain. Bradan didn't even flinch: he just stood there, frozen.

Goddammit. I pushed Olivia towards Danny. "Take her," I told him. Then I raced back across the lawn, wincing as bullets hissed by me.

I sprinted up to Bradan and grabbed his arm. "*Come on!*" I yelled. "*Go!*"

He turned to look at me, but he didn't see me. It reminded me of Olivia, waking from her nightmare. He was somewhere else.

Then he blinked once, twice, and seemed to shake it off. We ran together into the trees, bullets chewing up the ground behind us.

We had to really push to catch up to the others, and by the time we did, I was huffing and panting. I wished again that I'd run more in prison. As we pushed on, not daring to stop, Olivia started to struggle, too. I took her hand again and pulled her along. She was doing great, considering she'd probably never had to run so far or so fast in her life.

The sound of gunfire behind us faded and then stopped. They'd lost sight of us. JD slowed to a stop and we all pulled up. The elderly Dr. Guzman leaned against a tree, his chest heaving.

"Someone want to tell me what happened?" asked Cal.

Colton glowered at the sky. "That joint-toking son of a bitch ran home to mommy and left us high and dry, is what happened!"

"But how did the cartel find us?" asked JD. "They hadn't caught up to us by last night. And we didn't show any lights, so they didn't find us in the dark."

I was suddenly really glad Olivia and I had stuck to the rules. This wasn't our fault. So how *had* they found us? Everyone looked at each other in confusion.

An Irish accent broke the silence. "There's one way," said Bradan. He seemed normal again, as if nothing had happened on the lawn. "If they detected the chopper early enough, they could have worked out where it was heading and sent their guys there."

"That means they have radar," said Danny. "How does a drug cartel get *radar?!*"

"Good question," said JD. "I don't know. For now, let's focus on getting out of here." He brought out a map and spread it out on the ground, and we gathered round. I was beginning to warm to the guy, even if he was kind of a boy scout. He was calm in a crisis and he was good at keeping us on task.

The map didn't have good news for us. We were still deep in cartel territory, and between us and civilization was hundreds of miles of jungle. "Can we get another pilot?" asked Olivia.

JD shook his head. "Gantz is going to go back to town and tell everyone how he got shot at. No pilot's going to fly in and get us after that."

We all stared at the map despondently. Olivia looked terrified and I didn't blame her. We were cut off with no rescue or backup, and it was only a matter of time until the cartel found us. *Think of something,* I told myself angrily. *Think of something or we're all dead, including her.*

And finally, I did.

I stabbed at the map with my finger. "Here. It's a military base. We go there, hand ourselves in."

JD stared at me as if I'd gone nuts. "We're conducting an illegal operation in their country. They'll throw us in jail."

"Not necessarily."

JD looked confused. Then he crossed his arms and gave me a look I hadn't seen since Mrs. Martinez, my school principal, asked me to explain why all the vending machines were suddenly empty of snacks and their coin banks were full of Slovakian pennies.

"When I used to move stolen goods through Ecuador," I explained, "there was a guy I used to bribe to look the other way. He had a real weakness for vintage Rolexes. Well, these days he's the deputy minister of defense. We give ourselves up, persuade the military to let us call him...I'm pretty sure I can still cut a deal with him."

JD let out a long sigh and shook his head. Bribery and backroom deals clearly didn't sit well with him, but: "I'm beginning to see why Kian wanted you on the team," he admitted. "Okay. It's the best plan we've got."

Cal looked at the map. "That's a full day's march," he warned. "We're almost out of food. Running low on water, too."

"The sooner we get there, the better, then," said JD. "Move out."

As we moved off, I nodded JD aside. We fell into step at the back of the group.

"Bradan froze," I told him. "Just stood there out in the open. I need to know what his story is."

JD grimaced and shook his head.

"JD," I said gently, "we're in the shit here. And we can't work together if we don't trust each other."

We looked at each other. I was as surprised as he was: *where did that come from?* For the first time, I didn't sound like a loner who'd been press-ganged onto the team. I sounded like I actually wanted to make this thing work.

JD's face softened. "You remember that thing in California with the cult? The town that got raided by the FBI?"

"Sure. *That's* his story? He was FBI, and something happened with—"

I broke off because JD was shaking his head sadly. He stared at me, waiting for me to make the leap. I felt my jaw fall open. "He was—"

JD nodded. "The cult took him when he was just a kid. Brainwashed him. Trained him to kill. He was one of their best assassins. That's all he knew, for *years.*"

I stared at Bradan, up ahead. That's where his skills came from. And that's why he was a little...*off,* like never having been to a party as a teen. For a good chunk of his life, he'd been practically a machine.

"Kian and his other brothers found him and got him out," JD told me. "They broke the cult's hold over him. He's been out of it for years now. But..."

But he'd still killed people. A *lot* of people. Was that why he was freezing, was he having flashbacks? My distrust of him melted away. *The poor guy must be wracked with guilt.*

I nodded my thanks to JD and we marched deeper into the jungle.

23

OLIVIA

WE WALKED ALL MORNING, AND AS THE SUN ROSE, IT GOT STEADILY hotter. The tree canopy shielded us from the direct sun but the dense jungle meant there was almost no breeze. "Hotter'n a goat's butt in a pepper patch," muttered Colton.

Our faces shone and dripped with sweat: just moving was exhausting. But we had to keep up a brutal pace because we didn't know how far behind the cartel were.

We had another problem, too. The heat meant we burned through our water more quickly. I'd been sharing Gabriel's canteen and when he shook it to see how much was left, it sounded worryingly close to empty.

He offered it to me. I shook my head. "You first." He was carrying a pack, after all, and I wasn't.

Gabriel raised the canteen and took a slug, then held the canteen out to me.

I just stood there staring at him. I'd been watching his throat and it hadn't moved. He'd just mimed drinking: he was saving it for me.

He must have read my expression and known I'd caught him because he looked away guiltily for a second. Then he stubbornly offered me the canteen again: *I don't care, take it.*

He'd risked his life for me, come all the way here to rescue me and he was *still* protecting me. As I finally took the canteen and drank, my chest ached: how could I possibly give this man up?

You don't have to, a little voice told me. *You could go on the run with him.*

But that wasn't me: I couldn't spend the rest of my life looking over my shoulder. I couldn't never see my mom again. I cursed myself for not being more like him.

We marched on and then, around noon, we came to a cliff. Far below, we could see an open area with large, blocky buildings: the military base.

A cool breeze was blowing against us, a relief after the heat. But while the rest of us luxuriated in it, Cal stopped and frowned. He picked a handful of undergrowth and then tossed the stalks into the wind, watching how they blew. "That storm's coming," he muttered.

We all looked up at the sky: it was still blue all the way out to the horizon. But JD nodded soberly: he obviously trusted the big guy when it came to nature. "How long?"

"Late tonight," said Cal. "Or early tomorrow morning."

JD grimaced. "Great."

We stopped and ate the last two ration packs and shared out the last of the water. I caught Gabriel's eye: *not good.*

"Don't worry," he told me. "When we make it to the base, they'll have food and water."

It took almost two hours to pick our way carefully down the cliff and make it through the jungle to the base. Finally, in the middle of the afternoon, the trees thinned out and we saw the base's gleaming metal fence in front of us.

"They're getting ready to go somewhere," said Colton, frowning. Inside the fence, a convoy of a dozen vehicles stood waiting and soldiers were hurrying back and forth, loading them with gear.

"I'll go first," said Gabriel. He gave his weapons to JD and then the rest of us waited at the edge of the jungle while he walked towards the base's front gate with his hands in the air. When the guards pointed their guns at him, he stopped and called out in Spanish:

American! Friendly! He turned slowly around, letting them see he was unarmed, and they cautiously called him forward.

JD and I exchanged reassured looks: *so far, so good.*

The guards talked into their radios, and a few moments later, a jeep drove out to the main gate. An officer climbed out and stepped forward to talk to Gabriel.

I squinted. There was something—

Oh God. I recognized him. The silver stubble. The wrinkles at the corner of his mouth.

I spun to face JD. "We've got to get Gabriel out of there!"

He frowned. "What's the matter?"

I realized I was the only one of us who'd seen him without his bandana. "That officer: that's the guy who kidnapped us, the guy who was running the camp!"

24

GABRIEL

THE OFFICER INTRODUCED HIMSELF AS MAJOR ZAMORA, HEAD OF A UNIT based at this base. He didn't specify what sort of unit but something in the way he held himself, and the fancy assault rifle he carried, screamed Special Ops. When I'd explained our situation, he nodded towards the jungle. "And your friends, and the doctors you rescued?" he asked. "Out there?" He scanned the tree line. "Please, tell them to come out. We won't shoot."

I nodded, smiled, and turned to signal the others to come out of the trees. But then I frowned. They were *already* coming out, and Olivia was right out in front, running and waving her arms. "*Get out!*" she screamed at the top of her lungs. "*Get out!*"

Major Zamora's smile disappeared. He unslung his assault rifle and brought it up to point at me. *Oh crap.* I was unarmed and defenseless. I winced and waited to die.

Bullets kicked up dirt right at our feet. Zamora and the gate guards dived for cover. The team was advancing, firing, and JD was waving for me to get out of there.

I bolted over to them, and together, we retreated back into the cover of the trees. I grabbed Olivia's hand and then we were off and running, back into the jungle. We ran until we couldn't run anymore.

I collapsed against a tree, feeling like I was going to burst a lung. The others weren't doing much better. "Will someone please tell me what the *fuck* is going on?" I panted.

"The cartel guys who kidnapped the doctors," panted JD, "weren't cartel. They were these guys. Soldiers, dressed up to look like cartel members. The guy you were just talking to, with the silver in his hair?"

"Major Zamora," I told him.

"He was the guy running the camp!"

I groaned. When they'd interrogated me, he'd stayed in the shadows and he'd had that damn bandana over his mouth, but I still felt like an idiot for not recognizing him. My clever plan had taken us right to the lion's den. If Olivia hadn't warned us, we would have handed ourselves over to the very people we'd been running from. "That's why they were so well-organized, at the camp. They weren't cartel thugs: they were fucking Ecuadorean Special Ops!"

Danny was bent over, huffing for air. "Explains why there weren't any drugs in the camp."

"And why they've got radar," managed JD between pants.

"It's a false flag operation," said Bradan. "Kidnap the doctors, blame it on the cartel."

"But why?" asked Olivia.

No one had an answer. Cal said he'd check our tail and loped off into the trees. However far we ran, that guy never seemed to get tired.

"If the military's in on it," said JD, "that means someone in the government's in on it. That's why they wouldn't go in to rescue the doctors. That's why they wouldn't let the US help. They were behind it all along." He looked at me. "What the hell have we walked into?"

I shook my head. "Whatever it is, they don't want any witnesses."

Colton's voice was grim. "So what you're saying is..." He ticked points off on his fingers. "The guys hunting us aren't cartel thugs, they're a fully trained Special Ops group. We're hundreds of miles from civilization with no goddamn ride. We've got no food, no water," —he nodded at Marcos—"one injured, and we're in the middle of some deep state, deep throat, black ops *conspiracy* shit we don't even fucking understand." He looked around: no one argued. "This job's FUBAR," he muttered.

I caught Olivia's eye and gave her a weak smile. "...up beyond all recognition," I translated.

At that moment, Cal jogged out of the trees. "We need to move. Soldiers: a *lot* of them, one click back."

JD spread out the map again. "There are more military bases here, here and here. We've got to figure they'll send reinforcements. The only way we can go is this way, through the jungle."

"For how long?" asked Bradan quietly. "We can't stay ahead of them forever."

JD looked at him. "You got a better plan, I'm listening. But if we don't move now, they'll box us in."

I nodded to myself, thinking. Then I heard myself say something I never thought I'd say. "JD's right. We don't have time to debate it. We've got to go."

JD looked at me in surprise. I gave him a quick nod of respect. I was starting to realize that this was what JD was good at: making quick decisions under pressure, even when all the options were lousy. We had to trust him, or we were screwed.

We got moving. I sidled up beside JD. "Bradan's not wrong, they'll catch up to us eventually. We've got no food and no water, and they can keep throwing fresh men at us. We need an extraction. There's a river, maybe twenty miles ahead of us. A chopper could get in there."

"But no pilot's going to come out here and get us," said JD. "Not after Gantz spreads word of what happened to him."

"I can think of one who might. Let me borrow the sat phone."

25

GINA

I was four in the afternoon, and I was in a hammock with a Frenchman.

It had been one of those nights that started with red wine and steak and ended with dancing and tequila. He'd wanted to take me out and treat me like a lady, which was pretty hilarious but he was hot as hell, so I'd agreed. We'd gone to bed with the dawn and not gone to sleep for some hours after that.

Now I felt like my head was an eggshell and someone was pounding on it with a hammer. The only way I could cope with the hangover was to press myself even closer to the naked man who was stretched out next to me. Jean was the son of a smuggler and he was bouncing around South America looking for new opportunities. He had big, brutish shoulders that I'd loved clinging onto and the six pack of an underwear model. Most of all, he had a French accent that was pure sex. It was like he took normal words and dunked them in molten gold, leaving them addictively smooth, warm and gleaming. I could have listened to him for hours.

Someone opened up on my skull with a pneumatic drill and I groaned and tried to bury my head under Jean's shoulder. *Make it stop!* But the drill kept going. It took me a while to figure out that it was the ancient landline phone in my apartment. *Who the hell is calling on that?* I hadn't used the phone once since moving into this place six months ago. It was on Jean's side of the hammock, so I prodded him until he woke up and grabbed the handset. Mercifully, the noise stopped.

"Allo?" asked Jean. It was almost worth the pain just to hear the accent. Then the cool plastic of the telephone handset pressed gently against my ear. "Is for you, *ma cherie.*"

I frowned, my eyes still closed. "Yeah?" I asked grumpily.

"My name's Gabriel Kain."

The accent was smooth and sexy, with just a hint of southern gentleman, and I recognized it. "The guy from the bar."

"Things didn't go so well. Gantz left us stranded out here in the jungle."

"I'm *stunned,*" I deadpanned.

"Look…" His voice changed in a way that made me half open my eyes and pay attention. There was a ragged edge to it: he sounded honest, even vulnerable. "I came here to bring someone home. Someone special. Now I got her, but something's happening out here. The military's in on it, probably some people in government, too. We got Special Ops on our tails. We need a chopper out of here."

"So you want me to become part of an illegal, unauthorized op, fly into a hot LZ, and have Ecuador brand me a terrorist in the process? There isn't enough money in the world."

"What if I wasn't just offering money?" said Gabriel. "What if I said I could get the charges against you dropped?"

I sat up, which set the hammock swinging and nearly made me throw up, but I toughed it out. My heart was suddenly thumping in my chest and I tried not to let the emotion into my voice. "How do you know about that?" I asked gruffly.

"Because before I called you, I called the bar and the bartender gave me your name: she knows you pretty well." He said it without judgment. "Then I called our guy back in the US and got him to look up your file. Gina Novak, formerly of the 160th Special Operations

Airborne Regiment." His voice became gentle, almost like he understood. "You had some trouble, down Mexico way. Enough trouble that you're still wanted in the US. Gina, we have a connection in Washington, and believe me when I say it's at the highest level. If you help us, I can get those charges dropped. You could go home."

Home. My chest ached. I hadn't set foot in the US in almost three years.

I cursed under my breath and wished I wasn't making this decision with a raging hangover. The reasons to tell him to go to hell were easy. I could get shot, I could go to jail. But if I did do it, and this guy was for real...

I looked down at the dozing Jean. I was having fun out here in South America. One-night stands, drinking, a few quasi-legal flying gigs to pay the bills. But life used to be more. I used to be part of something.

"You get the charges dropped *and* I want the money you would have given Gantz," I told him. "And I'm only giving this one shot. You aren't there, I'm not waiting."

"Fair," said Gabriel. He gave me some coordinates, which I scrawled on my hand. "We'll be there at ten tomorrow morning. See you soon."

I hung up the phone and lay there for a while, staring up at the slowly turning ceiling fan. One way or another, my life was about to change.

With a sigh of resignation, I leaned down and kissed Jean on the cheek. "Time to go," I told him. "I've got to work."

"Oh..." He reached for me and kissed down my neck. "*Non, non, non, ma cherie,*" he mumbled into my shoulder. But we both knew it was only a one-time thing, and eventually I hustled him into his clothes and out the door.

Then I walked into the bathroom, turned the shower on ice cold, and stood under the spray, cursing and shivering, until my head cleared. I toweled off, dug a khaki flight suit out of my closet and pulled it on. I dug around in my kitchen cupboard, found some energy bars and slid them into the flight suit's pockets: when you spend a lot of time hanging around airfields at 3am, waiting for a fuel truck to show up, you learn the benefit of always having food with you. Then I put on a pair of sunglasses and headed out into the day.

I needed to find a helicopter, some painkillers, and some coffee... not necessarily in that order. It was time to sober up.

26

GABRIEL

WE MOVED AT A PUNISHING PACE FOR THE REST OF THE AFTERNOON, jogging for long stretches and only slowing down when the jungle got too thick. Everyone was exhausted but we had to stay ahead of the soldiers. We could hear vehicles in the distance, probably trucks using logging roads to drive deep into the jungle and drop off their soldiers close to us. We were being boxed in, just as JD had predicted, and if we didn't keep moving, they'd be right on top of us.

The thirst was becoming a problem, too. All of us were sweating hard and there was nothing replacing the lost fluid. My mouth was desert-dry. Danny had passed around a pack of hard-boiled sweets and sucking on one of those had brought a little relief, but now I was starting to get lightheaded. We'd all stripped off to the waist to try to cool down. I'd given Olivia one of my tank tops so that she didn't have to walk around in just her bra, and I was trying not to stare at her lush curves and the way her breasts bounced as she walked. I was goddamn crazy about this woman. How the hell was I going to leave her behind?

As we reached a clearing, JD called a break and we all dumped our packs for a moment and leaned against trees, panting. Colton wiped sweat from his forehead. "I'd give a month's paycheck for an ice-cold beer, right now," he muttered. "Or a swim in the lake. Hell, both at the same time."

I cracked a smile. I was getting to like Colton. I was getting to like all of them, despite my best efforts. They were a good bunch of guys. I was even warming to JD.

When I'd handed the sat phone back and told him Gina would be coming to pick us up at ten the next morning, he'd given me a look of genuine respect. I'd felt a stab of guilt because he didn't know about another call I'd made while I'd had the sat phone, to my friend back in Quito. I'd managed to rearrange my escape. The guy wasn't happy: he'd waited an hour for me at the airfield, only to see Gantz arrive home alone. I'd had to double his fee to $200,000 and he'd made it clear that this was my last chance: if I wasn't back at the airfield at noon tomorrow, tough, he'd be gone for good. And without him, I'd have to hand over the gold and stay with Kian's team for ten long years. *No. No way.* I'd worked too hard. I *deserved* that gold. I'd do anything to get it.

I glanced at Olivia and forced myself to harden my heart. *Anything.* Even give up the one woman I cared about. She was using the break to check Marcos's wound, her hands quick and efficient as she worked. Marcos saw me looking and stared coldly back at me. No doubt he'd heard Olivia's cries of pleasure the night before and he'd picked up on how we seemed a little more distant with each other, since. He thought I'd used her and dumped her. Well, maybe after all this, he could get together with her. He was good-hearted, decent, respectable...he was the sort of guy she *should* be with.

So why did it hurt so much, to think of me getting the gold and him getting her?

A roar of gunfire tore the air apart. You could tell in a heartbeat who'd seen action before: every single member of the team *moved,* before their brains had even consciously registered what the noise was, diving for the nearest cover. Olivia, Marcos and Dr. Guzman flinched and looked around.

I dived at Olivia and Marcos with my arms outstretched, knocking them both down behind a log. I heard bullets zip over our heads.

Danny and JD returned fire. I lay there panting, holding Olivia and Marcos down so they weren't tempted to lift their heads. The gunfire stopped. "Three of them caught up to us," Danny said breathlessly. "We got 'em, but more are right behind them."

I let Olivia and Marcos up. Marcos was blinking at me in shock, the coldness gone from his eyes. "Everybody okay?" I asked. "Anyone hit?" Everyone looked at each other, worried, but we all seemed to be—

"Oh God." Olivia ran over to where Dr. Guzman was sitting against a tree. He had both hands clutched to his stomach and his face was rapidly turning gray. When Olivia pried his hands away to look, blood spurted, and she cursed.

"We've got to move," said JD. "Those three were just scouts, the others will home in on the gunfire. Colton?" He nodded at Dr. Guzman.

"Got it, boss." Colton heaved the groaning Dr. Guzman over his shoulder, handling him as if he weighed nothing at all. We ran together into the trees.

But only a few seconds later, Olivia suddenly stopped dead in her tracks and then bolted back the way we'd come. I grabbed hold of her as she passed me. "What are you doing?!" I demanded.

She'd gone pale with fear. "The medical bag! I was using it on Marcos, it's still back there on the log!"

"Leave it! There's no time!"

"I need it! I need it to treat Guzman!" She was in a full-on panic, scared *and* guilt stricken. She thought Guzman was going to die and it would somehow be her fault. She tore out of my grip and sprinted back to the clearing where we'd taken the break.

"Olivia!" I yelled. I cursed under my breath and sprinted after her.

I arrived in the clearing just in time to see her grab the medical bag. She turned, about to run back to me...but at that second, two more soldiers arrived from the left: between me and her. I brought my rifle up but I didn't have a clear shot: if I missed, I'd hit Olivia.

Another three soldiers ran into the clearing from the other side. One of them saw Olivia and raised his gun—

She darted into the trees on the far side of the clearing and ran. I started firing at the soldiers and managed to draw their attention from her, but then I had to fall back as they advanced. I was outnumbered...and being pushed further and further away from Olivia.

I felt a cold dread settle into my bones. My chest went tight and my stomach knotted. She was all alone in an area thick with soldiers. She didn't have a gun or even a pack with any survival gear. And it would be dark soon. How the hell was I going to find her?

27

OLIVIA

I RAN HEADLONG INTO THE JUNGLE, DODGING AROUND TREES AND leaping over undergrowth, not daring to look back. I had to put some distance between the soldiers and me but with every step, I was getting further away from Gabriel and the team.

I finally slowed to a stop and pressed my back against a tree, listening. No footsteps. I was alone. But I had no idea where I was or how to get back to the team. The jungle looked the same in every direction and even if I did know which way to go, there were soldiers between me and Gabriel.

I looked around. The shadows were deepening and spreading, joining into black pools. The sun was going down and soon, I wouldn't be able to see at all. *What the hell am I going to do?*

The prison camp had been frightening but at least I'd been with the other doctors. There's a special kind of fear that comes from being entirely on your own. The jungle seemed to expand around me: I was a tiny speck in the middle of hundreds of miles of wilderness. Even if I could avoid the soldiers hunting me, I wasn't equipped or trained to survive out here.

I cursed myself for going back for the medical bag. But Dr.

Guzman would die without it. *Yeah, like it's going to do him a lot of good now.*

I froze. I could hear voices, off to my left, talking in Spanish. I closed my eyes. *Please don't come this way, please don't come this way.*

The voices grew louder. *Shit!* I had to move. But as I crept away from them, I saw someone moving through the trees ahead of me. They were coming from both sides!

I stood there looking around wildly. *Think!* What would Gabriel do? Something unexpected and tricksy. The voices came closer and I pressed myself protectively against the tree—

The tree! Growing up with three brothers, I'd learned to swarm up trees like they were ladders. The trees here in the rainforest didn't have branches: they were smooth and skinny as telegraph poles. But the birch tree in our neighbor's yard had been like that and we'd learned to climb that, too. I just had to hope I was still strong enough.

I hooked both hands around the trunk of the tree and leaned back, taking my weight on my arms. Then I gingerly lifted one foot onto the trunk.

The trees behind me rustled. They were coming.

I pulled with my arms and managed to get my other foot onto the tree. I bent my knees and took a little step up the trunk, keeping my arms taut. *This was a lot easier when I was twelve.*

I glimpsed the glow of a flashlight ahead of me, moving closer. *Move!*

I hitched my hands higher up the trunk and took another little step, then another, walking my feet up the tree. After just a few steps, I was panting and sweating but I kept grimly on because I didn't have a choice. I forced myself into a rhythm. *Hands step step. Hands step step.* I had to get as high as I could before—

Voices below me. I looked down and saw two soldiers step out of the trees. I froze where I was, about ten feet up the tree.

The pair of soldiers walked beneath me and I started to relax. But just as they were about to disappear into the jungle, they stopped, hearing the other group coming towards them. A moment later, another two soldiers emerged from the trees and the four of them started talking...right at the base of my tree.

I was exhausted from climbing and my body wanted to heave in big lungfuls of air. I had to force myself to only take tiny, quiet breaths. I hung there motionless, terrified. How long until one of them looked up?

28

GABRIEL

WHERE IS SHE?!

I crept through the darkness, staying low. The dark made it easier to hide from the soldiers but it made it harder to see, too. I didn't dare call her name. What if I walked right past her?

In some ways, it reminded me of my old life as a thief. No team, no one giving me orders, just me on my own against the odds. It should have been a relief.

But it didn't feel that way. I'd gotten used to the feeling of having good people around me. I wished I had Cal to lead the way: he'd have moved more silently than I ever could. I wished I had Danny or Colton to cover the sides. I wished I had Bradan or...hell, even JD to watch my back.

There was another reason this felt different. When I was a thief, I'd been after a *thing:* a painting, gold, jewels... I'd gone through hell for some of those scores, spending hours shivering on mountaintops or hiding in storm drains, waiting for the right moment, and I'd thought that meant I'd cared about them.

But I hadn't. Not like I cared about her. The fear I felt now was like nothing I'd ever experienced: someone had my heart in their fist and was slowly crushing it. At any second, I expected to hear a gunshot, a shout of triumph from a soldier, and that would be it, she would be dead.

If I could have traded everything I'd ever stolen just to have her there beside me, I'd have done it in a heartbeat. And when that thought went through my head, I realized how stupid I'd been. If I could just get her back, I'd hold onto her forever...no matter the cost.

I crept deeper into the darkness. *Olivia, where are you?!*

29

OLIVIA

THE SOLDIERS WEREN'T MOVING ON. BUT THEY HADN'T GLANCED UP, either. My hopes rose: maybe I could wait them out.

The problem was, the trick I'd used to climb the tree was made for climbing: it wasn't designed to let you just hang out halfway up a tree. Most of my weight was hanging from my arms and they were starting to weaken. Even as a kid, I'd have shimmied down the tree by now, or made it to a branch and sat on it. And I wasn't a kid anymore.

I checked below me again. Muted laughter and chat: they were talking, but not so loudly that they'd fail to hear me if I made the tree creak by moving. I couldn't adjust my position at all, couldn't even shift my grip on the trunk to rest my fingers.

I closed my eyes for a while and tried to imagine I was somewhere else. I blocked out the chatter from below, I ignored the ache in my shoulders and forearms. I thought about walking hand-in-hand along a beach with Gabriel, the wet sand squidging between our toes, warm water washing over our feet. I could feel the sun on my back, the wind toying with my hair. He'd slow, his hand tugging on mine, bringing me to a stop. Then he'd pull me closer and bring his lips down on mine—

My shoulders were a solid, throbbing ache now, one I couldn't ignore any longer. I didn't dare move them because it felt like they'd set like concrete and if I moved, they might go into spasm and I'd lose my grip completely. The soldiers *must* have moved on by now.

I opened my eyes and looked down. The moon had gone behind a cloud and everything was in shadow. I couldn't see anyone and there were no voices. For a wonderful second, I thought they'd gone. I actually started thinking about how best to get down.

Then I saw a tiny, orange circle. A moment later, it split into two. Then one of *those* split into two. They were smoking. I felt my chest contract in fear. How long would that take? Five minutes, ten? *I can't hang on that long!*

My legs were starting to shake now, not used to being bent and strained for this long. And my fingers were beginning to go numb. There was no breeze and the smoke from the cigarettes rose straight up, enveloping me. I held my breath.

Three of the soldiers seemed to be listening as the fourth told a story: something sexual, from the few words I could pick up. I was getting desperate to breathe. I twisted my head around, trying to escape the cloud, and couldn't. Lungs bursting, I finally gave in and tried to inhale slow and steady, but the smoke was rough and stinking, and my chest spasmed. *Don't cough, don't cough.*

The story finished, and one by one, the orange circles disappeared as the men put out their cigarettes. *They're going!* Another thirty seconds and they'd be gone. The cough in my chest swelled and swelled. I clamped down hard on it, eyes watering—

It burst out of me, and even with my lips pressed hard to my shoulder, a loud, rasping cough filled the air. Instantly, the soldiers jerked to attention and looked up, jaws dropping when they saw my silhouette above them. Their guns came up to fire and I screwed my eyes shut.

There was a long burst of gunfire but the pain didn't come. I opened my eyes...

The moon had cleared the clouds again and I could see the bodies of the soldiers on the ground. Then another figure stepped out of the trees and looked up at me.

I've never been so glad to see someone in my life. *Gabriel!*

At that moment, my numb hands finally gave way and my grip slithered down the tree. My legs swung away from the trunk and I dangled from my arms, ten feet up.

"Drop!" Gabriel told me.

I was panting, trying to swing myself back up so I could wrap my legs around the trunk.

"Drop!" Gabriel insisted. "I'll catch you!"

My stomach lurched: fear of falling plus my old insecurities coming back: I was too heavy to catch—

"Olivia," said Gabriel firmly, "*drop!*"

I let go. The sky shot away from me...

And strong arms caught me and cradled me. He gave a groan of relief and crushed me to his bare chest. I felt all of the fear slowly melting away. We were still in danger, still being hunted, but nestled against him, I could cope with that.

As I relaxed, I became aware of the tension in *his* body. He was gripping me as if he never wanted to let me go, rocking me gently against him as his chin rubbed the top of my head. Then he gripped me hard by the shoulders and pushed me back so that he could look at me.

"Don't *ever do that again.* Okay?"

I nodded quickly, the raw emotion in his voice making me go weak.

He grabbed me by the waist and tugged me to him, kissing me hard and quick. He broke the kiss and spoke from an inch away, the word a hot little gust on my tingling lips. "*Ever!*" he repeated.

He gazed into my eyes and suddenly, I couldn't breathe. Something had changed since I last saw him. The need in his eyes... He grabbed my hands and took a deep breath, about to say something. Then he looked around at the jungle and cursed under his breath. "Not here," he muttered. "Come on."

He led me off into the jungle. But after just a few feet, I pulled on his hand to stop him. A shaft of moonlight had broken through the trees and was making something gleam in the undergrowth, something metal. Only ten feet from the tree where I'd hidden, there was a wire fence. Who would build a fence, all the way out here?!

The jungle had fought back against it: the humidity had rusted it, the trees had pushed their roots under it, and undergrowth had climbed all over it until it was a broken, sagging mess. A metal sign hung lopsided on the fence: a symbol, two black triangles side by side.

"I've seen that before," I told Gabriel. "At the camp."

He frowned at it, then tugged on my hand. "We'll figure it out later," he told me. "We gotta go."

And we hurried into the jungle.

30

GABRIEL

IT TOOK US ALMOST AN HOUR TO FIND OUR WAY BACK TO THE OTHERS. The jungle all looked the same and we had to keep taking detours to avoid soldiers. Three times we had to lie flat in the undergrowth and wait while patrols passed by, their boots just a few feet from our heads.

When we did reach them, I almost walked straight by them. We were saved by Cal, who saw us coming, intercepted us and guided us in. I wanted to hug the big bastard.

JD visibly slumped in relief when he saw us. "Thought you two were gone for good." He slapped me on the shoulder almost affectionately. Then he saw the conflict on my face and frowned at me. "What's eating you?"

I shook my head and turned away. Was I really going to do this? Give up *four hundred million dollars?*

I looked at Olivia. She hadn't taken a second to rest, she'd walked straight over to where Dr. Guzman lay and was using the medical bag to tend to him. She was dressed in army fatigues and one of my tank tops, her face was smudged with dirt from hiding in the undergrowth, there were bits of twig and sticky tree sap in her hair...and she'd never looked more beautiful.

Yes. Yes, for her, I'd do it. I was aching to tell her, but first we had to get somewhere safe.

I looked up and saw Marcos staring right at me. At first, his face was full of relief that she was back, and gratitude to me. But then, as he saw what was in my eyes, his expression shifted. The jealousy flared again for a moment...and then finally, he lowered his eyes and sighed, accepting it.

When Olivia had finished working on Dr. Guzman, she came over to JD and me, her face grim. "I've done what I can," she told us. "But he'll die without a hospital."

"We'll have to carry him," said Colton. "That'll slow us down."

"We're behind as it is," said JD. He looked at the map for several seconds, silently figuring out distances and speeds. Then he sighed and shook his head. "We're not going to make it. The soldiers will cut us off before we can get to the river."

Everyone looked at each other. We were all close to breaking: exhausted, dehydrated, and hungry. I felt an unexpected pang of something I hadn't felt in years: belonging.

I'd been doing my best to push those feelings away until now, knowing I'd be running out on them. But now, if I was going to abandon the gold and stay with Olivia...I'd have to stay with the team, too. That was the deal I'd cut with Kian. So, finally, I let the feelings creep in.

We'd come into this not even knowing each other but now, after going through hell together, these guys were actually starting to feel like a team. *My* team.

I straightened up, feeling the fatigue drop away. It was up to me to save them. We needed a miracle and that was my department: the sneaky plan no one else would think of.

I stared at the map with fresh eyes. Then I stabbed at a thin line that wound through the forest. "This logging road. It leads almost all the way to the river."

JD shook his head. "The soldiers are all over that road. That's how they're getting men into the area, they're bringing them in in trucks."

"That's what I'm counting on," I said. I looked at Bradan. I hadn't trusted him at first, with his lack of military background, the way he froze up, and the blank spots in his personality. But if we were going to get out of this, we needed to start relying on each other and Bradan was the stealthiest son of a bitch I'd ever seen. "Let's go steal some transport."

31

GABRIEL

A HALF HOUR LATER, BRADAN AND I WERE STRETCHED OUT SIDE BY SIDE on our bellies looking down a steep slope to where a road curved through the jungle. Two trucks were parked there, and we could see three soldiers lit up by the flames of a campfire.

"You don't trust me, do you?" muttered Bradan, not taking the binoculars from his eyes.

I went to speak and then closed my mouth again. We had to get this stuff out in the open so we could get past it. "I know you went through some bad shit," I said quietly. "Maybe did some stuff you're not proud of."

"I'm fine," said Bradan stiffly.

I waited a moment, then said gently, "Sometimes, just now and again, it seems like you're somewhere else. Remembering things."

"I told you," said Bradan. "I'm fine." He passed me the binoculars and suddenly he was off, creeping down the slope towards the soldiers.

I cursed, taken by surprise, and scrambled to find him with the binoculars. Even knowing where he'd be, it was difficult to follow his moves. I'd never seen anyone move so stealthily: he seemed to melt into the shadows and then slide out of them somewhere else, graceful and silent as a cat. I watched one soldier fall, tumbling soundlessly backwards into the jungle, Bradan's arm around his neck. Then another. The guy was incredible.

And then...nothing. Bradan just disappeared.

Minutes ticked by but there was no sign of him. *Shit.* He must have frozen up again and there was a third soldier somewhere down there. Maybe this had been a bad idea...

A rustle of clothing behind me. I rolled over onto my back and saw the third soldier standing at my feet, his gun just coming up to point at me. I scrambled for my rifle but there was no time—

Bradan stepped out of the shadows and cut the soldier's throat in one quick move. The body fell to the ground right beside me and I recoiled, gaping up at Bradan.

"Saw that one wandering up here so I circled back," Bradan said casually. "C'mon."

He set off down the slope again and I raced after him. A moment later, we were sitting in the cab of one of the trucks. I stared at Bradan in wonder as he started it up. "Thanks," I said at last.

Bradan glanced across at me...and something happened. He gave a little nod and a shrug, like saving my life was nothing, but I saw him relax just a little bit. Like this was the first real connection he'd made in a while. I suddenly felt even more sorry for the guy. Leaving the cult must have meant leaving everything he knew behind. That adjustment would be hard enough but he'd had something much worse to deal with. As he was counseled or deprogrammed or whatever they called it, he must have become aware of what he'd done, what the cult had made him into.

How do you cope when you wake up and realize you're a killer? How many deaths did he suddenly have on his conscience: five, ten, a hundred? How hard would it be to make friends after that? You'd either have to lie to everyone, or tell the truth and have them be scared of you.

And suddenly, I knew what I had to do.

I'd learned it from my dad, the barber. Sometimes, his clients talked and talked and sometimes they sat there in silence and he could tell they wanted to let something out, but if he started talking to them, they'd just clam up or talk small talk. He had to give them silence, but the right sort of silence. Not the uncomfortable, cold silence that makes people nervous and twitchy. A warm, soothing silence that expands to fill the room, that feels like sliding into a hot bath. The sort of silence that draws out the poison people are keeping inside, the way a warm poultice on a wound can draw out the splinter. With a slow snip-snip of his scissors, my dad could create the sort of comforting silence that therapists, with their couches and book-lined offices, could only dream of.

So as we pulled away and drove, I just...stayed...quiet.

And after a few minutes, Bradan muttered, "I've started getting memories. Out of nowhere. Something sets it off: a voice or a smell or something I see, and suddenly I'm back there." He swallowed. "Killing someone."

I thought of his girlfriend, back in Colorado. "You talk to Stacey about it?"

"Stacey has her own problems. She's from LA, she had a business there, and she followed me all the way to Colorado, to this tiny little town. She hasn't found a job yet, she doesn't know what she's going to do there. She's done enough for me."

"Not sure that's how it works, when you love someone," I said gently. And suddenly, without meaning to, I was thinking about Olivia. I felt myself flush.

"When I froze up," said Bradan haltingly, "back on that lawn...it was because I saw that fountain. I'd seen one just like it before, in Colombia. There was this guy, a politician. Young guy, people liked him. I shot him. Made it look like one of the cartels did it. He died slumped over the fountain." Bradan glanced across at me and in his eyes, I could see the scared kid who'd been taken by the cult as a teenager. "It's like I'm waking up, remembering a nightmare. Only all of it's real."

"You sure you're ready to be out here?" I asked.

"Only thing I *am* sure about," he said. "I've got a lot to make up for." He drove in silence for a moment. Then he sighed. "You're right.

Stacey would help if I told her. I just don't want to. I don't want that stuff near her."

I understood. A lot of soldiers felt that way. You bottled stuff up because you didn't want it to hurt the people you loved. But it was also about wanting to keep them clean and untainted, so you had one pure, innocent thing in your life. Thing is, though, you have to let this stuff out to *someone,* or you go crazy.

"You can talk to me about it," I said. "If it helps."

Bradan gave me a long, appraising look...and then nodded. And we drove on into the night.

32

OLIVIA

I WAS PACING. I'D MADE DR. GUZMAN AS COMFORTABLE AS POSSIBLE, I'D checked Marcos's wound again, I'd even helped Cal, as he fashioned a stretcher from lengths of bamboo and one of the sleeping bags. Now there was nothing to do except wait and worry about Gabriel and I found myself pacing, unable to keep still. What if he and Bradan had been caught? What if they'd been killed? What if he was out there somewhere, in need of medical attention, and I didn't know—

The rumble of a truck engine in the distance. Cal loped off into the jungle, and a few moments later, he came back beaming. "It's them."

We grabbed our gear and hurried through the trees, carrying Dr. Guzman on the stretcher. We reached the road just as Bradan and Gabriel pulled up in an army truck. Gabriel jumped down from the cab and I was hugging him even as his boots hit the ground. He clutched me tight, pressing me to him, and as his stubble rasped against my cheek, he gave a sigh of relief in my ear. "Missed you, too," he whispered.

I unwound myself from him and stepped back. Those hazel eyes were burning, desperate to tell me something...but at that moment, JD walked up. "Good job," he said with feeling.

"Bradan did all the hard work," said Gabriel. Bradan looked sweetly embarrassed.

We loaded Dr. Guzman's stretcher into the back of the truck. Danny climbed into the driver's seat and patted the steering wheel lovingly: I'd learned he was the team's driver and it was obvious that he was happiest behind a wheel. JD rode shotgun to navigate and the rest of us all piled into the back. We set off through the night, following the road up through the hills. The truck wasn't fast but it was much, much faster than walking and we didn't have to dodge soldiers or stop for breaks.

The only problem was thirst. My head was throbbing and I could feel my heart racing, despite the fact I was just sitting slumped against the canvas wall of the truck. From the look of the others, they weren't feeling any better.

We made good time, and near dawn, JD announced we were close to the river. We pulled the truck off the road and hid it as best we could, then heaved out Dr. Guzman's stretcher and headed into the jungle for the final hike to the river.

The air felt different: there was a freshness to it, a breeze that hadn't been there before. When I looked up, the entire sky was covered with thick clouds that had rolled in while we'd been in the truck. I remembered what Cal had said about the storm. "Oh, please, please," I begged.

We started marching. Everyone looked up when the first roll of thunder echoed overhead. A few minutes later, there was another one, then another. A cloud of birds rose from the treetops and flew away, squawking.

I raised my cracked lips to the heavens. *Please!*

There was a long rumble of thunder and then...

Dr. Guzman felt it first: lying in the stretcher: he had more surface area than the rest of us. He yelped as a spot of rain hit his leg. Then Colton got hit on the head. And then it was falling all around us: big, weighty droplets of rain, falling like precious jewels. We put down the stretcher and just stood there, arms up and mouths open, trying to catch even a few drops. But then the rain intensified, becoming a constant, hissing stream and we whooped and threw our heads back, letting it fill our mouths. Nothing in the world had ever felt so good. We let it soak our clothes, washing the days of dirt from our faces. Cal stretched out a tarp and we used it to collect the rainwater and channel it into our water bottles, refilling them one by one.

Only one person wasn't enjoying the rain. JD was standing apart from the group, a grim statue, head bowed as rain drummed on his shoulders. No one else seemed to have noticed. "JD?" I said gently, but my voice was lost in a roll of thunder.

I walked slowly over to him, moving until I could see his face. "JD...?"

I stopped in shock as I saw his face. His eyes were closed and he was silently quaking as if trying to hold back tears. There was so much rain running down his face that I couldn't tell if he was succeeding. My chest contracted: I'd never seen someone in such agony. And this was JD, the stoic, craggy leader of our group. I'd thought he was made out of rock.

A hand brushed my arm, and I looked up as Danny padded silently past me. He nodded to me: *I've got this.* As I watched, he slipped an arm around JD's shoulders and began to talk to him in a low voice. I couldn't hear what he was saying but I got the tone: serious and heartfelt, words drawn from down deep. As rain streamed down his face, Danny touched foreheads with JD, then roughly squeezed his shoulder. JD nodded. Danny seemed to know the words that would work...because, I realized, this wasn't the first time he'd done this for his friend.

I crept away, giving them some privacy. I'd picked up on the fact that the two of them were close, but I hadn't realized *how* close. Whatever JD was going through, it seemed like hell and I was glad he had his best buddy there. Seeing them together made me a little sad, though: I'd never had a friend that close, not even back at the ER in Phoenix. I wondered if I ever would.

~

We marched on, and an hour later, we came to the river. At first, we couldn't see anything: the storm clouds covered the moon and the stars, and there was barely any light at all. But when lightning split the sky, we caught a glimpse of what was in front of us.

The land dropped away in a sheer cliff until it met the water a hundred feet below. Swollen by the rain, the river was as wide as a football field and was flowing terrifyingly fast. Entire trees were being washed downstream and torn to matchwood as the current smashed them against jagged, dark rocks.

JD pointed downstream. "The landing point for the chopper is a few miles that way, on the far side."

"How do we get across?" asked Gabriel. "There's no way down on this side. Even if there was, no way can we swim across that."

JD pointed in the other direction. On the next flash of lightning, we saw a rope bridge a little way upstream. "We use that. But not yet. There's no cover on the far side of the river and when the sun rises, we'll be sitting ducks until the chopper arrives. I don't want to be there any earlier than we have to be. We'll spend the night here and then cross at dawn, hike downstream and we'll still be in good time for the chopper."

We found a clearing a little way from the cliff edge and set up camp there. The moon broke through the clouds, lighting up the pounding rain so that it looked like thousands of glittering glass spikes stabbing down from heaven. I checked on Dr. Guzman and gave him another shot of morphine. When I'd finished, I looked up... and saw Gabriel standing there gazing down at me. Rain was trickling down his forehead and his hair was plastered into black knives on his forehead. His eyes were locked right on me and they were gleaming. I'd never seen someone with such singular purpose.

I swallowed and looked around. Cal was tying a tarp to some branches to make a shelter and Colton was helping him. Danny and JD were at opposite ends of our little camp, on guard duty. For the first time since we were reunited in the jungle, Gabriel could finally have some privacy.

Gabriel offered his hand. When I took it, he hauled me to my feet, then pulled me gently but firmly into the jungle.

My heart was thumping. This was *it*: whatever he'd been wanting to say, he was finally going to say it.

33

GABRIEL

I didn't go far. I pushed through the trees until we were screened from the camp and then I led her a little way along the cliff, to where the gray rock rose above us and formed an overhang that would shelter us from the rain. That would do. I couldn't hold onto what was bursting up inside me any longer.

I turned her to face me and took hold of her other hand. I took a deep breath.

What the fuck are you doing? Are you insane? You can't do this! I was raging at myself, furious. *Seriously, Gabriel, what the fuck?!* Everything I was, all those layers of personality that had formed in prison, as a criminal, as a hustler in the Marines...all the way back to when I was stealing the candy my mom couldn't afford to buy me, *everything* was telling me not to do this.

But there was a new part of me...or maybe a really old part, buried deep, one that hadn't seen light or air since I was that poor kid in Chicago. A part that she'd coaxed out into the daylight and nurtured. It was awkward and unfamiliar and a pain in the ass but I liked it. And that part wouldn't be silenced.

"I need you," I said. "I need you with me. You—" I gazed down at her. Water from her rain-soaked hair was running down her cheeks like tears and I cupped her face and brushed them away with my thumbs. "You're *who I needed to meet,* who I always needed to meet, I just didn't know it until I met you. I nearly lost you once. I can't say goodbye to you again. And that's why...I'm not going after the gold when we get back."

Her wet cheeks moved under my fingers as she cocked her head to one side. "Wh—*What?*"

"I'm not running away," I said. "I'll show the Justice Department where the gold is. They can—" Suddenly, the words got hard to say. *Am I really doing this?!* But I bulled on through. "They can have it. The four hundred million."

I'd braced myself but, in the last three words, it hit me. The pain was unbelievable, like someone was slicing deep into my chest.

But then the realization broke across her face like the dawn and the hope I saw there made the pain worthwhile. Jesus Christ, it felt good.

"You'd do that?" she asked in a tiny voice. "For *me?*"

"I'd *only* do it for you," I told her. And then, as the pain hit again, I leaned down and kissed her. I immersed myself in her soft, warm femininity. I drowned my sorrows in the goodness of her, in that irresistible, buttoned-down innocence and that secret streak of urgent lust. The pain didn't shrink, but I felt myself growing and maybe, with her help, I'd *keep* growing and so the pain would hurt less.

She melted against me with a little sob of pure joy. Her soaking body pressed full-length against me, her arms wrapped around my shoulders and her head tilted back. Her lips opened and her tongue brushed mine, tentative and light. I teased the tip and felt the need inside her wake: she moaned and pressed against me harder, her tongue dancing with mine. I growled. We rotated on the spot, neither of us able to keep still, my fingertips rubbing slowly over her wet skin and the edges of that tightly pulled-back hair, her hands roaming over my shoulders and back.

She broke the kiss. I grudgingly opened my eyes, breathing hard, and looked down. Her eyes were heavy-lidded with lust and I'm guessing mine looked the same. The tank top I'd given her had turned almost translucent in the rain and her bra wasn't much different.

"What will you do?" she asked, stepping back. Her voice, normally so serious and precise, had gone throaty with need and it was the hottest thing I'd ever heard.

"This," I said hungrily, my lips still tingling. It wasn't a line: I honestly couldn't think of anything in my future more important than kissing her. I stepped forward.

She dodged out of the way, but with a soft little groan of regret. I was wrong, before: *that* was the hottest thing I'd ever heard. "I meant where will we go? What will we do?"

I frowned and tried to clear the lust fog from my head. "I'll join the team," I said. "I've got to, that's the deal. Ten years. They're based in Colorado, in this little town, so I guess we'll live there. We won't have much money: they seized my assets when I went to jail and what I managed to hide, I spent on my lawyer. Once I give up the gold, I'll be down to the shirt on my back." I looked into her eyes. "What do you say: you want to come live in the mountains?"

She blinked up at me, eyes shining. Tears joined the rainwater running down her cheeks. "*Yes,*" she croaked, and ran back into my waiting arms.

34

OLIVIA

HE WAS STILL TOPLESS, HIS RAIN-SLICK CHEST STRONG AND wonderfully warm as I pressed against him. He crushed me so close I could feel his racing heart. We were one, inseparable.

His stubble rasped against my cheek and then he nuzzled my ear and kissed the side of my head. He wrapped me in his arms and I'd never felt so secure. "I guess I'm a good guy now," he mused.

I nestled into his chest, my cheek against the firm slab of his pec.

It started small. I was in dreamy, warm contentment, a lake with a surface as calm as glass. And then there was a flicker, like seeing a tiny fish, deep under the surface.

A good guy.

I tightened my arms around him and he tightened his arms around me. This was heaven.

A good guy.

This time, the fish made a ripple, expanding outwards, disturbing the pristine surface. *No. No!* I'd found my happy place. I wasn't going to give this up, not for—

A good guy.

Surfacing in my mind again before the ripples had faded. Waves formed, breaking together chaotically, getting higher and higher until they couldn't be ignored...

I pushed back from him but his arms were tight around me. I pushed again and felt him look down at me, confused. I shook my head, and he released his arms, his chest filling as he drew in a worried breath. "What?" he asked.

I stepped back, staring up at him. I didn't want to give it life by saying it, but I had to.

"You're not a good guy," I whispered.

He frowned. Shock, then hurt. "But—"

"You saved me," I said. "You risked your life for me. You did all this, joined the team for me. But you're not a good guy. You're a thief. You always have been, you always will be. You're a thief who does good things. And the gold, that's your big score. If you give it up for me, you'll wind up resenting me."

"*No!*" He grabbed my hands. "No, never!"

"You spent three years in jail planning how you were going to spend that money."

He shook his head slowly, gazing at me. "But I spent my whole life waiting to meet someone like you."

"*Four hundred million dollars.* No one could give that up for another person: it's too much to ask. A year from now, or ten years from now, you'll wonder and it'll grow until it cracks us apart."

"*No!*" he was begging now. But he wasn't just begging me. He was begging for it not to be true, because he knew it was.

"I can't let you do it," I said. "Not for me."

It hurt too much to look at him. I turned away and walked out from under the overhang. As I walked over to the cliff edge, the rain sluiced down my face leaving me gasping.

I'd never been sure of much in my life but I was sure about this. I wanted to be with him, but I *needed* him to be happy. For his sake, I had to give him up.

I drew in a breath but my lungs jerked and it turned into a sob. I was letting go of all that beautiful, safe warmth and all that was left was bitter cold and an eternally gray sky. Going home alone was so much worse, now that I'd had those few glorious minutes of imagining the fairy tale.

Another sob rose, spasming my chest and prickling my eyes. Then another, and another. I heard him walk towards me but then his steps faltered and stopped. He'd realized that holding me would only make it worse. He was right, but that reality—that from this moment on, being together would only bring us more pain—was too much, it was sandpaper on my soul. *This isn't fair,* I kept thinking, little-girlish and stupid. *This isn't fair!*

I descended into wracking, ugly sobs. I cried until my chest ached, until I couldn't breathe and couldn't see. I stepped back from the cliff edge to be safe, and then gave a bitter little laugh. Even when I was crying my eyes out, I was pathetically sensible.

And that's when I remembered something.

That's when I remembered there was a third way.

I'd been too cautious before, too scared. But coming so close to death had made me realize that you can waste your whole life, being cautious. And coming so close to saying goodbye had made me realize that nothing was as scary as the thought of losing him.

I turned around, sobs still shaking my chest. "I can't let you give up the...the money for me," I began.

He stared at me, his eyes shining with tears.

I took a deep breath. "So I guess I'm just going to have to run away with you."

35

OLIVIA

For a second, he just stared, his mouth open in shock. Then he cocked his head: *did I hear that right?!*

I nodded firmly. I could feel a ghost of cold panic creeping into my chest: we'd always be on the run, I'd never see the US again, *this wasn't me!* But as I watched Gabriel's face fill with pure elation, a warm rush chased the cold away. I'd face those fears...for him.

He grabbed me by the shoulders and pulled me to him, hugging me tight and then leaning down to kiss me fast and hard. I closed my eyes and molded myself to him, elation blossoming in my chest and expanding to fill every part of me. I stroked his stubbled cheeks, then tangled my fingers in his wet hair. Still kissing, he walked me back under the overhang so we were out of the rain.

When he finally broke the kiss, I gazed up at him, eyes half-closed, drunk on him. He grinned and went to kiss me again, then stopped himself, his hands already on my cheeks. "You *sure?*"

I nodded again. I could deal with the flickers of panic, as long as he kept kissing me like that.

He gave a wicked chuckle and then his lips were on mine, tasting and exploring me as if discovering me for the first time. His hands roamed up and down my back, then along my sides, tracing the shape of me through my soaked clothes. He kissed my cheek, my jaw, the base of my neck, and I squirmed and moaned. "I want to show you Rio," he told me. "And Hanoi. And Havana."

"Mmm-hmm," I managed. Every time his lips found a new place, I writhed harder against him. My hands slid over his wet back, his muscles deliciously hard and warm under my fingers.

He drew back for a second to look at me. "You're going to make a great outlaw," he told me with feeling.

I gave him a shy smile and he growled, grabbed my ass and lifted me into the air. I yelped in shock and something happened: the feeling of being so easily handled, of giving up control and just letting him lift me, triggered something. It bubbled up inside me, a release—

I giggled. I couldn't remember when I'd last done that. It felt alien but Gabriel's eyes lit up as if he liked it. I felt suddenly better, *lighter*.

He was good for me.

He pulled me to him. My legs slid either side of his waist and I caught my breath as his torso pressed between my thighs. He started kissing me again, open-mouthed and hungry, and I kissed him back even harder. He squeezed my ass, lifting and lowering me a little with each squeeze, and that rubbed the washboard of his abs against my groin. I began to pant into his kisses and *me* getting turned on turned *him* on more, so he ground against me even harder... It became a feedback loop, both of us spiraling upward until we couldn't take it anymore.

He walked us over to the rear wall of the shallow cave formed by the overhang and pressed me against it. Even with the rain hissing down outside, the air was still hot and the rock wall felt wonderfully cool against my body.

Gabriel cupped my head in his hands and just looked at me intently. A lock of hair had escaped my bun and was plastered to my forehead: he pushed it away with his thumb. "I got lucky, that day in prison. I'm glad I got knifed."

"Well, try not to let it happen again." I tried to think of something funny to say. I wanted to be one of those witty women who can banter but that wasn't me. I wound up just saying what I felt. "I couldn't take it if something happened to you."

He leaned forward and kissed me tenderly. Maybe me just being me was okay.

He kept kissing me and it became slow and deep, setting up a rhythm that radiated through our whole bodies until we were writhing together against the wall. His hands fell to my shoulders, then skimmed down my sides to the hem of my tank top. I drew in my breath as he peeled it slowly upwards, lifting my arms so that he could get it over my head. Then he reached behind me, unhooked my bra and pulled it off over my arms.

My breasts throbbed at the sudden shock of the air. He gazed down at me and his eyes narrowed in lust. He suddenly cupped my breasts, taking me by surprise, and I stared up at him, panting, as he squeezed them and then started to strum my nipples with his thumbs. "God, I love your body," he murmured, and I felt myself lift inside, all my old insecurities falling away.

I ran my hands over the huge swells of his shoulders, tracing over his biceps and the chiseled hardness of his forearms, then letting our fingers tangle together. We stared into each other's eyes and something passed between us. He finally set me down on the ground and then we were both scrambling to shed our boots, pants and underwear. Naked, we ran back into each other's arms. He picked me up and spun me around, kissing my neck, and I groaned at how good his warm body felt against mine.

We kept turning and walking, spinning around and around as he inched me higher and higher in his grip, until my breasts were level with his mouth and he could lash at my nipples with his tongue. I cried out and tangled my fingers in his hair, clinging to him—

Suddenly, I felt water hit my back. Not raindrops, this was a solid mass of water, like I was standing under a faucet. I looked up...

Gabriel had walked us out to the edge of the overhang that had been shielding us from the rain. Inside the little cave, it was dry. Outside, the rain pounded the rocks. But just at the edge, the rain that hit the cliff and washed down it formed a solid curtain of water a few feet wide, a miniwaterfall. The water was deliciously cool after the days of heat, refreshing without making you shiver.

Gabriel gently lowered me and maneuvered us so that both of us were in the stream. The water pummeled our shoulders and rushed down our bodies, washing away the grime and stress of everything we'd been through. I turned my face up to the water and let it pound me. Then I felt Gabriel's fingers in my hair, sliding out my hair clips. My hair slid free, and the water drew it out into long, soaking tresses. Gabriel grinned, his eyes lighting up, and he ran his fingers through it. "I didn't get to see it properly last time," he muttered reverently. Then he slid his palms down my slippery body, lightly squeezing my breasts, stroking my hips, my ass. I shook the water from my eyes and blinked up at him.

He ran his hands up and down my flanks, relishing the shape of me. Then he took hold of my hands and stepped back, out of the water. He kept moving back until our arms were stretched out, my fingertips only just hooking onto his.

"Look at you," he said. The same words he'd said the very first time he met me. "Somebody ought to paint you, dammit." He looked hungry, possessive...but there was something else, too: *victory*.

He was a planner, a schemer. Sitting in his jail cell, all those weeks ago, he'd had a simple, elegant plan to do his time and get rich. Then our lives had collided and since then, everything had been chaos: the prison riot, me going to Ecuador, him coming after me, the gold being at risk, the mission going wrong. But one thing had worked out just the way he'd wanted it to. I was his.

And the way he looked at me, it was as if that was all he really cared about.

I gazed at him. Water was trickling down his body from his soaked hair, making the caramel slabs of his pecs shine and running in rivulets over the deep ridges of his abs. My eyes roved lower, to the diagonal lines of his adonis belt and then down to—

I watched as his cock lifted and hardened. I could feel his eyes on me and the knowledge that it was me that was doing that to him unleashed a rush of sparkling, silver excitement in my chest.

His cock was rock-hard now, and standing to attention. He grinned at me in the way only he could, wicked and proud. And beckoned me closer.

I walked slowly towards him, the rock floor cool on my bare feet. I was falling under his spell all over again, his raw badness hypnotic. I wanted him, *needed* him, all the time, but this was on another level. This was instinctual, almost primal, something deep in my soul reacting with something deep in his, just as it had in prison. Good and bad. Innocent and filthy. The maiden and the highwayman. Heat was throbbing at my core, and with every step I took towards him, it grew stronger and stronger. By the time I reached him, I was breathy and twitchy, my mind clouded.

I closed the gap between us and put my palms on his chest. He stroked my breasts, and I felt his cock weighty and hot against my inner thigh. His lips twitched into a devil's smile and he leaned down and kissed me.

I closed my eyes and gave myself up to that seductive lower lip and the ruthless, hard upper one. Then suddenly they were gone, and the warmth of his body against mine disappeared. I opened my eyes, confused, just in time to see him on his knees in front of me. I blinked dumbly down at him for a second and then—

At the first touch of his tongue on my folds, I cried out. All of the heat that had been building inside me suddenly tightened and spiraled into a dense, glowing coil. He ran his tongue down the seam of my lips, licking jewels of water from my sensitive flesh. I trembled and gasped and heard him chuckle.

His tongue flicked up to my clit and began to caress it. Silver streamers of pleasure radiated out, wrapping around me and rocketing me upward. I grabbed hold of Gabriel's head, sinking my fingers deep into his thick, dark hair as his tongue circled and feathered. Now I was *sure* he'd done a deal with the devil: he'd been given a forked tongue, that was the only explanation.

Gabriel nudged my legs a little further apart and I shuffled my feet wider. His hands squeezed my ass hungrily, bringing me forward to meet his lips. I felt myself opening under his expert touch and then his tongue was parting my folds and pushing up inside—

My fingers played piano scales on his head and my toes tried to dig into the floor of the cave. *Oh my God oh my God oh my God*— The pleasure was like nothing I'd ever felt: it pulsed through me, making my whole body vibrate to its rhythm. And the most amazing thing was *how* he was doing it, the mood he created. With past boyfriends, it had sometimes felt like this was a duty for them, but Gabriel was so obviously enjoying himself and enjoying my reactions. I'd moan and he'd increase the pace; I'd cry out and rock forward and he'd move from my clit to my lips so that I didn't come too soon.

The pleasure built and built, strumming through my body. I needed to move to contain it but I *couldn't* move, not if I wanted that heavenly contact to continue. So my toes danced, my fingers twisted in his hair and my back arched, face tipped back to pant at the ceiling, but my groin stayed rock steady against his mouth, his strong fingers kneading my ass.

He licked faster and I began to mumble wordless pleas, my eyes screwed shut in ecstasy. That made him growl in satisfaction and the sound vibrated through his lips against my slippery flesh. My jaw opened in a silent scream of pleasure. I could feel the orgasm thundering towards me, the sensations drawing inward and becoming dense and weighty. "I—*Ahh!*" I managed.

Gabriel gave a wicked chuckle and his tongue traced my lips and swirled over my clit...but he kept the touch too fleeting to take me over the edge. He kept me teetering on the brink, each swipe of his tongue making the pleasure swell even more. My hands clutched his shoulders and my breath came in helpless gasps. I couldn't talk, couldn't think. The whole world had narrowed down to the white-hot, coiled pleasure that was pulsing at my core, aching to explode. I started babbling: just like the first time. I needed it so much that I pushed all my hang-ups aside. "Oh God *please* Gabriel, *please*—"

The cave echoed with his words, hot little rushes of air against my sopping folds. "I'll catch you."

He'll catch *me?!*

He leaned forward and fluttered the tip of his tongue against my clit. The coiled pleasure *shook,* dense as a collapsed star...

And then it detonated. The wave of pleasure slammed into me and carried me up and out of the cave, up beyond the clouds, somewhere up near the stars. I felt everything tense, and for long seconds I rode it, shaking and yelling, and then the wave subsided and my whole body went limp and rubbery.

I felt arms encircling my waist. I opened my eyes, still panting... and I was back in the cave, flopped forward onto Gabriel's shoulder, my legs twitching and floppy beneath me. *He caught me.*

Gabriel gently eased us down to the ground. He grabbed his clothes to use as a pillow and laid us down with him on his back and me lying on my side with my head on his chest.

He cuddled me close while I recovered. Then he started gently stroking my back, and then my leg, and then my ass, until I began to press myself up against him. He kissed me and then rolled me onto my back, my head on the makeshift pillow.

He retrieved something from clothes wadded under my head, then stood up. He backed off a pace, until he was standing between my ankles. And then he just stood there and gazed at me.

I swallowed. Gabriel was big but from my position on the floor, he was a colossus. Utterly naked, his caramel skin still glistened from our waterfall shower. With his feet planted apart, he formed an X, from the hulking, broad shoulders and strong pecs down to his tight waist and then out again, to his thickly muscled hips and thighs. And rising from between those thighs...

His cock was rock hard and standing straight up against his stomach. I felt my groin pulse, just looking at it. The balls, heavy and loaded. The thickly perfect shaft, rising to the purplish-pink, jutting head. I started to breathe faster.

Then his hand came down and his fingers wrapped around his shaft. He began to slowly stroke himself, his eyes locked on mine. I saw his chest tremble, his breathing ragged.

He wanted me. He *needed* me.

My eyes flicked down to the head of his cock as it emerged from his hand. Then back up to his burning hazel eyes. A hot ripple went down my body, leaving every inch of skin throbbing. I'd never had this before, never had a man want me so much that he'd—

I nodded. I wanted it too.

He stepped forward, his cock bouncing. Then he was kneeling between my legs, and I heard him roll a condom on. He lowered himself, taking his weight on his elbows so he didn't press me into the rock floor. With one hand, he guided his cock to me. With the other hand, he cradled my cheek, his fingers sliding into my damp hair. He stared deep into my eyes, watching my reaction as—

I inhaled as I felt the head of him against me. God, the intoxicating hot throb of him. My eyes widened as he spread me wider, wider...then my chin lifted and my eyes fluttered closed as he filled me with a long silken push.

He came to rest with his groin nestled against mine. I panted, adjusting to the size of him, feeling the heat of him so deep inside. He gave me a second but he couldn't wait for long, couldn't bear to: I could see it in his eyes...

He needed to fuck me. *Now.*

He began to move, slow pumps of his hips, his ass rising and falling between my thighs. Every time he drew back, the slick, perfect friction sent silvery streamers of pleasure dancing to my core. There was a second's ache of needing him, then he'd thrust into me and the silver pleasure would compress into heat.

He cupped my breasts, squeezing lightly, his big thumbs rubbing across my nipples until I gasped and moaned. Then his head dipped, and the hot wetness of his mouth enveloped first one and then the other. The slow pumping of his hips never stopped but, as the heat inside me built and I began to thrash and buck under him, his thrusts started to speed up. The more turned on I got, the faster and harder his cock slammed into me, until I was a gasping, breathless wreck.

He growled and lowered himself onto me and the weight of him felt *good*, savage and primal, his body pinning mine to the cave floor and pressing my thighs open wider. But his hands were gentle as they cupped my face and he stared into my eyes as he fucked me towards my peak. My hands found the tattoos of thorned vines on his back, and I traced them over his shoulders and down to his biceps, going weak inside at the raw need in his eyes, at the wickedness of him. He reached down between us for a second, stroking my clit, and when my mouth opened into a pink O of shock and pleasure, he moaned in lust and his cock twitched inside me. He was getting drunk on my innocence, just as I was getting drunk on his sin.

He sped up again, pounding me for long minutes, his chest rubbing against my nipples on every stroke. Oh *God,* I was *close,* the heat glowing and scalding inside me, desperate to be released. I pressed my hips up to meet his thrusts, arched my back and ground my breasts harder against him. Then my legs came up and hooked around his body—

He thrust deep. His body tensed. He stared into my eyes, and his face was open and honest, all tricks put aside.

"Dammit, Olivia," he panted. "I am never letting go of you. *Ever.*"

And I felt him come in long, shuddering jets just as I spasmed and trembled around him.

We rolled onto our sides, arms and legs intertwined, and stayed that way until the sun came up.

36

GABRIEL

THE RAIN HAD STOPPED AND IT LOOKED LIKE IT WAS GOING TO BE A beautiful day. We wrung out our clothes and put them on damp, which actually didn't feel so bad, given the heat. As we walked back to camp, I was still in a post-orgasm state of bliss and childishly excited about the plan. In just a few hours, I'd be back to doing what I did best: tricking everyone and running off with the loot. But for the first time, I wouldn't be doing it on my own. I squeezed Olivia's hand and she squeezed back.

When we reached the camp, the others were just getting up, stiff from another night sleeping on the ground and grouchy with hunger. All of us were exhausted and even my happiness couldn't mask it completely. But then we smelled something that broke through the tiredness. All of us rushed over to where JD had built a campfire. He'd just poured a metal pot of boiling water into a mug, and it smelled like—

"Is that *coffee?*" I asked with rising hope.

"Saved a packet from my MRE, when we started running low," said JD. "Figured we might need a lift, about now." He offered me the mug.

I took it, speechless. He really *was* a great leader: he cared about his team so much. "Thanks," I mumbled.

We all sat in a circle around the campfire and passed the metal mug around, sipping. We made sure to save some for Colton and Cal, who were on guard duty, and the injured Dr. Guzman, who we were trying to move as little as possible. That meant we only got a few mouthfuls each, but it was enough for the smell and the taste to trigger that coffee high. It was about more than just the caffeine. It was about having a moment of luxury, far from home. And sharing it made our ragtag bunch feel like even more of a team.

It was going to be hard, leaving them.

We packed up, Colton and Cal rejoined us and we set off, with Danny and me carrying Dr. Guzman on the makeshift stretcher. It was only a mile to the bridge but most of it was through thick forest. There was no path and Colton had to go in front, hacking through the dense undergrowth with a machete. He muttered as he worked, swinging the machete every few words.

"When I get *home*...I'm gonna go to Kansas City and get myself the biggest plate of *ribs*...you've ever seen. All sticky with *sauce*...and a whole plate of burnt *ends*..." He panted. "And beer. A lot of beer."

"Steak," said JD thoughtfully. "A good thick piece of beef, with gravy, and a pile of mashed potatoes. Gotta be proper mashed potatoes, cooked in chicken broth and then mashed with cream cheese and buttermilk." He inhaled as if he could smell them.

"There's this ice cream," said Olivia, "called *Gingerly Does It*. It's chocolate, but with swirls of caramel. The caramel stays solid until you put it in your mouth, then it melts on your tongue. And there are these nuggets of gingerbread mixed in, really sticky and moist and they smell like Christmas. I'm going to buy an entire tub of that and eat it with a huge mug of coffee."

She squeezed my hand in a way that said *two spoons*. And something about that, the simple romance of it, just hit me deadcenter in the chest.

"My wife's cooking," said Dr. Guzman from the stretcher.

"Is she a good cook?" asked Olivia.

"Terrible," said Dr. Guzman. "But I want to eat it anyway."

Olivia patted his shoulder. "We'll get you back to her."

Marcos spoke up. "There's this breakfast place in Quito that does the best llapingachos. They're little fried potato omelets stuffed with cheese. You get a few of those, a fried egg, some avocado and meat and a little peanut sauce..." He looked at Olivia and his expression turned sad. It must have been something he had planned for her, before I showed up. Then he rallied and he spoke to Olivia but looked at me. "You make sure you try them, sometime," he said. *Make sure she does,* his eyes demanded.

I nodded. I would. Then I turned to Cal, who was watching our right. "What about you? Some home cooked stew, made with berries and some deer you shot?"

Cal rubbed at his beard, thinking. "I do like venison. But I ate a lot of it, while I was in the woods." He went quiet for a while, long enough that with anyone else, you'd start to wonder if the conversation was over. But I was used to Cal's quietness now. Eventually, he said, "You know what I really want? A pizza. A really big, thick pizza, with a lot of pepperoni and melted cheese that I can share with Bethany. And I want to be able to just pick up the phone and order it and have some guy bring it to my door. And a steak for Rufus." He looked sad for a moment: you could feel how much the poor guy missed his girl and his dog. "What about you?"

I'd been thinking about it ever since I'd gone to prison, dreaming of that first meal as a free man. "*Teritas Pescado,*" I said. "It's fish: red snapper, or maybe marlin, sliced into thin strips and marinated with lime juice, onions and chilis. You load some of that on a tortilla chip, with a glass of crisp chenin blanc from the Loire, maybe a ten-year-old Stéphane Bernaudeau *Les Terres Blanches*..." I closed my eyes for a second, imagining Olivia and I sitting on a yacht, just off the coast of Mexico, a refreshing sea breeze caressing us as a waiter refilled our glasses.

"A curry," said Danny. "No, *two* curries: a lamb pasanda: golden, *creamy,* thick with coconut and almonds. And a chicken jalfrezi: light, spicy, heavy on the onions. And a naan *this big.*" He held out his hands to indicate a naan bread the size of a bathtub. "And a bottomless pint of lager."

Colton gave a final hack of the machete and stopped, sweating and panting. "You'll get it," he managed. "We're through."

We looked down the path he'd cleared and saw open grassland ahead of us. We sped up, everyone pushing harder now that we knew this was the final stretch. A few minutes later, we saw the rope bridge ahead of us. We hurried towards it...and then faltered and stopped.

The thing was a piece of crap. There'd been no way to tell when we saw it last night in the distance, but the ropes were old and fraying and it sagged on one side, so the planks you were meant to step on were sloping. The planks that were still there: about one in four were missing so you could see straight down to the river below.

"We could climb down," said Colton.

"That'd take hours, it's a sheer cliff," said JD. "Plus, the river's flowing too fast to cross, especially with the stretcher." He thought for a moment. "Cal, you go first to keep us covered. Once you're across, Colton and I will take the stretcher over. Then the rest of us will go one at a time, so there's not too much weight. Danny, you go last so you can watch our backs."

Everyone nodded. Cal stepped onto the bridge. There was a slight creak, but everything seemed fine. He took another step—

There was a crack like a gunshot and the plank he'd stepped on fell away. Cal fell through the hole and only just managed to catch himself in time. He hung there panting, his whole lower body hanging in space, a hundred feet above the rock-strewn river.

I ran forward to grab him but Cal waved me back. "I'm okay! I'm okay!"

I froze...then nodded and stayed off the bridge. The less weight we had on it at once, the better.

We all held our breath as Cal climbed back up. Colton looked especially pale.

Cal started to move again, this time testing each plank and skipping the ones he didn't like the look of. The bridge creaked worryingly when he reached the middle: you could hear the ropes straining, but they held. A few moments later, Cal made it across and we all let out a sigh of relief.

"Okay," said JD. "Colton, let's get the stretcher across."

He picked up the front end of Dr. Guzman's stretcher. Colton walked around to the back. But with each step, the big guy moved slower. He bent and picked up the stretcher's bamboo handles and when he straightened up, he'd gone sheet-white. JD, facing away from him at the front, didn't see.

"Let's do this," said JD. And he started forward towards the bridge. Colton followed, walking like a man on the way to his own execution. I got a bad feeling.

JD stepped onto the bridge and started across. Colton walked up to the edge...and then he just stopped.

JD was taken by surprise and almost dropped the stretcher when it suddenly stopped moving. He turned to look back over his shoulder. "Colton?"

Colton shook his head once, twice. Olivia hurried forward and took the stretcher from him and she and JD reversed course and carried it off the bridge.

Colton paced, scowling at the ground and cursing. "Colton?" I asked gently. "What's up, buddy?" But I was fairly sure I already knew. I'd seen that look on people's faces before, that primal fear.

Colton didn't answer at first, too busy cursing up a storm. But when he saw everyone looking at him, he violently shook his head. "I don't like heights." And then he started cursing himself again, telling himself how stupid and pathetic he was. The poor guy was humiliated.

JD came over and waved the rest of us back. We all gave them some space. JD sat Colton down on the ground and talked to him, quiet and relaxed. I couldn't hear what he said, but I got the tone: fatherly, gentle. He didn't yell at Colton or make him feel dumb. And when Colton looked at the bridge and shook his head—*I can't do it*—JD put his hand on his shoulder and nodded. *Yes you can.* And while we waited, no one bitched about it, or made fun of Colton. I liked that about this team.

After a few minutes, Colton nodded and got to his feet and he and JD picked up the stretcher. I could see Colton muttering to himself, psyching himself up, and I found I was digging my nails into my palms, willing him on.

"Eyes on me," JD reminded Colton. And then they were off across the bridge, carefully testing each plank as they went. With the weight of three people on the bridge, the ropes creaked even more, and it felt like the whole thing stretched and sank as they reached the middle. But as they passed it, the bridge rose again and a few minutes later they reached the other side. Colton slumped in relief: I thought he was going to kiss the ground. Everyone relaxed. If the bridge held for them, it should be fine for the rest of us, if we went one at a time.

Bradan crossed to the other side. Then I nodded to Olivia. "You next."

She started across. This time, I watched the bridge more carefully and my stomach knotted when I realized it was definitely hanging lower now. Some rope had stretched or some knot had loosened. We'd just have to hope it held for the rest of us.

Olivia was about two-thirds of the way across when Cal suddenly snapped his rifle to his shoulder and started firing. A second later, JD and Colton did the same. I followed their fire and saw soldiers pouring out of the jungle on their side of the river. *Shit!*

I waved to Olivia. *"Come back!"* We'd have to retreat across the bridge and find some other way across the river.

Olivia nodded, turned around and started back as fast as she dared. But she was only at the midpoint when gunfire erupted behind me. I spun around and saw Danny firing at soldiers behind us. They'd caught us between two patrols. And we were massively outnumbered.

We had to regroup and fight together. I thought fast. There were five people on the far side of the bridge and only three on my side, with Olivia halfway across. Plus, carrying the stretcher across made us sitting ducks, plus Colton might not be able to handle coming back. We had to join JD and the others on the far side. "Go!" I yelled to Olivia. "Go across!"

As she hurried back towards JD, I joined Danny in shooting. We held off the soldiers while Marcos hurried onto the bridge, then I followed, walking backwards, still firing, and Danny brought up the rear. I checked over my shoulder to see if Olivia had made it across yet.

She was frozen, still near the middle of the bridge. Why wasn't she going across to JD?

Then I looked up and saw JD with his hands up. Cal, Colton, and Bradan were doing the same. They'd been overrun and soldiers were surrounding that end of the bridge. Olivia had nowhere to go.

Danny, Marcos and I were all on the bridge now. With Olivia, that made four of us, more than when the stretcher had gone across. And the bridge was weaker now. I could feel the whole thing sinking. "Back!" I yelled to Danny. "Go back!"

But we couldn't: the soldiers had already reached the edge of the bridge and were pointing their rifles at us, yelling at us to throw down our guns. And the bridge kept sinking. The ropes let out a long, faltering creak.

We had no choice. We had to give ourselves up and get the hell off the bridge before it gave way. I threw my rifle at the feet of the soldiers and Danny did the same. "Let us off," I yelled in Spanish. "Bridge—" Dammit, what was *weak?* "Bridge dying!" I tried.

But either the soldier I was talking to didn't understand the danger or he didn't believe me. He pointed his rifle right at me. *Stay there!*

I checked over my shoulder. Olivia was right in the middle of the bridge, looking frantically between the two sides. "Come to me!" I yelled.

She started towards me.

The creaking became continuous, rising to an ear-splitting shriek. *"Run!"* I yelled.

She managed three running steps, the bridge sinking with each stride. Then there was a cracking sound from JD's side of the bridge. For a second, I thought one of the soldiers had fired. Then I saw the snapped rope falling free.

The floor under my feet went vertical. I grabbed hold of a rope, more by luck than anything else. My eyes went straight to Olivia. She was dangling from the center of the sideways bridge, her legs kicking in space.

I started to climb sideways along the bridge towards her. Behind me, I glimpsed the soldiers grabbing Marcos and Danny and hauling them off the bridge. Luckily, I was too far away for them to reach.

I can do this. It was just climbing along a rope. Just like the assault course in basic training. "Hang on!" I yelled to Olivia. "Hang on, I'm coming!"

I could see her panting, hanging on to the rope with all her strength. I climbed like I was possessed. Another thirty seconds and I'd reach her. Another twenty. Another *ten.*

"Just hang on!" I yelled breathlessly.

She nodded, pale-faced but holding it together. *Attagirl!*

I reached out to grab her.

There was another hard *crack.*

The other rope on JD's side gave way and the bridge dropped. I was suddenly weightless, gasping and flailing as we fell. Then the bridge started to swing sideways, towards the side that was still attached to the cliff. I looked down and saw Olivia, her body stretched out like a flag as she was pulled through the air. I watched the rope slip free from her fingers—

No!

And she fell screaming, a hundred feet to the river below.

37

GABRIEL

I JUST HUNG THERE, STARING AT THE SURFACE OF THE WATER, MY BRAIN refusing to accept what I'd seen. My hand was still outstretched to grab her. I'd been no more than a foot from taking her hand.

No. No, she can't be— No!

I panted in fear, scanning the river frantically. But she didn't surface.

I was barely aware of being hoisted upward. The soldiers were hauling the remains of the rope bridge up onto the cliff, and me along with it. I didn't resist as they pulled me roughly up onto solid ground, my eyes still locked on the river. It was only when they zip tied my hands behind my back that I finally looked up and stared at Danny and Marcos. Their faces were as slackly pale as mine must have been.

It was real. She was gone.

It felt like a black hole was growing in my chest, sucking everything in until there was nothing left. Going home, the gold, us being captured...none of it felt like it mattered, anymore.

The soldiers loaded us into the back of a truck and we set off along a dirt road. Not long after, we stopped to pick up JD, Cal, Bradan and Colton. They laid Dr. Guzman's stretcher on the floor of the truck and sat us in two rows on either side, facing each other. Guzman was fading fast: he'd die if we didn't get him to a hospital soon. Not that it made much difference now: once he'd found out what we knew, Major Zamora would kill us all.

As the truck moved off again, we all stared at each other's boots, grimly silent. There was nothing to say.

We'd lost her.

The woman we'd come here to rescue, the reason why this team had been thrown together in the first place, the sweetest, most innocent member of our little family. All of us had bonded with her. But as we sat there, brooding and miserable, I could feel the attention turning my way: little glances, sideways looks. They knew it was way worse for me.

They knew I'd been in love with her.

I saw Cal watching me with those eyes that saw everything. He'd known, even right back in Mount Mercy, when he'd asked why we were doing this mission. And he knew what it was like to love someone, to need someone: I'd seen the way he missed Bethany.

Danny, directly across from me, shook his head. "Sorry, mate," he said, his voice tight with emotion.

Bradan gave me a sympathetic nod, then turned away, looking ill. Relationships, like everything else, were new to him. This was probably the first time he'd imagined losing Stacey.

Marcos was tending to Dr. Guzman. He looked up and caught my eye, then gave me a nod, solemn and heartfelt. I nodded back. All the anger between us was gone: we'd both lost her.

Colton just silently seethed, scowling at the floor in fury. Given how much the guy cursed out loud, I couldn't imagine what he was saying about himself in his head. The poor guy thought it was his fault: if he hadn't been scared of heights, if that hadn't delayed us on the bridge...but the truth was, it was only one person's fault.

Mine.

If I hadn't flirted with her in prison, she wouldn't have stood up to the governor to save me and she would never have come to Ecuador. She should be back in America, safe, instead of—

Someone pressed their shoulder against mine, the closest thing to a comforting pat that we could manage, with our hands tied. I glanced to my right and saw JD. Just a few days ago, I couldn't have imagined him offering me any kind of comfort, or me accepting it. But now I'd seen him in action, I realized he was one hell of a leader. And he was *decent,* in an old-fashioned way I didn't think still existed, and that was exactly what a bunch of reprobates like us needed, a moral compass to keep us pointing in the right direction.

I nodded to JD in thanks...and saw something in his eyes, a deep sadness. I'd only seen it once before, when Olivia had mentioned family around the campfire.

My stomach flipped over, and I stared at him in shock. He looked away, but I knew what I'd seen.

He understood how I was feeling because he'd lost someone, too.

The truck rumbled deeper into the jungle, carrying us to our fate.

38

OLIVIA

MY FACE BROKE THE SURFACE AGAIN AND I SNATCHED A MOUTHFUL OF air. Then the current dragged me deep down again, tumbling me over and over along the bottom, my arms and legs picking up fresh bruises as I pinballed off rocks. I was completely at the mercy of the river: the current was far too strong to swim against and even if I wanted to try, I couldn't use my arms because I had to keep them wrapped protectively around my head. If my skull hit one of the rocks, I was dead.

I didn't know how long I'd been in the river, only that I'd spent most of the time near the bottom with only a few quick chances to pull in a breath as the current took me briefly up to the surface. I couldn't see, either: the river was moving so fast, it had torn tons of soil from the banks and they'd turned the water cloudy and brown. All I could do was hold my breath and pray for it to end.

Just as I was running out of air again, I felt the current slowing. I tentatively unwrapped my arms from my head, dreading that any second, I'd feel cold stone smack into my head. I began to claw at the water, hauling myself up, and at last, I surfaced.

I heaved in air, then dissolved into rib-shaking coughs. I was still spinning around like I was on a fairground ride, and my eyes were full of water and grit so I couldn't see, but I was alive.

When I could finally breathe again and my eyes had cleared, I looked around. The river had widened...a lot. That's why the current had slowed. The nearest bank was at least a couple of football fields away. I struck out for the bank and that's when I realized how banged up I was: my body felt like one big bruise and I was scraped raw in several places.

At first, the bank didn't seem to be getting any closer. Ninety percent of my effort was spent fighting the current that was dragging me downstream. But I kept mechanically dragging myself through the water and after what felt like hours, my hand hit dirt. I didn't so much climb out as slither up onto the shore, and then I collapsed face down with my feet still in the water, too exhausted to go any further. The medical bag was still tangled around my body, the strap half-strangling me, and I shrugged my way out of it and dumped it on the ground.

I was absolutely broken. Bruised and bleeding, lungs sore and chest aching from coughing, soaked and more tired than I'd ever been in my life. I had no idea where I was, but I knew I'd been carried downstream a long way, far from Gabriel and the others. I was alone in the jungle, with no supplies and no training.

But worse than any of that, they were gone. The whole team captured. Even now, they were probably being interrogated, and once the soldiers had found out what they knew, they'd kill them. The other two doctors, Colton, Danny, Cal, Bradan, JD...and Gabriel.

I started to sob. I was too tired, too broken to curl up, or put my hands to my face. I just lay there, my cheek pressed into the cold mud, and cried and cried, my chest heaving against the ground.

He was gone.

Happiness, real happiness, for both of us had been within touching distance and it had been snatched away.

Tears coursed down my cheeks, the cold ground swallowing their warmth. Gabriel Kain. Rogue. Scoundrel. Charismatic master thief. He'd survived all those heists, all those gun battles and knife fights, picked up all those scars. And now he was going to die because for once, he'd tried to do something right. Because of me.

I couldn't understand why fate, or destiny, or God, had done this. Someone had *screwed up!* They'd taken someone incredible and brave and cunning and left *me*: normal and boring and too serious for her own good. What really hurt was that if the situation was reversed, if I'd been the one captured and he'd been the one still free, I knew he'd come up with some clever plan to save me.

That thought sent me into wracking sobs, my body twitching against the ground. It went around and around in my mind: *he's going to die because I'm not more like him.*

Until, eventually, the thought flipped inside out.

He's going to die unless I'm more like him.

My mind rebelled against it. *That's crazy.* I wasn't Gabriel. I wasn't even a soldier. I had no idea what I was doing or even where I was.

But I was all he had.

My tears slowed and stopped. I gave a long, shuddering sniff. And then I lifted my face out of the mud and started pushing myself up. My arms were like rubber, all their strength used up by the swim. My legs ached and my ribs, elbows, and hips were covered in purple bruises from banging into rocks. But eventually, I got myself up to standing and looked around.

I was on a narrow riverbank of red-brown soil. The river was behind me, and in front of me, the jungle stretched on for mile after mile.

What would Gabriel do?

He'd try to find me. I looked around. I had no map, not even a compass. But I knew the current had carried me downstream. Gabriel and the rest of the team were somewhere back upriver.

I looked down at the medical bag. It was soaked through and stained. When I lifted it, river water drained out. But most of the contents were individually packed in plastic and should still be okay.

I hefted it onto my shoulder, turned upstream and started walking.

39

GABRIEL

THE TRUCK JERKED TO A STOP. A SOLDIER OPENED THE TAILGATE AND motioned for us to climb out.

We emerged blinking into the morning light. Whatever the place was, it wasn't an army base. Just a small clearing in the jungle with a few white prefab cabins. It looked more commercial than military.

Soldiers surrounded us. I recognized Major Zamora, the Special Ops guy who'd been in charge at the "cartel" camp. But there was someone else there too, a civilian in a spotless white shirt and black slacks. He had fancy, blue-and-silver-framed glasses and he was sipping coffee from a travel mug.

"This is all of them?" the stranger asked. His accent was American. *What the hell?*

"All that's left," Major Zamora told him. "The woman died."

He practically shrugged as he said it. I felt my hands curl into fists behind my back.

The stranger looked at us. "Who's the leader?" He looked at me. "You?"

"Me," growled JD.

I looked at JD in shock. If no one had spoken up, they would have had to interrogate us all. JD had just ensured that only he took the pain. I'd been on my own so long, I'd forgotten that kind of self-sacrifice existed.

The stranger definitely wasn't former Special Forces: I was pretty sure he'd never served at all. But he attempted a swagger as he strolled over to JD and got up in his face, enjoying playing the badass. "You're going to tell me what you know," he told JD with a cocky grin. "And who you've told."

JD lifted his chin a fraction of an inch and just stared silently back at the guy, telling him without words exactly how little he thought of him, exactly how easily he could kill him, even with his hands tied behind his back, if the guy didn't have a squad of soldiers to hide behind.

The stranger's grin crumbled. He looked away, embarrassed, then waved angrily towards one of the cabins. "Take him in there," he ordered Major Zamora. "And start beating it out of him."

40

OLIVIA

I STOPPED FOR A SECOND AND LEANED AGAINST A TREE, PANTING. I'D been walking for a solid hour, following the river upstream, but I wasn't sure how much distance I was covering. The jungle was especially thick here, and without Colton and his machete to hack things out of the way, I had to climb over branches and twisted vines almost constantly. My thighs burned from crouch-walking under things and my arms were covered in scrapes, adding to the ones I'd picked up in the river.

I tried to walk on the riverbank as much as possible because the going was so much easier there. But the bank kept petering out and I'd have to head into the jungle again, sometimes walking for minutes before I could find a way on. Every time I lost sight of the river, my chest contracted with fear. Everything looked the same and it was way, way too easy to get turned around and wind-up walking in the wrong direction: it had happened twice already. As the sun rose, the air was heating up and I was already dripping with sweat. The doubts started to multiply in my mind. *What if I can't find the river again? What if I run into the soldiers? What if it's just too far?* I had no food or water, no gear to survive out here.

I pushed off from the tree and staggered on. There was no time for *what ifs,* not if I wanted to save Gabriel.

I ducked under a vine that stretched between two trees. As I looked up, I saw a man right in front of me.

I gave a startled yell and jumped back, my heart thumping. He was no more than ten feet away. He was stripped to the waist and was wearing a pair of loose cotton pants the same color as the undergrowth. He blended so well with the jungle that I'd almost walked straight into him.

In one hand, he carried a spear. But the tip was pointing up towards the treetops, not at me.

I swallowed. "Hi. *Hola.*"

There was a tiny rustle behind me. I turned and saw another two men. Where the hell had they appeared from? I must have walked right past them.

The man in front of me said something in a language that wasn't Spanish and I heard one of the men behind me mutter something. They seemed a lot more relaxed than the ones we'd run into before. I guess an unarmed woman is a lot less threatening than six heavily armed men.

"Estoy perdido," I tried. *I'm lost.* I had no idea how I was going to find Gabriel but getting to the bridge would be a start. Except...I couldn't remember the Spanish for *bridge.* I pointed in the direction of the river and mimed walking. Then I tried miming crossing the swaying rope bridge, and they got it and motioned for me to follow them.

The men seemed to slide through the jungle effortlessly and I had to walk fast to keep up. I had no idea how they navigated but a half hour later, we emerged into a cleared area with dozens of small wooden buildings and one big one. Children were chasing after a ball on a soccer field, and through the open door of the big building, I could see more children sitting in rows: a school. The sun was high in the sky now, but a soft breeze was blowing. People carried baskets of squashes and bunches of plantains, a little girl was being followed around by a flock of ducks, and two old men sat mending shoes.

There were no cars—there wasn't even a road—and the chatter of people was the loudest sound by far. The place was idyllic.

The conversation paused as I passed: It didn't feel hostile, just intensely curious and a little cautious. The men took me to a small building at the center of the community, where a man in a soft pink shirt sat behind a table. His hair was silver but it was difficult to peg his age: he could have been anything from fifty to seventy. The men introduced me in their own language and he smiled warmly at me. "American?"

"Yes," I said in relief. "*Si!*"

He introduced himself as Antonio, and between my patchy Spanish and his shaky English, I managed to explain how the soldiers had captured my friends. He spread out a map on the table and showed me where we were, and where the rope bridge had been, another mile or so upriver.

When I told him what had happened and that something shady was going on, possibly involving the government, he nodded grimly. The government, he told me, was too friendly with big corporations. He pointed to the map, where several areas were highlighted in red pen. "Oil," he told me, almost spitting the word out. "Under our feet." Then he pointed out of the window.

At the edge of the cleared area, amongst the trees, there was something ugly and man-made. A fence, sagging and half-overgrown.

"Welamco. One of the big oil companies. They want to drill," Antonio told me. "But we protest. And the journalists, they help. Newspapers. TV. We stopped them."

I walked over to the window, a chill creeping up my spine. I shielded my eyes from the sun and squinted at the sign hanging on the fence. Two triangles, side by side. A stylized *W*, I realized now. A logo I'd seen before.

"Oh my God," I whispered. Suddenly, it all made sense.

Welamco, the oil company, had found oil, but couldn't drill it because the Shuar were on this land. So, Welamco had made a deal with someone in the government. Major Zamora and his men had posed as cartel members and kidnapped me and the other doctors.

That had scared everyone out of the area: journalists, charity workers...anyone who might be a witness.

I let out a groan of horror as I remembered the military convoy we'd seen being prepared at the army base. Major Zamora and his men were coming *here,* to wipe the Shuar out. The government would blame the cartel and there'd be no witnesses to say any different. And with the Shuar gone, the oil company would be free to drill.

I turned to Antonio and explained as best I could. His face paled and I followed his gaze to the window: to the children on the soccer field, to the little girl with the ducks.

A noise from outside made us both look up: the clattering drone of a helicopter. Antonio looked panicked. "¡El ejército!" *The army.* Were they here already?

But I hadn't seen a helicopter at the army base. I thought hard... then I realized what time it was.

I ran out of the hut and sprinted through the village, drawing curious looks from the locals. I plunged into the jungle, barely slowing down, ducking under vines and scrambling over fallen trees. My legs, still rubbery from all the swimming and walking, screamed for relief and my lungs burned. But I kept going. I could hear the helicopter getting louder and louder, it would be there in minutes, and if I missed it, it was all over.

I stumbled out of the trees and onto the riverbank just as the helicopter descended. It was an old, green-painted thing that looked like it had come straight from the Vietnam war. I staggered to a stop and shielded my eyes as the rotor blades kicked up dust and spray from the river. As the engine shut down and the blades slowed. I walked over to the cockpit, my legs shaky and my chest heaving.

The woman inside pulled off her headset and massaged her ears. She had black hair in a bob cut and was wearing a green flight suit with about a thousand pockets. She opened the door and frowned at me. "You the one he was trying to rescue?"

I nodded and grabbed hold of the helicopter's door frame to support me, panting too hard to speak.

"Where's the rest of them?"

She had to wait a moment before I could form words. "They got captured," I wheezed.

She cursed.

"I need your help," I told her. "We've got to go and rescue them."

"*What?!* Nooo. I had one job: come here at the right time and ferry you guys home." She sighed and her voice became a little more gentle. "C'mon, get in and I'll take you back to Quito."

"No! He came thousands of miles to save me. I can't let him die!"

For a second, the woman's face softened. Then she shook her head. "It's bad enough that I'm not going to get paid. I'm not getting shot too." She nodded to the rear of the helicopter. "Park your butt, buttercup, we're leaving." She turned away and pressed some switches. The helicopter's engine roared into life.

I looked at the seats in the back. All I had to do was sit down and I'd be back in civilization in an hour.

I shook my head. "No."

She looked round at me in horror. "*No?!*"

"I...I have to try and help him."

"*By yourself?* You're going to get yourself killed!"

"I have to try."

She stared at me for a moment, then sighed, shook her head, and put her headset back on. "Fine," she said. "I did my part."

She slammed the door, and I stepped back as the rotor blades spun up. The roar from them became deafening. The woman put her hand on the control column, about to take off—

She stopped and just sat there for a moment, her hand flexing on the control column. She glanced at me for a second, then turned to face front.

She started talking to herself. No, not talking, *cursing*. I couldn't hear but from her expression, she was unleashing a white-hot flood of curses that would make even Colton blush. Then she flipped some switches and the engine shut down.

I watched in shock as she pulled off her headset and opened the door.

"Okay," she muttered. "What did you have in mind?"

41

OLIVIA

AN HOUR LATER, I WAS LYING ON THE GROUND, PEEKING THROUGH THE trees at a collection of white prefab cabins. It hadn't been too hard to find the team. Antonio had only had to look at his maps for a few moments before he'd stabbed a finger at the disused oil company site. It was the only place in the area where the soldiers could take them. He'd offered his help but I'd shaken my head: he was needed in the village, where the Shuar were scrambling to prepare for the soldiers' attack.

I had no idea what I was doing. I could see soldiers patrolling back and forth around the edge of the clearing, rifles ready in their hands. If even one of them saw me, I'd be killed or captured. And even if I got into the clearing, what then? How the hell was I going to get them out?

What would Gabriel do? I thought frantically. *He'd plan.* He'd study everything and then come up with some cunning scheme.

I stayed in the trees and sidled around the clearing to get a better look. I stopped when I heard voices coming from one of the cabins.

"Who do you work for? Who knows what we're doing out here?" The voice was American and tight with anger. No answer came. Then there was a sound that made me flinch: the crack of bone hitting bone as someone was punched.

A second later, there was a low, Texas rumble I recognized. "That the best you can do?" *JD!*

I crept closer, pressing myself against a tree and praying I was invisible in the jungle's shadows. Through the window, I could see the oil company guy with the glasses, the one I'd seen at the prison camp. He was pacing back and forth as he asked questions, but he wasn't the one doing the punching. There must be a soldier in there, maybe more than one. I stepped sideways and peeked through the open door. The other team members were sitting on the floor with their hands tied behind their back. I glimpsed Cal and Danny and...*there! Gabriel!* My heart soared. *He's alive!*

What now? I couldn't just run in there. I wasn't even armed.

I moved on, circling around the clearing. In the next cabin, I could see a military backpack on the floor. It was Colton's: I'd walked behind him often enough to recognize his bedroll and the dark red steel cup tucked into a pocket. I craned my neck and saw a rifle leaning against the wall. That cabin must be where they'd put all the team's gear. I stared at the rifle, thinking hard. The cabin was only about eight feet from the edge of the jungle. I might be able to sneak in there and take one of the rifles. But then what? I'd never shot a gun in my life.

Then I saw something else: a belt that had been taken from one of the men. Hanging from it was a pistol in a holster and three dark green metal balls that dangled together like a cluster of fruit. Grenades. Maybe I could create a diversion, and then try to help the team while everyone was distracted.

I crept forward and hid behind a tree, right at the edge of the clearing. There were three soldiers patrolling and there always seemed to be one looking at the door I needed to get to. I waited and waited and then it happened: all of them looked away at the same time. I took a deep breath...and went for it.

It was the scariest thing I'd ever done. I had to just focus on the door and *walk*. Not run, or I'd make too much noise. Not creep, or I wouldn't be there before the soldiers turned around. I had to walk, a spot on the back of my neck itching, knowing that at any second there could be a shout, a gunshot...

I stepped through the door of the cabin and ducked down inside, heart pounding and sweat dripping off me. For a second, I just sat there, panting, letting the cool of the wall soak into my body. Then I gingerly unhooked one of the grenades from the belt.

Where to throw it? Somewhere far enough away that it wouldn't kill me. How far was *that?*

I peeked my head out of the door. At the end of the clearing furthest from the team, there was a generator and some big tanks of propane. Would that work?

I could hear the oil company guy yelling in the cabin next door. More questions, then more punches. Then I heard another voice I recognized: Major Zamora: he must be in there, too. "Enough," he said in English. "He's not going to tell you anything. Let's just kill them."

Oh Jesus. I ran outside and stared at the grenade. I'd only seen them do this in movies. I knew you were meant to pull out a pin and then throw. There was a safety catch and I fumbled with it. Then...*here? Pull this ring?*

I pulled and the ring came free in my hand, trailing a shiny metal pin. *Is that it?* Then the sickening realization: *oh God that's it, it's going to explode!*

I turned towards the generator. I'd always been lousy at sports. Memories of a thousand school softball games rose up in my mind, the other girls laughing at me. *Oh God oh God oh God—*

I threw. And for once, I got it exactly right. The grenade flew in an arc that would have made my Phys Ed teacher proud and landed among the propane tanks.

I ducked and winced in anticipation. But nothing happened. *Did I do something wrong? Was there something else I had to—*

There was a quick, sharp *bang* that hurt my ears. Then a massive explosion shook the ground and a shockwave of heat and air lifted me off my feet and slammed me into the cabin's wall.

42

GABRIEL

THE SOLDIERS HAD FORCED US TO OUR KNEES AND LINED US UP FACING the wall. JD was thrown down next to us. His nose was broken and one eye was swollen shut.

Major Zamora flexed his fingers, wincing, his knuckles raw from beating JD. Then one of his men tossed him a gun.

This was it. I looked left and right, taking in the team's faces. We were all going to die, far from home, and it was my fault: I'd gotten them into this.

I heard Major Zamora cock the gun. I'd imagined dying in all sorts of ways: shot by a guard during a theft, shanked in prison by an enemy, double-crossed and left for dead by someone I'd done a deal with. But I never would have dreamed, a few weeks ago, that it would end like *this:* with me in a team again.

I looked left and saw Cal and Bradan. I looked right and saw Danny, Colton, and JD.

I was going to die. But not alone. I wasn't ready for the deep swell of emotion that brought.

Major Zamora walked over to JD, who was first in line, and pointed the gun at the back of his head. So that's how this was going to go. I'd have to wait my turn, I'd have to hear three gunshots, hear JD, Colton, and Danny taken from me before merciful oblivion.

I screwed my eyes shut.

The floor heaved upward and everyone fell forward. A huge explosion blocked out all other sound: for a second, it was just dark chaos: bodies thumping against each other and lots of sharp little pains.

I opened my eyes, stunned that I was still alive.

The floor was a sea of groaning bodies: the team, the guy in the white shirt, Major Zamora and a couple of soldiers, all mixed up together. I realized that the explosion must have rocked the whole cabin for a second: that's what had knocked everyone over. The windows had blown out, too: we were covered in broken glass.

Major Zamora had dropped his gun. He lunged for it, but I struggled to my feet and shoulder-charged him against the wall. The rest of the team did the same, hurling themselves at the two soldiers and using shoulders and knees to take them down.

The guy in the white shirt gave a moan of fear and bolted for the door. JD body slammed him into the wall and he went down hard. JD gave a grunt of satisfaction.

We stood there panting for a second, looking at each other in confusion. *What the hell just happened?* What caused the explosion?

Footsteps outside. We all spun to face the door—

I will never, as long as I live, forget that moment. I was breathing hard, desperately trying to free the zip tie around my wrists, ready to launch myself forward as soon as a soldier stepped into view—

And then *she* stepped into view instead. Her white tank top had black-edged holes where falling embers had singed it. Her fatigue pants were soaked and mud stained. Her arms were scratched and bleeding and her cheeks were crusted with mud but her hair was still drawn back into that tightly efficient, prim little bun.

I'm not often lost for words, but I was then. "O...Olivia?!" I managed at last.

She gave me a shy little smile, and that's when I knew my brain wasn't playing tricks on me.

She was alive.

She was *alive!*

"This way," she said, and nodded to her left.

Everyone ran out the door, moving as fast as they could with their hands tied. Outside, everything was in uproar: a fire was burning down at the other end of the camp and the soldiers were all trying to put it out. Olivia pointed us to the cabin next door and we all rushed in. Our backpacks, guns, and other gear lay on the floor. Olivia grabbed a knife and cut through the zip tie holding JD's wrists. Then she freed Danny, while JD grabbed his own knife and freed Cal, and soon we were all free. Everyone started pulling on their backpacks and grabbing their guns.

Everyone except me. I just stood there staring at Olivia, barely aware of what was happening around me.

She's alive.

Losing her had taken me to the darkest place I'd ever been. It felt like my heart, my *soul,* had been crushed under cold rock. Now I could feel everything lifting.

Colton passed me my rifle but I didn't take it. I just stood there staring.

She's alive.

I could breathe again. I could feel again. The future I'd thought was gone was back, within my grasp, and a thousand times sweeter for almost losing it.

"Gabriel?" asked Colton. Everyone else was ready and I was just standing there. "Gabe?"

I walked right past him, grabbed Olivia and hugged her to me, my arms like iron around her. My head knew she was standing there, alive, but I needed to feel her warmth against me, smell her scent: my *heart* had to know she was really there. "I thought I lost you," I croaked. I knew the others must be able to hear the raw emotion in my voice and I didn't give a shit. "I thought I lost you."

The others gave us a few seconds, facing outwards to cover us as best they could. But eventually, JD patted me on the arm. "Gotta go," he muttered. He sounded extra-gruff, like he was trying to hide the emotion in *his* voice.

I nodded and pushed back from Olivia, but I stayed close as I pulled on my backpack and finally grabbed my gun from Colton. I made sure I stayed right beside her as we moved out of the door: I wasn't losing her again.

The soldiers saw us this time, and started shooting. We had to shoot our way over to the truck, where Dr. Guzman and Marcos had been left. I cut Marcos's wrists free and Colton threw Dr. Guzman over his shoulder.

"Which way?" Danny asked JD.

But before he could reply, Olivia pointed, her voice confident. "That way."

JD nodded. "Go."

We ran into the jungle and started scrambling up a small rise. Danny and Cal covered our rear but more soldiers were coming, drawn by the explosion. We'd soon be overrun.

The hill steepened, and a few moments later, we emerged from the trees on a clifftop, with nothing but a sheer drop ahead of us. JD looked at Olivia, worried. "Dead end."

"No it's not," said Olivia. And at that moment, a helicopter rose into view. It was an old Huey, its paint worn and fading, and at the controls was Gina.

We jumped in and before the doors were even shut, we were lifting away from the treetops. Soldiers raced out of the trees and fired up at us, but we were already out of range.

Gina looked round from the pilot's seat. "Next stop, Quito," she yelled over the roar of the rotor blades.

We all slumped in relief. And then, as things sank in, we exchanged amazed looks. *We did it.* Everyone was still alive, and we were on our way home. Something occurred to me and I checked the time in panic. I hadn't even thought about the gold since Olivia fell from the bridge, but—

My heart soared. *There was still time!* Just. If we flew full speed back to Quito, Olivia and I could still make the rendezvous at the airfield. We could slip away from the Justice Department and go and get the gold. It could all still work!

I turned to look at Olivia, grinning...only to see her watching me, her face tight with worry. *What's wrong?* I mouthed.

She motioned me to the very front of the passenger area, away from the others. There was nowhere to sit and the ceiling was too low to stand so we crouched awkwardly. I pressed close and she put her lips to my ear: it was the only way I could hear her without her yelling.

"We can't leave yet," she told me.

43

GABRIEL

She told me everything. My stomach churned. I'm no saint, but slaughtering a whole village for *oil?* It was that special level of callousness that you only got from dictators and CEOs.

"We've got to save them," said Olivia, her mouth still pressed to my ear.

I nodded.

I mean, I went to nod, I tried to. But...my head stayed still.

Olivia pushed back so that she could look at me. She frowned, confused. *What?* She mouthed.

I gazed back at her, unable to speak. I couldn't put it into words, I didn't want to say what was in my head, but...

I saw the realization dawn in her eyes and I braced myself for the anger. But she didn't look mad. She looked disappointed, which was worse.

"The gold?" she asked in my ear.

I felt myself folding inward, shrinking. Just a week ago, I'd strode into her infirmary feeling like a king. Now I felt like something she'd scraped off her shoe. I grabbed her and held her against me, my lips brushing her ear as I tried to explain. "We have to go *right now.* We can have it, Doc, we can have all of it, the four hundred million, the new life, it's all right there!" I pointed out through the windshield, towards Quito. "But we gotta go now, *right now,* the guy won't wait, and this is our last chance."

I pushed back, looking into her eyes, needing to see her reaction. Jesus, of all the conversations in my life, why did this one have to be in a deafening helicopter?

Tears were welling up in her eyes. *They need us,* she mouthed.

I grabbed her hands. My mouth moved but I couldn't think of what to say. I *knew* they needed us. When I thought of what the army was going to do to them, I wanted to throw up. But...

It was *four hundred million dollars. My* money, money I'd sweated and bled for. I'd spent three years in jail for it. My whole career as a thief had been building towards it. I couldn't give it up. I leaned forward again and I spoke into the delicate, shell-like ear. "When we get to Quito, we can tell people what's going on," I tried.

"Tell *who?!* The government? The government is in on this!"

"The UN, then!"

"And what will they do? *Sanctions?!* Gabriel, those people don't have days or weeks, they've got *hours.*"

I caught myself wavering and scrambled to encase myself in cold, impenetrable rock. I was a criminal, goddammit, a *thief.* I'd always put myself first, ever since I got kicked out of the Marines and I couldn't afford to go soft now. When we were rich and living on a beach, I'd donate to charity: hell, I'd start my *own* charity.

I drew back and shook my head.

Her lower lip shook and she pressed her lips tight together, then leaned forward for one final try. "There are children, Gabriel."

I closed my eyes. I could feel the rock I'd just built around me beginning to fracture and break. I sucked in air through my nose, huffed it out through my mouth. *Four. Hundred. Million. Dollars.* I couldn't give it up. I just couldn't. "I always told you I'm not a hero," I grated.

Tears were spilling down her cheeks. "And I always told you, you are."

I realized she could have just told JD instead, and he would have pulled rank. She wanted me to make the decision. She wanted me to be the man she thought I was.

Goddammit. I crouched there, eyes closed, battling with myself, for five more breaths. Then I slammed my fist against the ceiling of the Huey and turned to the others.

"Change of plan," I yelled. And started telling them about the village. It was difficult to speak, with the pain that was going on in my chest. It's impossible to describe the feeling of losing your fortune, your dream, your life's work.

But when I glanced up and saw the way Olivia was looking at me, the different sort of tears that were in her eyes...the pain eased a little.

When I'd finished bringing them all up to speed, JD looked around at the team. "I know what *I* want to do," he said. "But this isn't what you signed up for. If we're going to do this, I figure we should all be on board."

He looked at each of us in turn. One by one, we nodded.

JD gave a sober nod, but I didn't miss the look that crossed his face, like a proud father at his kid's baseball game. "Alright then," he said. "Let's—"

"Nobody asked *me,*" yelled Gina from the cockpit. "Don't just presume I'm okay with your little mercy mission!"

I rose and walked forward to her, then leaned over the empty co-pilot's seat to talk to her. "You gonna leave those people to die?"

She looked away, fixing her gaze on the horizon. For a long time, she said nothing. Then, "You better pay me triple." Her voice was sour and extra gruff. Just to make it clear that she didn't have anything as soft or vulnerable as a heart.

"Okay," I said, my voice neutral. "Triple."

She nodded. "Fine. Let's go be heroes."

And she swung the chopper around so fast that everyone standing fell over.

44

GABRIEL

As we approached the village, Danny whistled to get our attention, then pointed ahead and down. JD and I leaned over the co-pilot's seat and looked. "That's not good," I mumbled.

The convoy we'd seen at the military base was on the move, snaking through the jungle towards the village. "We've got thirty minutes," said JD. "Maybe less". We'd been hoping we'd have hours to prepare.

As we got closer, the soldiers in the convoy opened fire and Gina had to bank away, cursing. JD shook his head. "There's gotta be eighty men in those trucks," he said. "We're not going to be able to hold them forever."

I nodded, thinking hard. "The whole thing with kidnapping the doctors," I said at last. "That was all so that no one knew what was going on here. They're terrified of this going public." I turned to Gina. "How long to fly to Quito and get back here with a news crew?"

She pursed her lips, thinking. "Ninety minutes, if I go all-out."

I exchanged looks with JD. We'd have to hold the soldiers off for a full hour, while outnumbered more than ten to one.

A few moments later, we roared over the village and Gina brought us in for a perfect landing in the middle of the soccer pitch.

We jumped out, leaving only Dr. Guzman and Marcos on board: Dr. Guzman needed a hospital and Marcos would need to look after him enroute. I turned to Olivia and realized we were alone: everyone else had hurried off, following JD. She was looking up at me the way someone would look at a rock star: adoring but like she was worried she was in a dream, and might wake up. I sighed and nodded: *Yeah, I can't believe I did it, either.* I'd been shot, more than once, and I can say honestly that losing four hundred million dollars hurt more. After years of always finding a way: the cunning plan, the last-minute double-cross, the switcheroo no one saw coming—I'd *lost.*

Olivia threw her arms around me and pressed close, her breasts pillowing against my chest and her breath soft against my neck. I ran my hands all the way down her back to her ass and squeezed. And felt a little better.

"This place is about to be a warzone," I told her, and nodded at the chopper. "Don't suppose I can persuade you to go with them?"

She shook her head, stepped back and slung the filthy, soggy medical bag over her shoulder. "People are going to get hurt. Marcos can look after Dr. Guzman. You need me here."

She hurried off with the others. I went to close the door...and stopped when Marcos grabbed my wrist. Our eyes locked and something passed between us, man to man.

"Take care of her," he told me.

I gave him a solemn nod and gripped his hand. "Always," I promised.

I slid the door closed and watched the helicopter lift away. Then I ran to join the others.

Olivia introduced us to Antonio, the head of the village. "We're getting all the children into the school," he told us.

JD looked over to where the adults were hustling kids into a large wooden building. His gaze seemed to lock, and for a moment, he just...stopped.

I followed his gaze. A little boy was trying to hurry up the steps, but he was being weighed down by the weight of a backpack that was far too big for him. A woman who might have been his teacher was telling him to leave it, that it was too heavy for him, but he stubbornly struggled on.

I looked at JD again, my chest going tight. *Wait. Did he lose—*

JD looked away from the kid and caught my eye. He must have seen the concern on my face because he looked thrown, then embarrassed, and finally, firm. *Don't,* his eyes told me.

I nodded sadly.

All business again, JD started issuing orders. We huddled close to listen. "Cal, you find a perch, tell us what's coming and cover our asses. Bradan, Gabriel: they got us beat on raw numbers. You've got to find ways to slow them down. Give us as long as possible to get ready." He pointed to Colton and Danny. "We three are the welcoming committee: we'll try to pin them down and then fall back house by house, make them fight for every inch."

I found myself nodding. Just days ago, we were a bunch of guys, thrown together. Now, we all knew each other's strengths and weaknesses. And we trusted JD to know the best way to put us to use. We felt like a team.

"Go do your stuff," said JD. And the huddle broke as people hurried away to their tasks.

Olivia threw her arms around me and I kissed her hard and deep, then picked her right up off the ground and crushed her to me. I'd told myself that I'd never let her go again and here I was, running off into battle again. I looked down at her, worried.

She nodded firmly, as if she could read my thoughts. "Go," she told me, "Go! I'll be fine."

I reluctantly put her down...then I nodded to Bradan and we ran off to meet the enemy.

45

GABRIEL

As we'd flown in, I'd been able to get a feel for the layout of the village and the land around it. The military convoy was approaching from the north, down a winding logging road that cut through thick jungle. I ran with Bradan to the edge of the village and stopped in the middle of the road, staring at the point where the convoy would round the corner. If the convoy drove right into the village, the soldiers would be able to use their trucks and jeeps as cover while we'd be stuck sheltering behind flimsy wooden buildings. We had to even the odds. We had to somehow get them out of their vehicles.

"We're going to need an ax," I said at last. "No, two axes."

Bradan ran off and returned only a few minutes later with an ax in each hand. "You're going to cut down a tree so it falls across the road?"

"Mmm," I said, noncommittally. I was walking along the road, looking at trees, measuring distances and angles in my head.

Bradan followed patiently for a while. But then we heard the distant rumble of engines. "Maybe we should...you know, get chopping."

"Mmm-hmm." I was looking up at a tree. *Not that one.* I walked to the next. *Not that one either.*

The engines were getting louder. "They're going to be here any minute." Bradan watched as I examined a tree and then walked away from it. "What was wrong with *that* one?"

"Trust me," I mumbled, already frowning at another tree. "I did this with an armored car once, in France."

The engines became a roar. "Gabriel, seriously, just *any feckin' tree!*" His Irish accent got stronger when he was stressed.

"This one," I said triumphantly, slapping the trunk. I took an ax from him and started chopping. Bradan raced over and we got into a rhythm, alternating our swings. The tree was a big one, the trunk at least three feet wide. Each chop sent a shower of matchwood spraying out but the cut in the tree barely seemed to get any deeper and the engines were getting louder and louder: you could make out individual vehicles now. Maybe I *had* spent too long choosing. We pushed ourselves harder, swinging like madmen.

The engine noise changed, becoming clearer: they were only one corner away. We looked at each other in fear: we were only two-thirds through. I threw down my ax. "Push!"

Bradan and I hurled ourselves at the tree and pushed with everything we had. At first, nothing happened. But as we dug our boots into the soil and heaved with our backs, slowly, slowly, it started to tip. And then, with a cracking, tearing sound, it toppled, crashing down across the road. I pulled Bradan well away, back towards the village, and we hunkered down where we could watch.

The first truck came around the bend and stopped when the driver saw the tree. The convoy stopped and the soldiers in the first few trucks dismounted and fanned out cautiously, expecting an ambush.

They looked at the tree. There was a quick discussion. Then the truck driver drove slowly forward, butted the truck's bumper up against the tree and began to push. The tree held fast for a moment and then, as he gunned the engine, it started to slide along the road.

"Feck," muttered Bradan despondently. "After all that." He turned away.

I grabbed his shoulder. "Wait," I told him. "Watch and learn."

The tree slid along the road...and then it suddenly stopped, hard. The truck driver stopped and jumped out. The soldiers all gathered around the tree in confusion.

What I'd done was pick a tree that was tall enough that, once we cut it down, it would reach right across the road and stick out into the jungle on both sides. And I'd made sure there were other trees closer to the road so that when the soldiers pushed the felled tree forward, it would hit them and form an immovable obstacle.

"That," said Bradan, "was very bloody clever."

Major Zamora marched up to the front of the convoy. My jaw tightened. He was the one who'd kidnapped Olivia. He was the one who'd beaten JD. He'd cost me four hundred million dollars. Whatever happened here today, that guy was going down.

Major Zamora examined the tree, cursed in Spanish, and ordered everyone out of the convoy. We'd done it: we'd got them to abandon their vehicles. Now we had to slow them down as much as possible. "Go to work," I told Bradan.

As the soldiers started advancing on foot towards the village, Bradan slipped into the trees. I tried to keep an eye on him so I could cover his ass but in seconds he was just...*gone*. I couldn't see where—

A soldier fell, suddenly and silently, clubbed over the head with the butt of Bradan's rifle. I glimpsed Bradan for an instant, then he was gone again.

The soldiers found their fallen man and a shout went up: *someone's here!* They crept forward more cautiously.

Another soldier fell. And immediately, Bradan was gone again, disappearing into the shadows. When the soldiers found this one, they slowed down even more, yelling to each other to be careful.

A third soldier fell, right over on the other side of the road. I hadn't even seen Bradan cross. Now the soldiers were truly afraid. Someone was in the trees, hunting them, and Major Zamora had to yell at them to make them advance at all. Pale-faced and twitchy, they crept towards the village, and instead of taking two minutes to cover the distance, it took them more like fifteen. Eventually, though, they made it to the edge of the clearing and we had to fall back.

I slapped Bradan on the back as he rejoined me. We'd bought the village some time. We just had to hope it was enough.

As we ran for cover, three guns opened up. We looked and saw JD, Colton and Danny firing from the windows of a house. Bradan and I slid into cover behind the corner of a building and started shooting too. Together, we did our best to hold back the advance but the soldiers kept coming, an unstoppable tide.

Then JD yelled an order in Spanish. More guns started firing from other buildings and I looked around in shock. JD had used the time we'd bought him to organize the locals, helping them pick out good defensive positions. Now they were fiercely defending their homes. It evened the odds a little: instead of us six versus eighty soldiers, now it was maybe twenty versus eighty. For a while, it looked like we might actually be able to hold them off and the tension in my chest eased a little.

But then the soldiers got smart and started fanning out through the jungle, hitting us from multiple directions at once. Within minutes, we were overrun and the soldiers were in the village. The battle turned into a brutal, house-by-house fight of the kind we'd all seen too much of in Iraq and Afghanistan. We yelled to the locals to fall back but some of them weren't quick enough: I saw one Shuar man fall and then another.

That's when I saw Olivia on the far side of the street, feet thumping against the dirt as she sprinted from one house to another, the medical bag banging against her back.

My heart shot into my mouth. I forgot where I was, I forgot I was hunkered down behind cover, I forgot *everything*. I stood up and reached for her, even though she was forty feet away.

I heard a gunshot. At the same time, Colton slammed into my legs. I hit the ground on my back and lay there wheezing: when Colton tackles you, you go down *hard*. A bullet zipped over my head: if not for Colton, I would have been going home in a body bag.

Colton panted and shook his head, staring at me: *what's gotten into you?* Then he looked across the street and saw Olivia, crouched low behind a wall as she tried to reach an injured Shuar man. Colton's face softened. "At least *she* knows to keep her head down," he muttered.

Olivia's eyes were huge and her face had gone sheet-white with fear. But then she looked along the street to where one of the Shuar men lay clutching his chest, and her jaw tightened in determination. I winced as she broke cover again and sprinted closer to the man, then ducked behind a water barrel, pinned down by gunfire.

She was terrified, a thousand miles from home and completely out of her element, but she was still trying to help people. Something rose up in my chest, a huge warm swell of love and...I realized it was pride. I wanted to thank Colton for saving my ass but it was suddenly impossible to speak.

Every instinct was buzzing with the need to keep her safe. I wanted to run over there, pick her up and carry her to the school, tying her up if I had to, just as long as she stayed there. But I was just realizing that I couldn't do that. Saving lives was what she did: it was why she'd been an ER doc, why she'd come out here to Ecuador, why she'd saved me, in so many different ways. I couldn't stop her being her. All I could do was try to protect her.

Colton and I opened fire and managed to take out the soldier who had Olivia pinned down. "Go!" I yelled, and she sprinted to the next bit of cover, and then finally reached the man she'd been trying to get to. She dragged him behind a building and went to work with bandages, trying to stop the bleeding. I relaxed a little. But as soon as she'd stabilized him, Olivia was up and running again. Where was she going *now?!*

She disappeared behind a building. *Dammit!* I could work my way over there, but not until we'd secured this street. I'd never felt so helpless: I'd never had someone to worry about before. *Please, baby, be careful,* I prayed.

46

OLIVIA

I PRESSED MY BACK AGAINST A WALL, PANTING. I'D NEVER BEEN SO scared in my life. The village, so idyllic just a few hours before, had become a waking nightmare. The air stank of cordite. Brass shell casings littered the ground, and in every building people huddled, terrified, pressed against the walls in fear while others fired rifles from the windows. My hands and clothes were already stained with blood and I'd only managed to treat three people: there were so many more.

I'd seen news reports from wars on TV, seen reporters in flak jackets and helmets talking about how scary it was, but that had done absolutely nothing to prepare me for the real thing.

It felt like the air itself had become deadly. There were so many soldiers firing, all the time, that any open space in the village, anywhere where you were exposed, was death. You couldn't see the bullets, you certainly couldn't dodge them: by the time you heard the crack of gunfire or the hiss of the bullet, it was too late. You had to accept that if you were out in the open, you would die within seconds.

This is what Gabriel and the others had lived for years, in war zones all over the world. *How the hell do they do this?!*

I peeked around the edge of the wall, picking out the next bit of cover to run to, just like Gabriel had taught me. Every cell in my body was screaming at me to stay where I was, to stay safe.

I took a deep breath and *ran,* as fast as my aching legs would carry me, my whole body tight with tension, waiting for a bullet to rip into me. I slammed up against a stack of crates filled with fruit and crouched there, panting and shaky.

I risked a glance around the edge of the crates and my heart sank. I'd been trying to reach a woman who was lying injured in the middle of the street, having been hit in the leg, but I'd run out of cover, and she was still a good twenty feet away. How was I going to get to her and drag her behind something before I got shot? Worse, I wasn't in sight of Gabriel or the others, anymore. There was no one to protect me.

I heard footsteps behind me and twisted around to look that way. A soldier came around the corner, saw me and raised his gun to fire. I tensed, flinching—

And then the soldier just crumpled to the ground. The sound of a gunshot echoed off the buildings like a clap of thunder.

I had a guardian angel.

I shielded my eyes from the sun and squinted. Right down at the far end of the village, on the roof of one of the buildings, I could see the head and shoulders of someone lying full-length, a rifle in front of them. *Cal!*

He raised a hand in the air and then dropped it forwards, pointing: *go!*

I ran as fast as I could to the injured woman. When I was halfway there, a soldier came around the corner in front of me. I tried to skid to a stop, then yelped as a shot rang out and the soldier fell. It really was like being divinely protected. I muttered a prayer of thanks to Cal, grabbed the woman's shoulders, and started dragging her back the way I'd come.

But at that moment, four more soldiers came around the corner: more, maybe, than even Cal could handle at once. Two of them started firing up at the building where Cal was sniping from and the other two started shooting at us. I cursed, changed course, and dragged the woman towards the nearest house, almost running. She cried out in pain, clutching at her leg, and I winced in sympathy, but I didn't have time to be gentle.

I backed through the door and almost fell into the house with her, just as bullets tore through the front wall. The window disintegrated, spraying glass all over the room. I screamed and threw myself over the woman, trying to shield us both, feeling shards lance my arms.

Hunkered low so we were out of sight, I got a tourniquet on her leg and managed to get the bleeding under control. She was going to need a hospital, but first, I had to get her out of there. I peeked out of the window and saw soldiers flooding the street and firing up at the building where Cal lay. I watched as he was forced to abandon his sniper spot.

We were cut off, and I'd lost my guardian angel.

I crawled around the room, desperately peeking through windows and searching for a way out. But there was no cover nearby: we'd be seen instantly, out in the open. If I'd been on my own, I might have tried running for it, but the woman couldn't run, and I wasn't strong enough to carry her.

I heard shouted orders, doors being kicked open and bursts of gunfire: the soldiers were going house-to-house, gunning down anyone they found. Most of the houses at this end of the village had already been abandoned, but any minute, they'd try *this* house.

The woman was watching me from where she lay on the floor. "Déjame," she said at last.

I shook my head firmly. No, I wasn't leaving her.

The bursts of gunfire came closer and closer. *What would Gabriel do?* Something sneaky and unexpected. Can't fight. Can't escape...

Hide. He'd hide.

There was a square trapdoor in the middle of the floor. I hauled it open and found a space about the size of a double bed and only a few feet deep: just big enough for the family to store a small crop of root vegetables out of the sun. It was half full of cassavas and sweet potatoes.

I grabbed the woman by the shoulders again and hauled her into the root cellar, then lay down next to her on my back. When I eased the trap door down, its wood planks were only an inch from our noses.

The gunfire got closer. Then it seemed to die away. *Maybe they won't come in here. Maybe Gabriel and the others have pushed them back.*

Then I heard the door fly open and crash against the wall. It happened so suddenly, I had to stifle a scream.

There were enough gaps between the floorboards that I could see slices of what was happening. Two soldiers crept cautiously inside, weapons up and ready, their weight making the floorboards bend and creak. They fanned out, checking the corners. I held my breath. *See?* I thought desperately. *No one here. All gone.*

One of the soldiers stepped right onto the trapdoor, sending dust and dirt trickling down onto my face. I forced myself not to twitch.

The soldiers looked around, then one of them grunted something in Spanish and they started to leave. I dug my nails into my palms. *Another few seconds...*

They were almost at the door when one soldier stopped, tapped his buddy's shoulder and pointed at something on the floor. I couldn't see what it was at first. Then one of them picked it up and my insides turned to water.

The medical bag. *Why didn't I bring it with me? Idiot!*

The soldier marched over to the trapdoor and pointed his gun right at it: right at *us*. He snapped an order to the other one, who ran forward and grabbed hold of the trapdoor's handle, ready to pull it open. They nodded to each other. *Uno,* counted the one holding the trapdoor.

Dos, he mouthed silently.

I grabbed the woman's hand and squeezed it hard—

There was a crash as the door was broken off its hinges. Both soldiers turned to look.

Gabriel was the first through the door. He smashed into one of the soldiers, knocking his rifle away from us, then clubbed him in the side of the head with his gun. Colton charged the other soldier like a bull, knocking the air out of him and ramming him up against the far wall, then knocking him out with a punch to the face.

As both soldiers slumped, unconscious, Gabriel heaved open the cellar door. I gaped up at him, shaky and weak, incapable of speech.

He reached down, grabbed me around the waist and lifted me, then pulled me against him, my feet dangling a foot off the floor. I wrapped my arms around him and pressed my head against his. Nothing in the world had ever felt so good. I'd really thought I was going to die.

"I gotcha, Doc," he whispered. And I closed my eyes as he squeezed me tight.

Colton bent and scooped up the injured woman, cradling her in his arms. Gabriel reluctantly put me down and I grabbed the medical bag. "Is Cal okay?" I asked.

Gabriel nodded. "He had to move, but he's okay. C'mon. We've got to go."

He checked the coast was clear, and then we were off and running, with Colton carrying the injured woman. We ran into the jungle and skirted around the village, coming in from the back.

It was terrifying to see how far the soldiers had advanced. They'd taken almost the entire village: only the school was left, and the soldiers were massing at the end of the street, ready for the final push. I could see Major Zamora at the front, snapping out orders.

The Shuar, many of them injured, were positioned around the school, the last line of defense between the soldiers and their children. I saw them sharing out the last remaining ammunition between them: some of them had even put their rifles down and picked up spears. My chest contracted: this is really what it was going to come down to? A people fighting for their children's lives with spears, against a modern military?

Colton carefully handed the injured woman to her people, and we went to find JD, Danny, Bradan, and Cal. They'd erected a ramshackle barricade between the soldiers and the school and were kneeling behind it, ready to make their final stand. We knelt down behind them.

JD gave a quick nod of relief when he saw us, but I could see how worried he looked. He nodded down the street towards the soldiers, reloading his rifle as he talked. "They're regrouping. There's still fifty or so of them left and they'll be on us any minute. We don't have the numbers and we're almost out of ammo."

"How long until Gina gets back?" asked Danny.

JD shook his head. "At least another ten minutes." He looked at the soldiers massing, preparing to push forward. Then he glanced behind him at the school. When he spoke, his voice was rough with regret and shame. "We can't hold them," he muttered.

The school. The children. The whole village. It was all about to be wiped out, and us with it.

We'd lost.

47

GABRIEL

I LOOKED AROUND DESPERATELY. *THIS CAN'T BE IT.* THE FEAR FOR THE Shuar, for the children, swelled up inside me until I thought I'd burst. *No. No, it can't be, there's got to be something—*

I'd forgotten what it felt like, to be fighting for something bigger than yourself, to be ready to give your life for it. I'd had years of only caring about myself. On a heist, if things go wrong, you bail. You run and you live to fight another day. But this...

I hadn't felt this way since that day on the boat, seeing those refugees in the water. I'd finally come full circle.

"There's time," said JD quietly. "If anyone wants to make a run for it. If you head into the jungle, you might be able to slip away."

He looked around at everyone, but we all shook our heads. None of us were going to run and leave these people to die.

I looked at Olivia, who was hunkered down with her medical bag, ready to patch up anyone who got hurt. Up at Cal, now on the roof of the school. I looked at Colton and Danny and Bradan and finally JD, all getting ready to die, stoic and determined. *No. No, this can't be the end!* I couldn't let anything happen to Olivia, but it was about the others, too. These guys had become friends. And they were all going to die unless...

Unless someone did something heroic.

"JD," I said slowly, "thank you for giving me a second chance. You're a hell of a leader." I hugged him, wrapping my arms around him and patting him on the back.

JD froze, taken aback by the sudden show of affection. Then he sighed and I felt him relax. "Glad I was wrong about you," he muttered.

I let him go, grabbed Olivia and pulled her to me. I slid my hand into her hair and kissed her deep, one last time. Then, as I let her go, I said, "You...you take care, okay?"

Olivia frowned. "What—" She read my body language and started to scramble to her feet in panic. "Wait, *where are you going?!*"

"To be a hero," I told her.

And I jumped over the barricade and ran towards the soldiers.

48

GABRIEL

It's strange what goes through your head when you're running into certain death.

As I looked down the barrels of fifty rifles, I didn't think about the gold I'd lost. I didn't think about the heists I'd pulled off, the paintings and the cash and the jewelry. I thought of *moments*. My first kiss. Getting drunk with my high school buddy. Hugging my dad. Stuff that mattered.

And a lot of those moments came from the last few weeks. Like the first moment I'd seen Olivia. Comforting her when she told me about how she got fired. And that night in the mansion, touching her in the darkness.

Other moments, too. Like sitting in a stolen truck with Bradan as he told me his problems. Passing the cup of coffee around at dawn. Hearing what food everyone wanted when they got home.

Being a team.

It was a hundred feet to my target. I managed to cover ten while the soldiers just stood there staring at me in shock. They weren't expecting one of us to just run straight at them, unarmed and alone. But then they woke up and started shooting, and I heard the bullets zip past me. *Shit.* I covered another ten feet, but I knew it was only a matter of time before someone hit me.

That's when I heard gunfire coming from behind me. JD, Bradan, Colton, Danny...they all opened up. They had no idea what the hell I was doing, but they threw everything they had into supporting me, using their last few precious bullets to take down anyone who was shooting at me. I covered another thirty feet as the soldiers ducked for cover, and now I was halfway. Then I heard Cal's rifle fire and saw a soldier fall: he was clearing a path for me, shooting the ones who looked like they were about to fire. I sprinted on: forty feet to go, then thirty—

Pain exploded on my left side, level with my navel. I thought I heard Olivia cry out. I took another step and the pain got worse, but I was still running so I figured it couldn't be too bad. *Push on.*

Twenty feet to go. The soldiers were looming close, now, and they had panic in their eyes. They couldn't believe I'd gotten this far. I saw soldier after soldier raise his gun to take a shot...and then one of the team would hit him and he'd go down. Fifteen feet. *Come on.* Ten feet. *Come on!*

But the odds weren't in our favor. The team needed to hit every single soldier who tried to take a shot at me. The soldiers only had to get one good shot off...

There. I could see it happening in slow motion: a young-looking soldier snapped off a good, clean shot before anyone could hit him and—

All the strength went out of my right leg. A fraction of a second later, the pain hit, boiling up through my body like lava. *Jesus!*

I stumbled. Took another step. When my right foot hit the ground again, it felt like every bone exploded into dust. I cried out, and this time I was sure I heard Olivia scream. The pain was so bad I couldn't breathe.

But my target was only six feet away now. I was so close I could see the disbelief on his face: I was coming for *him?!*

I launched myself forward, and as my right leg collapsed under me, I slammed full-length into Major Zamora. We hit the ground together, me on top. We rolled over and over...but he wound up on top and as I lay there, bleeding and spent, he pulled out his handgun and pointed it at my head.

Then he frowned and looked down at his other hand. At the shining metal cuff that surrounded his left wrist and the jangling chain that connected it to mine.

I imagined JD watching this, cursing, patting the empty handcuff case on his belt and realizing why I'd really hugged him.

Major Zamora scowled at me, confused. "Take it off," he demanded. "Where's the key? Take it off or I'll shoot you and take the key from your body—"

"You shouldn't be worrying about *that* hand," I panted. I was in so much pain, I was going floaty, and I wondered how much blood I was losing. "You should be worrying about what's in *this* one."

And I showed him the hand grenade I'd pulled from my belt, while we'd been rolling over and over. Then I pulled the pin and tossed it away. "Oopsie." Now my thumb was the only thing holding the grenade's lever down. If I let it pop up, the grenade would start its countdown.

Major Zamora's eyes bulged in terror. He instinctively jerked away, but the handcuff chain snapped taut and held him in place. "Disparale!" he yelled. *Shoot him!*

"You sure?" I asked quickly. "They shoot me, I drop this. Five seconds later, it explodes. How far do you think you can drag my body in five seconds? Far enough?"

Major Zamora had gone pale. So had all of the soldiers close to us. They looked at each other uncertainly. Then one broke rank and backed off. Immediately, another one did the same, and another and another. In seconds, we were at the center of a widening circle.

"Tell your men to put their guns down," I told Major Zamora. "And I'll put the pin back in."

"You're *insane!*" snapped Major Zamora.

"Maybe. I'm definitely light-headed. Must be the blood loss. Any second now, I'm going to pass out and *then* what happens?"

Major Zamora stared at me, then at the grenade in my hand. He looked at his men, at the village. He cursed under his breath.

And then he yelled to his men to throw their guns down. He was a corrupt, merciless son of a bitch but, as I'd guessed, he wasn't willing to die for his mission.

As the guns hit the ground, JD and the others raced over to cover the soldiers. Olivia dropped to her knees beside me and started tending to my leg and the wound in my side, which was probably a good thing because I really *was* getting light-headed.

JD crouched on my other side. "You are a sneaky son of a bitch," he told me. "But you're *our* sneaky son of a bitch." And he patted my shoulder.

"All you've done is delay things," snapped Major Zamora. "The government will send another unit. They'll send the whole army, if they have to."

"No they won't," said JD quietly, looking up. I heard the blare of rotor blades, and a few moments later, Gina swept overhead in the chopper. I could see a woman leaning out of the open side door holding a video camera and a guy narrating into a microphone. She'd brought a news crew. By that evening, the whole country was going to be seeing pictures of the army invading a Shuar village. "Good luck covering *that* up," JD said.

Major Zamora stared up at the glass eye of the camera...and slumped in defeat.

"You're going to be okay," Olivia told me. "You're going to have a nice new scar on your side, and we need to get some blood into you, but your leg should heal fine, the bullet went straight through." And then she stopped being a doctor, put her arms around my neck and cuddled in tight.

The Shuar people who'd been guarding the school ran over to help, collecting up the guns and watching over the soldiers. Someone let the kids out of the school and they swept out in a wave, finding their parents and hugging them. And I grudgingly admitted to myself that even though I'd lost the gold, it kind of felt like winning.

I cleared my throat and raised my voice over the hubbub. "This is all great," I said. "But could someone please find the pin for this grenade?"

EPILOGUE

Gabriel

The next few days were busy.

Gina started shuttling the injured to hospital by chopper. By the time she'd made her third run, the story had broken in Quito and other helicopters were arriving, bringing police, government officials, and high-ranking members of the army. Major Zamora and his men were taken into custody by military police. Soon after, it was my turn to be ferried off to hospital. Olivia and the rest of the team came with me and we spent the night at the field hospital Olivia had visited, just before she'd been kidnapped. Olivia asked to borrow the satellite phone, and with shaking hands, she dialed her mother, back in Arizona. The tears started as soon as her mom answered, days of tension finally starting to release. I put my arms around her from behind and held her close. "Mom?" she sobbed. "I'm—I'm okay. I'm coming home."

The doctors had been in touch with Quito and told us both Dr. Guzman and Marcos were doing well. They gave me a blood transfusion, patched up my leg, and loaded me up with painkillers. At that point, I crashed and crashed hard. We all did: none of us had slept much in the last few days. The rest of the team bedded down in the spare room Olivia had used. Olivia curled up next to me on my hospital bed, and we all slept for nearly fourteen hours.

The next morning, we got to take the first shower we'd had in days. Then we ate an enormous breakfast: fried eggs, their yolks golden and liquid, slices of rich fried plantain, corn tortillas, and huge mugs of coffee to wash it all down. Then, as I hobbled up and down the room, practicing with my crutches, Olivia used the hospital's computer to check her email. The big US news networks were already filling up her inbox, many of them offering cash for an exclusive interview: her kidnapping had been big news anyway, and now she was at the center of the whole scandal that was unfolding involving Welamco and the Shuar. But Olivia shook her head as she sifted through the emails. "I don't want to be famous," she mumbled. "I just want to go home."

Then one email made her stop and frown. She showed it to me. It was from an investigative reporter on a New York newspaper. She was covering the story, but in a lot more detail than the others. She sounded earnest, like she actually cared about getting the facts right. Olivia replied and got an answer back almost immediately. The two had a phone call that lasted almost three hours, with Olivia telling her the whole story, all the way back to getting fired from the hospital. I sat with her, rubbing her back and bringing her cups of coffee, and when it was over, I pulled her into my arms and held her close. She sighed and slumped against me, emotionally spent. But after a few moments of me stroking her hair, she looked up at me. "I think I feel better," she said.

That afternoon, Gina flew us back to the airfield at Quito. Olivia had the medical bag on her lap. The doctors at the field hospital had said she could keep it: it was ragged and stained and definitely needed some TLC, but she said she wasn't parting with it now. All of us gaped out of the windows as we reached the city: it felt like weeks since we'd seen a car, a bus, or a high-rise building.

As we touched down at the airfield, I looked sadly at the building I would have gone into, if everything had gone to plan: *in there, out the* *back door, through the hole in the fence...*We could have been rich beyond belief.

But there was no one waiting in a getaway car for me now. Just a shiny black SUV and three very serious looking agents from the Justice Department. And standing beside them, Kian O'Harra. I saw the tension drop from his face when he saw that we were all okay. "Good job," he said with feeling.

The Justice Department guys weren't quite so friendly. A tall guy with a bald pate and gold-rimmed glasses stepped forward. "Agent-in-Charge Jackson," he announced. "Where's the gold?"

I'd told the rest of the team about my deal on the flight. It didn't feel right, anymore, keeping things from them. I let out a long sigh. "Utah," I said. "It's in Utah."

Agent Jackson produced a pair of handcuffs but Kian pushed them away. "The man's cooperating," Kian said in a low, menacing tone. "There's no need for that."

I nodded my thanks. The agents showed me and Kian to the SUV. Olivia stepped forward too, but an agent blocked her path. "Just him and Mr. O'Harra," the agent told her. "You and the others can fly straight back to Colorado."

Olivia looked him right in the eye. "Where he goes, I go."

The agent tried to stare her down but she stared right back at him, defiant, and my chest swelled with pride. At last, the agent sighed and let her pass.

Then JD stepped forward, along with Cal, Colton, Danny, and Bradan. "Whoah, whoah, *whoah!*" Agent Jackson said. "What the hell is this?"

"Where he goes," said JD, in a voice like granite, "we all go."

Jackson looked at Kian for help, but Kian quickly found something really interesting to look at outside his window. Jackson sighed, lifted his glasses, and rubbed at the bridge of his nose. "We're going to need another SUV," he told one of his minions.

〜

The Justice Department had chartered a plane and we all stretched out, luxuriating in the air conditioning and taking full advantage of the free bar. Five hours into the flight, after a couple of glasses of a pretty good Chardonnay, I dozed off holding hands with Olivia, the two of us side-by-side in our big leather armchairs. I only woke once, half-opening my eyes to see the cabin in darkness. Olivia was slumbering peacefully next to me, and I smiled sleepily, enjoying just gazing at her. Then I saw the door to the restroom cautiously open and Danny slipped out, grinning, followed by a blushing flight attendant still tucking her blouse into her skirt. I shook my head in wonder. Then I closed my eyes, rested my head gently against Olivia's, and went back to sleep.

~

"This is it," I told Agent Jackson.

We were standing on the main street of an abandoned mining town. We were only about fifty miles from the bustle of Cedar City, but you wouldn't have known it: there was no sound apart from the creak of the old saloon sign and the distant sigh of the wind. Our little group were the only people for miles.

Agent Jackson grimaced at the red dust that was already caked on his shoes and pant cuffs. "Where?"

I pointed. "The saloon. Down in the cellar." I hobbled forward on my crutches. "Let me go down there first, to disarm the booby trap."

"You think I'm letting you go down there alone?" asked Agent Jackson. "No. Two of my agents will—"

"*I'll* go down there with him," said Kian firmly. And before Jackson could argue, he was walking with me into the saloon.

Inside, I went slowly, letting my eyes adjust to the dark. I'd only been here once before, when I stashed the gold, but I'd been thinking of the place non-stop for three years and every detail was burned into my mind: the creak of the floorboards under my feet, the way you had to jiggle the cellar hatch to get it to open. I shone a flashlight down the wooden stairs. "Stay here until I tell you it's safe," I told Kian. Then I took a deep breath and walked down into the cellar.

There were rows of wooden casks that had once held beer. And beyond them, right in the corner, there was a pile of old, dusty lumber. I pushed it out of the way to reveal seven metal boxes.

There was no booby trap, of course. But I'd stuck to the story because it meant I got a few moments alone with the gold.

I wanted to look at it. Just once.

I hinged open each of the metal boxes and then laid the flashlight on the floor. Its beam lit up the contents and I was bathed in a warm, yellow light: literally a golden glow.

Four. Hundred. Million. Dollars. I gazed slowly around the scene. Bar after bar after bar of shining gold, the surfaces mirror-bright. The power to buy whatever you want, do whatever you want, go wherever you want, *right there*...I reached down and caressed one of the ingots, letting its coldness soak into my skin, stroking its smoothness and then running my fingers over the indented numbers and letters.

I sighed.

Then I turned around and walked up the stairs, leaving the flashlight where it was. "It's safe," I told Kian as I walked past him.

A moment later, Kian followed me out of the saloon, and a victorious Agent Jackson led his men in. I couldn't bear to watch as they loaded the bars into crates and then into an armored car. I walked around the town with Olivia instead, watching tumbleweeds spin and bounce down the streets, imagining the outlaws and gunfights the place had seen. But eventually, I couldn't stop myself turning and looking at my gold as they prepared to take it away.

Olivia squeezed my hand. "Regrets?"

I looked at her. The wind had teased a lock of that long, black hair out of her bun and it was fluttering across her face in the wind. I brushed it back and tucked it behind her ear. "None," I said truthfully.

Olivia

Five hours later, I was sitting in the back of another SUV, biting my lip nervously as we sped out of Boulder airport. I'd been traveling pretty much non-stop now for over twenty-four hours and between the jet lag and the culture shock, I was starting to feel a little panicky and unsettled. *What happens now?* I knew I wanted to be with Gabriel, but I'd spent my entire life in Arizona. What if I didn't like Colorado? And what would I do for work? I still couldn't get a job as a doctor.

Then Gabriel slipped his hand around my waist and tugged me tight against him. As I turned to look up at him, he palmed my cheek with his other hand, his fingertips stroking the edge of my hair. *Whatever happens,* his eyes told me, *I'll be right there with you.* And I felt myself relax.

The city dropped away behind us, and as the peaks grew bigger and bigger on the horizon, I started leaning forward in my seat. We passed through the foothills and started up a twisty road that snaked up into the mountain. We came around a corner and—

The sunset was turning the clouds into pink and orange cotton candy and spilling golden light through the lush green pine forests that blanketed the peaks. And as we climbed higher, the view just kept getting better and better. And then there was the sign: *Mount Mercy.*

Danny expertly fed the car through a series of turns, and then we saw the mountain the town was named after, looming over the little community, menacing but beautiful. We drove down the main street and my jaw fell open: it was a gorgeous, quaint old place with wooden buildings that weren't so different to the ones in the ghost town in Utah, just lovingly restored.

We drove a little way out of the town and came to a disused factory, the windows dark holes edged with jagged glass teeth. *This was the team's base?*

Gabriel rubbed my arm. "I know. It needs work."

Three women were waiting for us outside the building. The first looked a little like me, pale and curvy with long black hair. But she wore her hair down in long, tumbling tresses, giving her a dreamy, romantic look. It streamed out behind her as she raced over to Cal, covering the distance in just a few seconds. But someone got there faster: there was a blur of tan and black fur and then a huge German Shepherd was leaping and woofing, overjoyed, his paws on Cal's chest. The woman ruffled the dog's head as she hugged her man close. *Bethany. And Rufus.* They were the main thing Cal had talked about, on the rare occasions he *did* talk.

The second woman couldn't have been more different. She was trim and compact, with glossy dark hair. There was something about the way she wore her smart gray suit and three-inch heels that reminded me of the way the team wore their camouflage gear. Gabriel looked great in anything, but when he dressed like a soldier, he looked *right,* somehow: you were reminded that *this is what he does.* This woman wore her suit in the same way. She ran halfway to the SUV: her heels didn't seem to slow her down at all. Then, as she saw Bradan get out, she stumbled to a stop and just stared, *captured,* like she was seeing him for the very first time.

Bradan gave her a grin and held out his arms. And the woman ran, faster than I would have thought possible, and jumped into his arms. Bradan locked his arms around her and spun them in a circle, their heads pressed together and their eyes closed, both of them breathing hard. *Stacey.* Bradan had talked about her a little, when we were recuperating at the field hospital. How he'd met her the day he left the cult. How they'd fallen for each other, despite their very different backgrounds. How she'd helped him through the difficult process of adjusting to normal life, a battle they were still fighting every day. It was the sort of powerful, intimate love that took your breath away and I felt myself tearing up.

The final woman wore a light gray two-piece and she came with an important accessory: three guys in dark suits who stood at a discreet distance and kept a watchful eye on her as she raced over to the car, long mahogany hair bouncing and *wumped* into Kian's chest. He put his hands under her ass and pulled her in tight as they kissed like there was no one else there. I looked at her, then looked at the bodyguards. Gabriel had told me about her, but it was still a shock to see her in real life, not on TV. *That's actually her. Emily Matthews. The former President's daughter.*

I squeezed Gabriel's hand nervously as the women hugged and kissed their men. They were all so relieved to have them home safe. How were they going to feel about me, when I was the reason they'd been in danger?

I needn't have worried. As soon as Bethany unwound from Cal, she gave me a huge, warm grin and hurried towards me. Rufus ran along with her excitedly, then realized Cal wasn't beside him and ran back to him, woofing and jumping around him until he came, too: clearly, he wasn't letting Cal out of his sight for a while.

"You must be Olivia." Bethany had the most calming voice I'd ever heard. "How are you doing?"

I started to answer and then stopped. I wasn't sure how I was doing. One part of me was drunk on relief: it was over, I was safe and back in the US and with the man I loved. But there was also that panicky feeling: I didn't know anyone here and, the thought of starting a whole new life in a strange town was overwhelming, especially when I was feeling emotionally burned out. Everything was made worse by the jet lag. I froze, helpless.

Fortunately, I was talking to exactly the right person. "Oh, you poor thing," she murmured. And she gently put her arms around me and pulled me into a hug. I felt myself immediately relax. "Everything's going to be okay," she told me, and I believed her. Then Rufus started alternately licking my hand and butting his furry head up against it for scratches, and that made me feel better, too. When she released me from the hug and smiled at me, I knew I'd found a friend.

She introduced me to Emily and Stacey. "We've been planning, while you've been away," Stacey told me. "We're going to have a barbecue tomorrow to welcome you all home. In fact, I need to go talk to Colton about using his grill." And she hurried off.

Emily and Bethany shook their heads, grinning. "Stacey used to run a chain of bakeries back in LA," Emily told me. "She's still figuring out what she's going to do here in Mount Mercy, and I think all that organizational energy's been building up. This may be the best planned barbecue in history. She's had everything on standby each day, because we weren't sure...when you were coming home." She exchanged a quick glance with Bethany, and I realized this barbecue wasn't just a celebration: it was what the three of them had used to keep themselves occupied, while their men had been away. The team had only meant to be away for two nights, but in the end, they'd been away for double that. These women must have been through hell.

"It sounds great," I told them. Then I had a sudden thought and looked down at myself. I'd only taken a few changes of clothes to Ecuador. The clothes I'd been wearing when I was kidnapped were pretty much just rags: torn, soaked, burned, and blood-stained. When we got back to the field hospital, I'd been able to finally get changed, but I'd been wearing those clothes ever since, plus they weren't exactly party material. "Not sure I have anything to wear, though."

"Not a problem," said Bethany. "I can lend you something. Stop by our place before the barbecue."

Then Gabriel was slipping his arm around my waist, and Cal and Kian were not-too-subtly prying Bethany and Emily away, too. The message was clear: there'd be time for chat later. But for tonight, these guys needed to be with their women.

~

We walked in comfortable silence down the hill towards the town. The sun was just going down, and Mount Mercy was undergoing that magical transformation into nighttime, the sky changing from pink to a deep, cool blue, the strings of lights that hung across the streets starting to come on. I looked around in wonder and took a big lungful of crisp mountain air. The cooler summers would suit me and my pale skin better than the ferocious Arizona ones, although the harsh winters would take some getting used to. I wondered how deep the snow got up here.

We strolled into the town, past people taking their dogs for an evening walk or heading to the bar for an after-work drink. I saw an old garage, a little bookshop, a cafe...and it was *friendly*, people nodded to us in greeting, even though they didn't know us.

It felt like a good place to make a home.

As we turned a corner, Gabriel's steps started getting faster. When a small apartment block crept into sight ahead of us, they got faster still. His arm tightened around my waist, and by the time we were fifty feet from the door, he was marching as fast as he could without actually breaking into a run, towing me along beside him. It was only when I looked up at him and saw the determination in his eyes that I understood. For the first time since we'd met, we were going to have proper privacy. A deep, hot throb rippled down through my body and detonated in my groin.

He managed to control himself until we got inside the block's front door. Then, in the hallway, he groaned and pushed me up against the wall. His hands cradled my face, his fingertips sliding into my pinned-up hair, and he kissed me long and deep. His body pinned mine to the wall, the heat of him soaking through his shirt and the thin cotton of my blouse. The kiss turned urgent, his lips chasing mine. His pecs swelled against my breasts as he panted, and I went weak as I felt his cock hardening against my thigh.

He grabbed me around the waist and hauled me with him across the hallway and towards the stairs. We corkscrewed up them, still kissing, until we reached the third floor.

I broke the kiss for a second. Immediately, my lips throbbed, needing him back. "Which one?" I panted.

"3A," he panted back. And then we were kissing again, his hands on my ass, keeping my body molded to his as we moved. We stumbled down the hallway to 3A and he slid the key into the door. Then suddenly he was lifting me, drawing a startled yelp and a giggle from me, and carrying me towards the bed, kicking the door shut behind him.

"I hope you don't have anything you need to be doing for about the next eighteen hours, Doc," he told me. His hazel eyes were molten and glittering. "Because I've got *a lot* of plans for you."

I didn't trust my voice, so I just nodded hard. *"Mm-hmm!"*

He threw me onto the bed. And until noon the next day, he showed me how deliciously wicked he could be.

~

I stopped and stared. "Wow."

It was early afternoon and the parking lot of the base had been transformed. Music was playing. Tables groaned with enough food for at least twenty people: bread, rainbow and regular slaw, grilled corn salad, spinach strawberry salad, mac and cheese...and that was just the sides.

Colton was grillmaster, working an immense charcoal grill that he must have brought with him from Missouri. There were huge, dripping steaks, racks of sticky baby back ribs, and glistening, vinegary St. Louis pork steaks. Stacey was standing behind a table loaded with beer, liquor, fruit, mixers and a huge bowl of ice, mixing cocktails. "What'll it be?" she asked us, grinning.

I went for a Sex on the Beach: I'd always wanted to try one and I'd always been too self-conscious to order one in a bar. Gabriel went quiet for a moment, just staring at the bar, then asked for a bourbon on the rocks. He held it up to the light, swishing the liquor and making the ice cubes clink. "Three years," he murmured. "It's been three years since I had a drink with ice in it." He took a sip and sighed in satisfaction.

JD nodded to us as he passed by. It was the first time I'd seen him in his Stetson and it made me smile: I'd never seen anyone suit a hat so much. He put his empty glass on the bar. "Stacey, that was the best margarita I've had this side of the border." He turned to call over his shoulder. "Danny? What are you drinking?"

I followed his gaze and saw Danny in a black suit and white shirt, the collar unbuttoned. Anyone else would have looked crazily overdressed but he looked effortlessly cool. He had one arm around a blonde woman with boobs that made mine seem small and a full sleeve tattoo. His other arm was around a slender woman in a red dress with long, chestnut hair. "Beer," he told JD, and grinned at the women. "Times three."

I shook my head in wonder. *How does he do it?* I wondered if he'd ever settle down.

I looked back at Gabriel to find him looking at me over the rim of his glass, his eyes molten. I flushed. "What?"

He lowered the glass and his lips curled into the sort of smile a lion would give an antelope. "You. In that dress."

I looked down. Bethany had been as good as her word. We'd headed over to their place before the barbecue, and while Cal and Gabriel played with Rufus, we'd spent a very girly hour trying on dresses. I'd wound up in a thin, green cotton dress that hugged my curves and that Gabriel said brought out my eyes. I had a feeling he liked it just as much for the square neckline: I wouldn't have worn something so low cut a few weeks ago, or worn my hair down. But a lot had changed. I was smiling more, giggling more: especially when Gabriel picked me up. I'd finally learned how to switch off. I'd just needed the right person to unbutton me.

Gabriel slid an arm around me and pulled me close. He stared down into my eyes and just wouldn't look away. "Someday," he said at last, "I'm going to have to get someone to paint you." And he bent down and kissed me gently on the lips. Then came back for another kiss, as if the first wasn't quite enough. Then a third, and now his breathing was a little growly—

I surfaced, breathless, and put a calming hand on his shoulder: *down, boy!* Even after last night and this morning, he was insatiable. Not that I was complaining. From the secret smiles on the faces of the other women, their mornings had been the same.

A newcomer spoke from the shadows, just out of range of the fairy lights. "So who do I have to screw to get a drink around here?"

I felt my face light up. I'd have known that grumpy tone anywhere. I ran forward and grabbed Gina's hand. "I didn't know you were coming!" I hadn't seen her since the rest of us went to Utah.

She shrugged. "Kian wanted me to come. Figured I owed him,

after he got me back into the US." She looked around, glowering at the lights, the music, the people.

"Let's get you a drink." We led her over to Stacey's bar.

Just as Stacey was mixing her a John Collins, the shrill ring of a cell phone split the air. It took me a few seconds to realize it was the new one I'd bought at the airport in Utah: I wasn't used to the ringtone yet. I scrambled in my purse for it and managed to answer just before the caller hung up. "Hello? Hello?" I listened and frowned. "Why do I need to be sitting down?"

Gabriel

I took Olivia's hand, my brow furrowing in worry. But the call didn't seem to be bad news, just confusing and unexpected. She squeezed my hand as she mumbled a question. She listened for a long time... and then her eyes snapped wide in shock.

She ended the call but didn't speak, just stood there staring at her phone. I waited while she processed. Then, at last, she lifted her eyes to me.

"That reporter I gave an interview to?" she said, her voice shaky with disbelief. "She followed up on what I told her, about what happened at the hospital."

I nodded and waited.

"Three weeks ago, Bryce, the doctor who framed me, suddenly retired. The reporter dug into it." Olivia's voice went throaty with emotion. "*They caught him!* The hospital caught him, stealing oxy again. But they let him retire instead of calling the cops because they didn't want a scandal." She shook her head in disgust. "They knew that meant I was innocent, but they didn't contact me, or try to put things right, because they were trying to keep it all quiet. But thanks to the reporter, it's going to go public. Now they're scrambling to make amends."

I felt my jaw drop. I stared at her, praying that meant—

"*They're clearing my record!*" There were tears in her eyes. "I can work in a hospital again!"

I threw my arms around her and pulled her to my chest. She was quaking in relief, and I squeezed her tight.

"There's a hospital in Mount Mercy," she said. "It might be a while before something comes up there, but..."

I nodded quickly and touched my forehead to hers, grinning.

Bethany saw our faces and hurried over with Cal to find out what the good news was. When Olivia told her, Bethany pulled her into a hug. That brought Emily over, Stacey came out from behind the bar and soon Olivia was being hugged from three directions at once, while Rufus put his paws on her shoulders from behind, thinking this was a new game. I saw Gina hurry away clutching her drink, before someone hugged *her*.

I withdrew a little, giving the women space. I had a feeling Olivia had found a new group of friends. And I was beyond happy that she'd finally be able to do what she loved again. There was only one thing that was niggling at me.

I'd told Olivia I had no regrets about giving up the gold, and that was true. If I had to do it over, I'd choose her and save the village again in a heartbeat. But...

It was weird. All those years in jail, I'd dreamed and planned what I was going to do with the money. Houses. Yachts. Maybe even a private island.

But when I'd asked her to run away with me, those plans had changed. Suddenly, the money had become about making a future for us and sharing all the places I loved with her. It had made all the original plans I'd made seem empty and lonely. *That's* the only thing I regretted. That I couldn't share the gold with her.

The women were deep in discussion now, something about dinner at Stacey and Bradan's place next week, so Cal and I joined JD and Colton over at the grill.

JD was listening to Colton tell him about the boat he lived on, back in Missouri. "Best thing in the world, being rocked to sleep by the water." He scowled. "Going to have to sell it: no way to get it here."

"You could use the money to buy a new truck," Danny said as he passed. He nodded at Colton's pickup, parked nearby. It was at least thirty years old, and patches of rust had spread across so much of the bodywork, it looked as if they might join up at any second and the whole thing would just split in two. The driver's door was orange and the passenger door was green: neither of them looked to be original. The rest of the paint had been bleached bone white by the sun, so it was impossible to tell what color the thing had been originally.

"There ain't nothing wrong with my truck," Colton told him firmly. He flipped a steak. "Next time we do this, we'll build a smoke pit and get some brisket going. And we'll slow-cook some pulled pork, put it all on sandwiches..."

As Colton mumbled himself off into a meat fantasy, Kian came over in jeans and a t-shirt. I did a double take: it was the first time I'd seen him in anything but a suit.

"Things are getting interesting in Ecuador," he said. "The government are still claiming they knew nothing about the plot to wipe out the village. They say the whole thing was all down to a couple of corrupt ministers, one army general, and our friend Major Zamora."

"You believe 'em?" asked Colton.

"Not really. Neither do their own voters: they're marching in the streets. Looks like they're going to kick the bastards out at the next election. And Major Zamora is looking at a military tribunal and serious prison time."

"What about the oil industry guy, with the glasses?" I asked.

Kian pulled a rolled-up magazine from his back pocket and wagged it at me like a giant finger. "Now that's even *more* interesting. He's Hugo Bainbridge." And he tossed the magazine to me, narrowly missing the grill's flames.

I unrolled the magazine. It was a *Time* from a few months ago, and the cover was a group photo, taken in front of a mansion. *A Rare Look Inside the Bainbridges*. I looked closer: yep, that was Hugo in the second row.

"They're the one percent of the one percent," Kian told us. "Old money." He pointed. "She's in pharmaceuticals, he's in defense, he's in finance...and our boy Hugo, he's deep in the oil industry. Between them, they run half the feckin' world. But even their lawyers aren't going to be able to keep Hugo out of jail."

Colton took the magazine and studied the photo, glaring at each face in turn, then passed it back to Kian with a grunt.

"This job put us on people's radar," said Kian. "I've been getting calls all day. Some of them from Langley."

JD looked impressed. "The *CIA* want us to work for them?"

I looked at the base and smirked. "Better hurry up and fix the roof."

"Better think up a name too," said Cal.

Everyone looked at each other. That hadn't even occurred to anyone. The team needed a name.

"O' Harra's Irregulars," said Danny as he joined us.

Kian grinned. "That does have a ring to it." Then the grin became a grimace. "But if Emily's dad wins the election, my name's going to be a bit too well-known to be connected to what we're doing." I felt sorry for the guy: it was obvious he'd rather be coming with us on missions, instead of sitting behind a desk.

"Steel Talon," said Colton. "Sounds *badass!*"

"It does," I agreed. "But we may get mistaken for a death metal band."

Kian rubbed at his stubble thoughtfully. "When we were kids, my dad used to take us to this beach in Ireland. There used to be these black-and-white birds. Stormfinches. They weren't big. Didn't look like anything special. But my dad said the sailors used to be superstitious about them. If you saw them, it meant there was a storm coming."

I looked at our little group. It fitted. We nodded to each other, then clinked glasses.

I looked around to check on Olivia and found her deep in conversation with Stacey. I didn't want to interrupt so I just stood there for a moment, gazing at Olivia and drinking her in. She was the prettiest damn thing I'd ever seen in my life. With her hair down she looked wildly romantic, like she should be running up some windswept hill to meet her secret lover. And with that dress revealing all that tempting, pale cleavage...I couldn't work out if I wanted to kiss her slow and tender or just push her up against a wall. *I'll just have to do both.*

I glanced sideways and nearly had a heart attack: Bradan had appeared right next to me. *"Jesus!"* I hissed. "We need to get a bell for you!"

"Sorry," he muttered. He was gazing at Stacey in the same way I was gazing at Olivia. "We're two lucky bastards, aren't we?"

I nodded silently. Then, as we stood there watching, I started to pick up on something. He wasn't just waiting for them to finish talking, like me. He was hanging back, standing in the shadows rather than joining the party.

I frowned. I've always had a good instinct for people and for years, I'd used it to help me steal: lying and cheating and conning. Now I was getting this unfamiliar feeling, like I wanted to...*help.*

Is this what it's like having a conscience? I sighed. "What's up?"

Bradan didn't answer for a while. I stood there patiently, cultivating that perfect, warm silence...

"She's the best thing that ever happened to me," Bradan said. "When I got out of the cult, I was a mess." He looked away. *"More* of a mess. She put me back together."

I nodded. *Go on.*

"I'd crawl through hell for that woman," he said seriously. "But sometimes I think..." He sighed. "Sometimes I think it'd be better for her if I wasn't with her."

I understood. All those things he did for the cult, the people he killed: he was drowning in guilt. "You think all that stuff makes you... not good enough for her?"

He nodded sadly. "Not just that. Just, like...ah, I don't know." He sighed. "Look...what you saw on the news about the cult...that wasn't the full story. There was some stuff about the history of the cult that the government didn't want coming out. That's why they didn't look too hard into all the things the cult did." His jaw tensed. "Otherwise, I'd be in jail."

"From what I heard," I said gently, "you were brainwashed. You weren't *you,* when you killed those people."

"Doesn't make 'em any less dead though, does it?" Bradan said, his voice jagged and bitter.

I said nothing. I didn't have an answer to that.

Bradan sighed. "It's just...look, I'm not saying I believe in karma, or any of that shit. Just...I feel like sooner or later, I'm going to have to answer for it. And that should be on me, just me." He looked at Stacey. "Not on her."

I thought for a moment. "All I know is, I saw the way you two looked at each other, when we got back. And..." Suddenly, the words came spilling out. "Look, when you find something *that real, that special,* you don't let anything break you apart. Not anything." I blinked, embarrassed. I'd been talking about him and Stacey, but I'd found myself looking at Olivia.

But it seemed to work. Bradan nodded, squeezed my shoulder and walked over to Stacey.

I frowned at my shoulder. *Is this how it feels to do good?* It bugged me that I couldn't do more. The guy needed to talk to someone about what he'd done, to get it all out of his system. I'd happily listen but I wasn't sure I'd be able to help him: I was a thief, I'd never killed except in combat. He needed to talk to someone who could really understand.

At that moment, I saw Gina walking past. I caught Kian's eye and nodded. It was time.

We caught up with her in a quiet corner of the parking lot, and she looked suspiciously between the two of us and then at her cocktail. "What is this, an intervention?"

"Listen to him," I told her gently.

She turned to Kian, eyes narrowed.

"I was wondering what your plans were," said Kian.

Gina caught on immediately. "Oh, no—"

"You need a job—" started Kian.

"Nooo, no no,"

"—we need a pilot—" Kian continued.

"Not for all the—"

"—you've got the experience," Kian finished, bulling through. "Night Stalkers. I've seen your record."

Gina scowled. "There are plenty of flying jobs that don't involve getting shot at. Stunt pilot. Cargo. Passengers. What makes you think I'd want to join your bunch of do-gooders?"

Kian leaned in. "I also read up on that incident that stopped you coming back to the US for so long. Smuggling medicine. Getting the cheap generic stuff to the people who can't afford the branded stuff. You probably saved some lives."

She snorted. "The money was good."

Kian glanced at me for help.

I looked Gina right in the eye. "You didn't have to come get us, when Gantz abandoned us. You didn't have to help Olivia rescue us. You didn't have to help us save the village. I think you did it because you still need *this*." And I touched her Night Stalkers tattoo. "You need to be part of something."

For a second, she just looked shocked. Then she looked at the grill for a second, staring hard at the flames. When she looked back at me, she was scowling. "*That's* your pitch? Appeal to my better nature?"

I watched her steadily. I'd glimpsed her heart enough times now, that I knew it was there, hidden beneath all those layers of grumpy armor. But she wasn't ready to acknowledge its existence.

"Also," I told her, "The money's *really, really* good."

She pursed her lips and thought for a moment. "*How* good?" she asked at last.

We had her.

As Kian led her away to talk specifics, I went to rejoin Olivia. As I marched through the party, eyes locked on her, a sudden rush of emotion caught me off-guard. I'd been away from her for just a few minutes but there was this wave of happiness, just from the anticipation of touching her again, holding her again—

I reached her and took her hand, but when I went to speak, my throat had closed up. She blinked at me in concern. "Everything okay?"

I nodded. "Yeah," I croaked and squeezed her hand. "Yeah. Everything's fine." God, the feelings I had for this woman...For the first time, I thought about how hard it would be, leaving her behind when we went on a mission. I'd never had that before, I'd never had someone to miss. But then I'd never had someone to come home to, either.

I stood there for a while, just gazing into her eyes and holding her hand, my thumb rubbing slowly over her knuckles. She balanced me. She was the good to my bad. The angel who'd nudge me back onto the right path if I strayed. And maybe I balanced her a little, too.

I wrapped her in my arms and held her close, my chin on the top of her head, rocking slowly to the music. I closed my eyes. *I'm at a small-town barbecue,* I realized. *Dancing with my girl.* Sitting in my jail cell, I'd never imagined anything so...wholesome. But...*I could get used to this.*

When I opened my eyes at the end of the song, I saw Kian standing watching us. "Follow me," he said quietly.

We followed, and he led us away from the party, not stopping until we were in the moonlit forest behind the base. Then he turned and held something out in both hands. It was about six inches long, wrapped in cloth. As I reached for it, he warned, "Careful. It's heavy."

I lifted it from his hands. It *was* heavy. Really heav—

Wait. Excitement rocketed up inside me, but I didn't dare to hope. I clawed at the cloth wrapping, trying to find the end, nearly dropping the thing—

The cloth slid back, and I stopped breathing. I was looking at mirror-smooth metal. The moonlight made it gleam silver, but I knew the real color was a warm, rich yellow.

"Oh my God," said Olivia in a strangled voice.

I looked from the bar to Kian. I'd left him alone in the saloon, just before Agent Jackson and his men had gone in there. He must have run down to the cellar and put one of the small ingots in his pocket—

"It's not four hundred million," Kian said. "But it's something."

I nodded, unable to speak. Kian patted me on the shoulder and strolled off to rejoin the party.

I stared at my own shocked face, reflected in the shining surface of the gold. We wouldn't be rich. But it was enough to put down a deposit on a modest house, with maybe enough left over for a cheap trip down to Rio. The emotion swelled in my chest, stealing my breath. I got to keep a little piece of the prize after all. And more importantly, I got to share it with her.

Another face joined mine in the reflection. Big, frozen-forest eyes blinking down at the gold. That cloud of black hair that had been pinned up for so long, now trailing down, all loose and romantic. I drank in her image for long seconds...and then I dropped the gold on the ground, spun around and pulled her to me. She yelped in surprise and then, when she saw the look in my eyes, her cheeks flushed.

I leaned down and kissed her. Soft and tender at first, but it quickly became open-mouthed and heavy, one hand buried in her hair while the other slid down to squeeze her ass.

Later, we could feel around in the dark grass and find the bar of gold. But I had more important things to do first.

The End

Thank you for reading! If you enjoyed *No Angel,* please consider leaving a review.

The story of how Kian O'Harra guarded—and fell for—the President's daughter is told in *Saving Liberty.*

The story of how Bethany saved an injured Rufus and was saved in turn by wild man of the forest Cal is told in *Deep Woods.*

Danny's book will be next. The British charmer meets the one woman who makes him want more than a one-night stand. But she's the one woman he can't have... To be notified when it's released, sign up to my newsletter at:

https://list.helenanewbury.com

You'll get a free book, *Brothers,* which tells the story of how Kian and his brothers save Bradan from the cult.